AFTER THE FALL

Visit us at www.boldstrokesbooks.com

AFTER THE FALL

by

Robin Summers

2011

ISBN 10: 1-60282-234-4
ISBN 13: 978-1-60282-234-4

This Trade Paperback Original Is Published By
Bold Strokes Books, Inc.
P.O. Box 249
Valley Falls, NY 12185

First Edition: July 2011

Credits
Editor: Ruth Sternglantz
Production Design: Susan Ramundo
Cover Design By Sheri (graphicartist2020@hotmail.com)

Acknowledgments

My first thank you has to go to Mrs. K., who saw the writer within and pushed me to find her. I know you said it's time to call you by your first name, but I just can't do it. You will always be Mrs. K., the most fabulous English teacher ever, who gave me extra homework and introduced me to Douglas Adams. I haven't seen the galaxy in quite the same way since.

To the fantastic folks at Bold Strokes Books, who have worked so hard to bring this novel full circle. Thanks to Radclyffe for many things but, most of all, for taking a chance. A special thanks to my insightful editor Ruth Sternglantz, who pushed me to dig deeper and challenged me to challenge myself, but who also listened when I dug in my heels.

Thanks to my colleagues in DC, whose enthusiastic support has meant the world.

Thanks to Cal and Nick, for making me drive 900 miles to your wedding, giving me a perfect landscape in which to envision the idea for this novel (plus the time to think it through). More than that though, thank you for being my rocks. Without you, I would not have had a back deck to write on or bonfires to pontificate in front of or card games or sledding at the Capitol or back surgery or Mr. Bill. And, Cal, thanks for gasping all those years ago when I said I wasn't writing anymore—it changed the course of history.

To my family, what can I say? You will find many pieces of us throughout these pages, and I hope that in reading them, you will know how much you all mean to me. To my parents, I thank you for pulling this family of ours together in the first place and for always supporting me in my endeavors, even when you didn't fully understand them. Dad, you have always been the best part of who I am. Deb, while you may not be my mother by birth, you have been and will always be my mom.

Finally, to K, my love, who dared me to follow my dream and pushed me when I would have given up. You were always willing to read another chapter or talk through another plot point or just listen to me ramble on about whatever randomness was going through my head (and let's be honest…there was, and still is, a whole lot of randomness in this brain of mine). I would never have finished this without you. Thank you for always believing in me, even when I did not believe in myself.

Dedication

For my parents—Dad and Deb—who taught me
about perseverance.

For Brian and Calaneet, who taught me about friendship.

For K, who taught me about love.
You are my heart, my hope, and my truest thing.

CHAPTER ONE

I feel the vibration in the air before I hear the rumbling. I slide the bat out from the makeshift scabbard with practiced ease and slip it down to my side. The bat's name is Mugsy, at least if you are on friendly terms with it. If you're not, then it is simply a bar of chipped aluminum coming at your head, and its name isn't of any particular importance to you.

For the last three months, as I have marched and slogged and pounded my way toward home, Mugsy has been my protector, my savior, and my best friend. Mugsy is comfortable in my hand, familiar and powerful and…safe. Safety isn't something you take for granted anymore, and I never take Mugsy for granted.

A gun would be better. Guns have become popular again, not that they had ever been particularly unpopular before. This new world has more in common with the Wild West than with the twenty-first century, at least if Billy the Kid and Wyatt Earp had owned semiautomatics. Everyone seems to have one, and I know that bringing a bat to a gunfight is a little like throwing a snowball at a forest fire, but still…I have a thing about guns. The muzzle flash igniting the pitch-black night, the sonic boom ringing in my ears, the acrid tang of gunpowder filling my nostrils. Yet all I see is a body falling in the woods, and all I hear is the strangled cry of a boy who died trying to save me.

"Well, Mugs," I say, looking down at the scratched and scarred maroon paint, "you ready?"

Mugsy winks at me. Yes, Mugsy is a girl, and she doesn't so much wink at me as reflect sunlight into my eyes, but I know that no matter what is about to crest the hill in front of us, we will be okay. We have come too far, seen too much, and are too close to our goal.

The lie sounds much better than the truth. These days, it always does.

Diesel chokes the air as the flatbed rises before me. Three silhouettes crowd the cab. I tighten my hand around Mugsy's rubber grip and spread my feet apart a little wider, which gives me a more balanced stance. Apart from that, though, you wouldn't notice any outward change in my demeanor. I learned early on not to give away too much. A threatening posture seldom serves any purpose but to make my ass a target for a thorough kicking, and I have found that my newly svelte frame deceives strangers into believing I'm not dangerous. It's an advantage I can use. Although I don't know the driver's or his traveling companions' intentions, I know full well what they could be, and that is enough to make the hairs on my body stand up and salute. I have met both good and bad on this terrible journey, and heard of worse and better. I figure I have a fifty-fifty shot of getting out of this unscarred and alive. I can't really ask for better odds than that.

The truck slows, and it is all I can do to keep my left hand from gripping Mugsy below my right. My mouth is a desert. My senses are sharper, heightened. I have been here before.

The truck stops, suffocating the mild September day. No doors open, no voices call out. Sunlight glints off the windshield, keeping me from seeing the faces of my would-be attackers or saviors. Then a shout, and a blur racing toward me. I bend my knees and tense, squinting to make out what it is that's about to try and do me in.

It skids to a stop in front of me, sizing me up with a swift head-cock. I stay still, not wanting to provoke the small-yet-powerful mutt, waiting for it to make up its mind about me. Then it is grinning up at me and rolls over onto its back, begging for a tummy rub. His tongue—I can tell the dog is a he now—is lolling out of the side of his mouth as he waits patiently. I start to reach down, but the familiar crack of a shotgun being chambered stops me dead. "Stop right there!" a gruff voice booms from behind the gun's barrel. The dog stops panting, looking up at me uncertainly. He is full of questions he can't possibly articulate.

"Rusty, come back here!" a woman shrieks. I don't know what threat she thinks I pose, but I don't blame the woman for being scared. Every stranger is a threat, an unknown force full of unknown intentions. I have more reason to be scared than she, however, what with the shotgun pointed at my chest and half a dozen people standing with clenched fists in a semicircle near the truck. I hadn't even noticed them.

So much for my heightened senses.

"Margie, let me handle this," the man behind the shotgun says. His eyes never leave me.

I look down again at the dog, who has exchanged confusion for fear. The people are yelling, which is never good. I lift both hands up in the air in the universal sign for "don't shoot my sorry ass" but keep my eyes on the dog.

"You better get back over there with your family," I say softly. "We wouldn't want them to get upset with you, now would we?"

The dog rolls to his feet, looking over to his humans and then back up at me. He swipes my hand once with his tongue, and then happily trots back to the truck. I turn my attention fully to the gun and the limited future I seem to have left.

"What's your business here?" the man shouts.

I look across the motley crew before me and start to think the man means me no real harm. Sure, he might kill me, but any man traveling with a woman, a dog, two teenage boys, and a grandfatherly type can't possibly intend the kinds of things I am afraid a group in a truck intends.

I decide to be honest with him. Mugsy will back me up if my judgment is wrong, or I will be dead.

"Walking, sir," I say. "Trying to get home."

He eyes me, like he's heard my story a time or two only to find out the hard way it's all a lie.

"Where's home?"

"Illinois."

"Where you coming from?"

"Washington, DC."

He falls silent, sizing me up. There is little left of Washington, and he knows it. Everybody knows it. Some people say DC is where the whole nightmare started, and maybe they're right. Lab rats in a maze. That's what it felt like, knowing the whole world was watching us to see what would happen. But soon there were others, other cities, other people. Eventually, everything just shut down. People fled, looking for God-only-knew what. Hope? Salvation? But there was none to be found, not for us, not for anyone.

Those of us who stayed watched the city crumble, figuratively at first, with the feds deserting us to set up command posts at undisclosed locations, leaving a vacuum of power and order and a great, seeping vulnerability. Then the metaphor went literal on us, because as with most vulnerabilities, someone figured out a way to exploit it. But I had left by then.

We'll never know for sure, I don't think, how it all started or why no one could stop it. There's no twenty-four-hour cable news to show us what happened, no Internet to feed us every scrap of information, relevant or not. Who cares now, anyway? The plague came, it took, and eventually it passed, leaving one hell of a messed-up world behind. Those of us who survived lived through every terrible second of it. No recap is needed or desired.

"The last refugees from Washington came through two months ago," he says. "When did you head out?"

"Five months, three days, a few hours. Give or take."

Another pause.

"You've been traveling all this time?" he asks. His words hold less accusation now. He's starting to put it together. But I'm still staring at a gun. I take a long, deep breath, trying to calm my nerves.

Just the short truth. No need for the long. Nothing there but pain.

"Yes, sir," I say. "I left just before the city went white. Waited too long, I guess, but I had friends there. Then it was time to go."

The man behind the gun prods me. "And you left?"

The rest of the story comes with practiced ease. "I made it

maybe one hundred fifty miles before the gas ran out. I waited for more in Pennsylvania, but it never came. So I started walking. Now I'm here."

He does the math in his head. I don't make him ask the question. "I had some…trouble."

The pieces all seem to fall into place. He nods curtly. He's heard the stories, maybe had his own experiences. He glances over at the woman he called Margie and closes his eyes, perhaps against the images I imagine are now ruining his mind. When he turns back to me, his face has softened and his eyes are shimmering.

I appreciate the empathy, but I will not be pitied.

"But I've got Mugsy with me now," I say with a mirthless laugh, slapping the bat against the palm of my hand, "and we won't tolerate trouble like that again."

The shotgun falls away. Concerned murmurs pass among the group, but a single glance back from him silences any dissension. The decision has been made.

"Can we offer you a ride?" he asks. "We've got a place not too far from here, some food, water, the basics. You're welcome to join us."

It could be a trap. Of course it could. The lowering of the gun, the softening of his voice, the confusion that flits between the others could all be an elaborate put-on designed to lure me in. I've met those kinds of people, the ones that set you up only to knock you down hard. But I've also met enough of the other kind to have a pretty good sense of which is which. So I nod, my stomach throwing a parade at the mention of food. He hands his shotgun off to one of the boys, who I realize will be watching me carefully even if the man has decided I am okay.

"Make room in the back, boys," he calls out as they load back into the truck. "Name's Buck, by the way."

"Taylor," I say. "Taylor Stone."

Chapter Two

The air was still, like it always seemed to be since the plague. It could be suffocating at times, the stillness of it all. At least that was how Duncan felt about it. Some days, it was like the whole planet was conspiring to choke him with its stillness, and Duncan had to fight just to keep breathing. Other days, it was a peaceful refuge, for with the stillness came the quiet. A soothing, consuming blanket full of quiet. He liked those days better than the ones where the earth was trying to kill him.

Duncan sunk his shovel back into the dirt, sending fine particles up into the stillness. He watched them hang for a moment before they lazily drifted back down. Ashes to ashes, dust to dust.

He was covered in dirt, more of a mud, really, as it mixed with his sweat. He wiped his brow with his forearm, smiling at the dark streak he could feel imprinting onto his skin. The dirt did not bother him. It made him feel useful, and Duncan liked feeling useful. It gave him something to focus on besides the stillness.

He glanced over his shoulder, watching the others sink the post into the ground, burying it deep. The men he was working with respected his work ethic. It was important to Duncan that these men respected him, even if they refused to accept him as a man. As one of them. To them, despite all the work he had put in since he had gotten here, Duncan was still just some local kid that Buck had taken in a couple of months ago.

He looked farther down the line of freshly cemented posts that they had been laying for close to a week. They had accomplished a lot in seven days, and he was proud. Only a few more posts to go, then they could start laying the crossbeams that would serve as the bracing for the heavy steel sheets that would make up the wall that would surround the entire property. The wall was important, and he was happy to be a part of its construction. Duncan figured they would have the wall finished in about two months, though he really did not know for sure. He had never helped build a fortress before.

The first snow should still be at least ten weeks off, just enough time to finish the wall, but the weather being what it was here, it could come sooner. If they were going to finish the wall before winter, they would need the snow to hold off and the ground to stay thawed. After that, Duncan was not sure what he would be doing, but he was not worried. There would be something to do, some new project for him to focus his attention on. There always was.

Duncan turned back to his digging, easing the dry dirt out of the hole and onto the pile beside it. He worked methodically, taking a moment after every third shovelful of earth to take a deep breath and rest. It was not particularly warm, but the midday sun beat down hard and heavy, making Duncan feel like an egg on the hood of a '69 Chevy. He could almost hear himself sizzle. So he worked short breaks into his work, although he liked to think of them more as pauses than breaks. Breaks implied laziness, while pauses were sensible, designed to prevent toppling over from heatstroke. Something his daddy had taught him when he was a kid.

Kid. Pfft. I ain't no kid. Not anymore.

He may have been only sixteen, but there was no way in hell or heaven he was still a kid. The plague had seen to that. When his parents had gotten sick, he had taken on every chore, every responsibility, everything that could or needed to be done. It had been too much, really, but he had done it because it needed doing. Then they were gone, and he was alone. But he had survived, and now he was here doing a man's work. He might still have a bit of a reckless streak, still have a touch of a wild side, still be a tad impulsive, and still crack a ridiculously disgusting joke from time to time, but these things were just traces of the boy he had been, not childish imperfections in the man he had become. Not in his mind, anyway.

It was during one of his pauses that Duncan felt an interruption in the stillness. He saw the plume of dust from the road to the north, the telltale sign of an approaching vehicle. The dust rolled over itself, closer and closer until he could make out the unmistakable sight of Buck's flatbed coming home.

Home. Such a funny word. A few months ago, he could not have imagined thinking of any place other than his folks' house as home, but now Burninghead Farm was his home, and he would do everything in his power to protect it.

"Buck's back," Tony called out from behind him. No more words were needed. Duncan and the rest of the men started packing up their tools and loaded them into the pickup. The gear stowed, they piled into the truck and headed toward the house to await what Buck had brought.

CHAPTER THREE

I sit on the back edge of the flatbed, my feet dangling above the road rushing beneath us. The others have tucked in near the back of the cab, putting a large stack of heavy metal sheets between themselves and the new girl with the bat strapped to her back. Only the dog is brave enough to come near me. He is hunkered down next to me, fast asleep. I laugh to myself. There are a lot of things in this brave new world to fear, and I'm not even close to being at the top of the list, but they don't seem to know that. I don't mind, really. Their fear means a wide berth, and that suits me just fine. I like the space, if not the quiet.

I used to crave the quiet. I sought it out, needing the freedom I found in it. Freedom to think, freedom to not think, freedom to breathe and rest and contemplate and, sometimes, freedom to just be. My head used to get noisy, polluted with the day-to-day and the what-ifs and the might-have-beens and the should-bes to the point that I needed the quiet like I needed oxygen. Without it, my brain would have imploded from the pressure. The quiet saved me.

But that was then, and now I hate the quiet like little else. Now it brings me chaos instead of peace, pain instead of relief. The quiet no longer saves me.

The truck turns, and I read the name above the gates as we pass through them. Burninghead Farm.

Buck Burninghead? That's unfortunate.

I don't know if this farm belongs to Buck, but it feels right. Not that it matters. Burninghead Farm is simply another stop on my journey, a brief pause to let me rest and gather my strength and then get the hell out. Buck is willing to give, and I am more than happy to take what his farm has to offer and then leave it behind. I am a john after a night of indecency, but it isn't the first time. And there will certainly be no money left on any nightstand.

That's Rule Number Three. No, not the money thing. Rule Number Three is Don't Get Involved.

People fall into two categories since the plague: helpful and not helpful. The usual distinctions you used to make about people, like good and bad, are largely irrelevant to the question of whether you are going to survive another day. Everyone has the capacity for evil when pushed to their limits, and trying to decide who's good and who's bad is rather pointless, considering that everyone has been pushed way too far.

It is much easier to simply decide whether someone is helpful or not. All you need to do is figure out what you need at any given point, whether the person has what you need, and whether they are willing to give it. That last one doesn't take a rocket scientist to figure out, either. The gun pointed at your face or the fist slamming into your jaw are pretty good indications that someone doesn't feel like sharing.

Yeah, Rule Number Three is pretty simple.

There are three rules in all.

Rule Number One: Keep Moving.

Just a little farther. Just a few more miles.

Rule Number Two: Keep to Yourself.

Just the short truth. No need for the long. Nothing there but pain.

Don't Get Involved makes the trifecta, and together these three rules are my guide, my conscience, and the only God I have use for anymore. Besides Mugsy, my rules are the only things I can count on as the flatbed comes to a stop in front of a large white farmhouse at the top of a hill half a mile inside the gates of Burninghead Farm.

The old farmhouse looks like something out of *Anne of Green Gables*. The television version of my childhood, anyway. Two stories high, wrap-around porch with antique-looking wicker chairs, green paint clinging to worn storm shutters. Although it has seen better days, in its own way, the house is majestic.

The truck doors protest on their hinges, and three sets of boots drop to the gravel. The flatbed lurches slightly as my traveling companions from the back follow suit. I sigh. I would rather pass the time looking at that old house than face what I am sure will be something akin to a suspicious, though hopefully not too angry, mob gathering in the town square.

Sure enough, a crowd is already gathering around the flatbed. No torches or pitchforks, though there are a large number of shovels accompanying the men jumping out of the back of the brown Chevy pickup that has just pulled up. I count about twenty in the crowd, including those I arrive with, but more are coming. Old ones, young ones, men, a few women…I wonder how many people are on this farm.

Most of the newcomers eye me with the aforementioned suspicion and maybe a little interest, but not with open hostility. The murmuring begins, whispered questions and too few answers. Everyone's looking at me. I feel like I should tap dance or juggle or something. Maybe I can sprout a second head for the crowd. Maybe I already have. I don't like being the star of the freak show, but I understand it. Anyone who doesn't meet a stranger with some degree of interest or apprehension is either short a few brain cells or a good actor.

No, what has my skin tingling and my right hand twitching at my side, itching to reach over my shoulder and withdraw Mugsy from her cocoon, are the three sets of eyes watching me from the back of the crowd, narrow and dangerous. More than watch me, they study me, sizing me up like prey in a springtime meadow. I am exposed, too out in the open. I want to bolt.

"Now quiet down, quiet down," Buck says. He waves his hands down, and the crowd falls silent.

"This here's Taylor," he says, laying a beefy hand on my shoulder. Funny how it doesn't spook me. "She's gonna be staying with us for a time, and I expect y'all to make her feel welcome."

I want to point out that "a time" is likely to be just one night, maybe two, but I keep my mouth shut.

The world grows silent for a moment. Then the questions come.

"How long?"

"Where's she from?"

"What's she doin' here?"

Buck smiles reassuringly and raises his voice above the din.

"You can get those answers yourselves later, if she feels like giving 'em. You know the rules here. Anyone is welcome, as long as they don't mean us any harm. Everyone's entitled to their privacy. Everyone pitches in."

Heads bob up and down. They have been through this before.

"For now, just know that I believe Taylor here means us no harm, all right? I give you the same guarantee that I've given you every time I've brought someone new to this place, and that is there are no guarantees. But I trust my gut, and I ask you to do the same."

The crowd seems to come to a kind of universal agreement, maybe not about me, but certainly about Buck. They've trusted Buck before. They will trust him again.

If I could still be moved by such displays, I might grow teary. Weepy, even. You don't often find this kind of faith in anything anymore, let alone in one man's intuition. But blind faith, I have learned, is easily corrupted, and therefore cannot be trusted. All I can trust is what I can see right in front of me, which right now is a siren blaring out a warning about the eyes in the back of the crowd still stalking me, and the set of the jaws of the men those eyes belong to.

CHAPTER FOUR

Duncan listened to the chatter die down around him as Buck started to speak. He had been pretty quiet since he and his crew had arrived up at the house. Everyone was focused on the new girl, though Duncan supposed she was not really a girl. She looked to be around thirty, though he knew she could be late- or even mid-twenties. Everyone looked older than they really were these days, and this girl—*woman*—gave off a sense that she had been through enough to make her appear twice her age.

Although he heard the chatter around him, Duncan tuned it out, as he usually did. He learned early on that whenever Buck would bring someone new to the farm, people would whisper and wonder and worry, indulging in idle speculation and pure fantasy until Buck gave his speech, the same one he was giving now. Besides, Duncan liked to make up his own mind about things, especially about people.

Taylor. That was what Buck had called her.

She was kind of pretty, Duncan thought, though in a hard, almost impenetrable way. The first thing he noticed were her eyes. They were the same silty brown as a river after a rainstorm. They were also small, though not narrow, and yet they seemed big and bold when they made contact with Duncan's briefly but forcefully, and he held his breath as her X-ray eyes scanned him, assessing what lay beneath his skin before moving on to the next person.

Her eyes were commanding. Yet despite their power, there was an emptiness there, a haunted hollowness born of pain and sorrow.

Duncan had seen the look before. They all carried a little of it now, like the sheer weight of their grief had sunk a hole in their souls, and Duncan wondered sometimes if those sinkholes would ever be able to be filled. But Taylor's hollow seemed far deeper than that of any of the others on the farm, like she was not just grieving for the people she had lost. Duncan wondered what horrors she had experienced out there on the road to make her seem so broken.

Duncan continued to make mental notes about her. Her hair was light brown, tucked back behind her ears in such a way that Duncan knew it would fall just a bit below her earlobes if it was let loose. It was also streaked with gray, which made him revise his earlier age estimate a little farther north. She wore a faded red Henley shirt and blue jeans that seemed to be falling off her. At what Duncan guessed to be five foot seven or eight, she was not a tiny girl, but she seemed fit and, well, shapely. He could not help but notice Taylor's breasts. Duncan felt the blood rising in his cheeks and shifted his gaze back up to her face.

For some reason Duncan kept being drawn back to her eyes, maybe because they told him about where she had been and where she was heading. Duncan wondered if Taylor knew her eyes told so much to someone who really looked. He somehow thought she would be surprised to find out, and maybe even angry.

That was when he finally noticed the scar beneath her left eye—a couple of inches long, shaped like a crescent moon, about an inch beneath her eye. It did not look like a surgical scar, it was not clean enough for that, though it was not exactly ragged, either. *Knife scar?* Duncan wondered. No, that was not right.

Duncan shrugged off the questions in his mind, dismissing them for a later time. He did not know why, but he thought he was going to like Taylor.

CHAPTER FIVE

O kay now. Go on and get back to whatever it was y'all were doing," Buck says. "I'll see y'all later tonight for chow."

The people of Burninghead Farm cheer and clap enthusiastically. I flash back to some old black-and-white movie I'd seen, where the unsuspecting adventurers smile gratefully as they're happily welcomed to dinner by the primitive tribesmen, only to find out they are meant to be the main course.

My brain really does go to some extreme places on occasion. When I was a kid, my dad took me to see *E.T.: The Extra-Terrestrial*. For weeks afterward, I was convinced E.T. was hiding out at the neighbor boy's house, all because the kid had a bag of Reese's Pieces on the playground at recess. I was also convinced that my uncle was one of the Bee Gees. I was crushed when I found out he wasn't. I was eighteen.

Nowadays, I'll be walking along and stumble across a shoe or a Twinkie wrapper or a body, and my mind will flash back to some memory about learning to tie my shoelaces or eating Twinkies on a swing set or my mom laying in a casket, and I get lost. I get so lost sometimes, I can't tell what's real or what's just in my head. I often like what's in my head better. But not always.

When I finally shake myself back to the real world, I wonder if I have perhaps gone just a touch crazy. Then I tell myself that *not* going at least a little crazy after the plague would be totally insane, which makes me feel better.

The crowd disperses, people heading off in seemingly random directions, a few moving to unload the flatbed. Except for my three hunters in the back. They wait, still watching, making me wish I had the power to turn invisible at will.

I remember as a kid doing things I shouldn't have just to make a point, even if by making the point I got myself into more trouble. Simple things, like taking a cookie before dinner after mom told me I couldn't have one, or staying out past curfew after dad threatened to ground me for being late the night before, or mouthing off to a teacher when my head was screaming at me to just keep my mouth shut. I always knew not to do it but often found myself doing it anyway.

So now, watching these three men watch me, I feel myself slipping down one of those childhood rabbit holes and unable to stop the fall. Their beady eyes and incessant stares are more than I can take.

I raise my head, directly challenging their collective gaze with my own. My chin juts out, and my jaw becomes a vise. I stand taller. My hands clench. I am the levee against the hurricane, and I will not be breached.

The man on the left and the man on the right both turn their heads toward their friend in the middle, awaiting his response. He is average in height but above average in build, with forearms bulging from beneath his rolled-up flannel shirt sleeves. His upper arms are like tree trunks, his hands meaty mitts. He has what I imagine could pass for a handsome face, if it wasn't so hard and pinched. Or if I went for that sort of thing. The guy reminds me of every evil drill instructor in every bad military movie ever made, though I fear there is more to him than that.

I wait, as his buddies do, for his reaction. When it finally comes, it is frighteningly familiar and chills me as if I am locked in a walk-in freezer in nothing but my bra and panties. The right corner of his mouth slides up into a cruel smirk. His teeth glint at me, evil diamonds refracting the sunlight. His pals each turn back toward me. I can feel the change. They sought an answer, and it was given by their leader. I worry what the question was.

A gentle hand on my shoulder distracts me for a moment.

"You okay?" Buck asks. I glance at him quickly. I'd forgotten he was even there.

"Yeah, sure," I say as smoothly as I can, my focus shifting back to my bigger concern. I let out a short rush of air as instead of those eagle eyes hunting me down, all I find is their backs staring at me as they walk away.

Relieved, I am finally able to focus on someone else. Buck. And the woman who has just walked up next to him.

"Hey there, Buck," she says, wrapping her arms around him with obvious affection.

"Hey, kiddo," Buck answers, embracing the woman like a father would his daughter.

For a moment I wonder if they are related, but then she turns her attention to me, and the thought dissolves as I get caught up in her eyes. They are the color of warm chocolate, with flecks of amber sparkling deep within. They are kind, open with compassion and gentle with wisdom. Yet there is a power in them, an intense strength that pierces right to the heart of things. I suck in a deep lungful of air, trying to calm my racing heart. Her openness unnerves me, yet I can't seem to turn away.

"Taylor, this is Kate," Buck says, his voice yanking me out of my introspection. "Kate, meet Taylor. She's been traveling for quite some time, heading home. She'll be staying with us for…well, for as long as she likes."

That last bit he adds with a smile and a wink in my direction, like he figures I think I'll be gone after a day or two but that he knows better.

Not likely, old man. But thanks for playing.

"Nice to meet you," Kate says, giving me a warm smile. She can't be more than twenty-six or twenty-seven, yet she holds herself with the confidence of a woman twice her age.

She reaches out to shake my hand. Her fingers glide across my palm, smooth and soft. I wish I had washed my hands. Something so perfect should never be touched by someone so unclean. Her eyes hold mine intimately, her head tilting to the side, as if something is telling her she should recognize me from some time long since past, but she cannot quite put her finger on the where or the when. I feel it, too.

"What do you say to the nickel tour of the place, Taylor?" he asks, smiling genuinely. "Kate, you mind?"

"Not at all," Kate says. I have to remind myself to breathe.

❖

I have to say, I am impressed. Except I don't say it. I swallow the words and forget I had ever thought them. But the truth is I am astounded by what these people have built.

Over the last hour we covered a lot of ground, most of it by pickup, though as I understand it from Kate, we barely skimmed the surface. From my vantage point near the south gate, Burninghead Farm sprawls north as far as the eye can see. I am glad this wasn't a walking tour.

Fields of crops spread out before me in various stages of growth. Horses and cows graze in a large pasture on the western end of the farm, oblivious to my scrutiny. The farmhouse which I'd first arrived in front of is little more than a doll house on the horizon, standing watch over the farm and its occupants. A picturesque barn stands near the western pasture and houses the farm's livestock. Two other large barns, if you could call them that, lie to the north and east, aluminum-sided monstrosities painted brick-red to match the barn.

One building serves as a makeshift cafeteria and meeting hall for the farm's residents. The other had been converted to act as a dormitory, currently holding forty-seven souls who now call Burninghead Farm home. Kate tells me that they have come from all over, many local, some from hundreds of miles away, all in need of a new home. A new family. Children, grandparents, men, women, couples, and singles. It is Noah's Ark come to Indiana, ensuring the human race will go on.

We park next to a large oak that looks like it has seen more than its fair share of hard winters. The oak rests atop a large hill, a rise not unlike many others that roll across the property.

"Pretty soon, we won't be using this gate anymore," Kate says, stepping out of the truck, pointing down the hill at the rusted iron gate that stands closed. I follow, landing in the soft earth with a muted thud, savoring the light breeze that kicked up not long ago. "Once the new wall is in, there will only be one entrance to the farm."

I don't ask why they are building a wall around the entire property. I don't need to.

Kate takes a few steps then stops, scanning the sky. She closes her eyes and breathes in deeply. "Rain'll be coming in soon."

I'm sure the look I give her is somewhere between *Huh?* and *Let me just get your measurements for your new white coat with the long, funny arms*. There isn't a single cloud in the sky.

She lets out a low laugh. It's a wondrous sound. "No, I'm not crazy," she says. "After a while, you just kind of know these things."

I'm still eyeing her a bit funny, not entirely sure she's in her right mind. Then again, who am I to talk?

"I grew up on a farm, not all that far from here. Trust me, we're going to have rain. Later tonight, after dinner."

I decide to change the subject. "So people seemed pretty enthused about dinner. Must be some good cooking."

She laughs again, and I wonder how suddenly a simple laugh can make me feel like I'm sitting at an outdoor café sipping a latte rather than standing on a hill in the middle of nowhere after the end of the world.

"The food is pretty good, and we're lucky to have it. The farm provides most everything we need. But no, I don't think it's the cooking."

"Then what?"

She doesn't answer right away. Instead, she walks a little farther, a little higher into the late afternoon air.

"The plague took too much, from all of us. But we're here. We survived, and we work hard all week, just trying to keep surviving. There are always chores to do, crops to tend, animals to care for, fences to build. Another task to complete if we want to stay alive. But the fact that we survived, that we're still here when billions aren't, is worth celebrating. So once a week, on Saturday night, we have a party. We gather in the north barn, we eat, we laugh, we play music, we dance, and we try and remember the joy in a world steeped in misery."

I wonder about the wastefulness of it, about how they can possibly think they will be able to sustain themselves if they use up their resources so indiscriminately. But then I notice how the sun is beginning to sink in the western sky, and how the first tendrils of evening creep across the landscape. Everything begins to soften as the light exchanges harsh yellow for a golden glow. My eyes flutter closed. My skin drinks in the gentle light of the setting sun, the whoosh of the breeze fills my ears. It is peaceful, this moment. It reminds me of home.

Home.

I curse myself for having let myself get caught up in the moment.

Left. Right. Left. Just a little farther. Just a few more miles.

I won't be here long enough to care whether these people waste away their survival.

Damn, I am tired.

Seeming to sense the shift in my mood, Kate starts walking back toward the truck. "Come on," she says. "Let's go get you settled in."

The joyous laughter of children trickles in through the truck's windows as we approach the two barns on the northeast end of the farm. The sound surprises me. I can only remember hearing prolonged laughter once since leaving Washington, and it had been neither joyous nor childlike. It had been cruel and mocking, with a hint of rage and a thread of desperation. This, though, is none of those things. This is cotton candy melting on your tongue and sticking to your chin. This is twirling in a field, your arms spread like wings as you spin round and round with your face turned up to the crystal blue sky.

It makes me want to cry. Instead, I find myself smiling.

The truck stops beside the north barn, where we will be eating dinner later this evening. Instead of taking me directly to the dorm, Kate slides out of the truck and heads around to the back of the north barn. I follow, not quite knowing what else to do and having no place better to be.

Kate rounds the corner and leans up against the side of the barn, her arms folded across her chest. Her head slips slightly to the right, and I can tell she would be content to stand there like that forever, just watching.

There are seven in all, five boys and two girls. None of them can be older than twelve, and most seem far younger. There are a few older kids too, teenage boys who appear to be acting in some sort of supervisory capacity but who are failing miserably at actually supervising.

They run with abandon, their little legs pumping furiously in a vain attempt to catch the one teenager who seems to be the object of their little game. The boy dodges and weaves, sidestepping and evading the tiny arms and bodies flying around him. He laughs heartily, urging the kids on in their attempts to catch him.

It seems as though the poor things will never catch up, until one little girl stops running and starts to cry. In an instant the teenager is at her side, checking for injury. He doesn't immediately see her crocodile tears, nor the devilish grin growing on her face just before she wraps her arms tightly around his leg, yelling, "I got him!"

The other children rocket toward the now-trapped boy, who can only laugh as the kids leap at him, grabbing baby fists of shirt and jeans, dragging him to the ground. Pretty soon the two other teenagers, who until now had remained on the sidelines, jump into the fray, joining the pile on the grass while being careful not to smush any of the younger children below.

It is demolition derby meets reverse tag, and it is wonderful.

Kate is radiant in the waning sunlight. Her eyes dance with merriment and a hint of wonder even as they work the scene, moving from one child to the next.

"Okay guys, time to call it a day," she calls out, her voice a rich symphony. A few heads shoot up from the pile of giggling and squirming children in the grass, the kids' faces lighting up as they find Kate. Clearly, she is someone special to them. I look at her again, wondering just who this woman is that she holds these children's hearts so.

Kate pushes off the barn. "Come on," she calls back to me as she heads into the fray. She stops next to the group, waiting as one by one they turn toward her. "Time to get washed up for supper," she tells them softly, as if she is just as heartbroken as they are that the game must come to an end.

There are a few disgruntled squeaks of protest and whiny *no*s, even as seven tiny heads and three larger ones peek up from the pile, obviously waiting to see what her reaction will be. She says nothing but begins drumming her fingers on one arm. Her right eyebrow arches to her hairline, daring anyone to protest again. She may have been sad to end their fun a moment ago, but she certainly isn't going to take any guff now. I bite back the grin threatening to erupt.

"Come on," one of the teenage boys says, rising up from the pile and helping some of the children to their feet. "You heard what she said. Time to wash up."

The children obey, offering little more than a few mumbled groans. They shuffle past her, heads hanging low in one final act of weak rebellion. A secret smile flashes across her face as she watches the last of the little soldiers marching past her.

I can't help but laugh. Her eyes lock on me in an instant, her eyebrow shooting up once again. My chuckle dies as quickly as it began. I clear my throat, my gaze landing everywhere but on Kate's face. I feel an urge to start kicking my shoe in the dirt like a ten-year-old who just got busted by my teacher.

Not that any of my teachers ever looked like her.

She can't hold the look in the face of my chagrin, and she laughs lightly as she heads back to me.

"Come on, let me show you where you'll be bunking." She tugs on my shirt sleeve and heads up to the dormitory.

CHAPTER SIX

"Most everyone has their own room right now," Kate says as we move down the wood-paneled hallway of the dorm. "Each room is set up with two twin beds, courtesy of the local-and-now-abandoned furniture store."

She shrugs at me over her shoulder, as if to say she normally wouldn't condone such a practice, but considering the circumstances...As far as I am concerned, anything abandoned is fair game, plus some things that are less than abandoned. You can't really steal something that doesn't belong to anyone anymore.

"Married couples room together, although there's only two of those right now. We put all the kids together in a cluster. One of the couples, Bruce and Diane, act as foster parents of sorts." She stops in the hallway and turns to me. The shimmer in her eyes echoes the sadness in her words. "They lost their daughter in the plague, not long before they came here. She was only five. But as soon as they arrived and saw the ones without parents, they offered to keep watch over the children who had lost their moms and dads." She shakes her head lightly. "I know we've all lost, but to lose your child and then willingly surround yourself with them when the grief is still raw...I don't know how they do it. I'm not sure I could."

"We all deal with grief differently." I speak without thinking, the sound of my own voice startling me. "Some of us isolate ourselves from anything that reminds us of what we've lost. Some go looking for such things, trying to fill the void by replacing what's gone."

Kate studies me, and I wither under her scrutiny. She nods her head and picks up where she had left off. "There aren't many women here, obviously. We've all kind of taken on the kids as our purpose here, making sure they eat properly and go to school and have playtime and such. Just generally keeping an eye out. It's not very feminist of us, I know," she says with another shrug. "I certainly never envisioned myself as a den mother. I guess our biological instincts are running on overdrive."

Her pseudo-apology intrigues me. I wonder why she feels it necessary, given her obvious affection for the children. I start to imagine myself as June Cleaver, complete with apron and pearls. As if I don't already have enough nightmares to keep me awake at night.

"Go to school?" I ask, trying to redirect my mind.

"Yeah," she says, stopping once again. "We managed to get some textbooks, a portable blackboard, and some school supplies from the local K through 12. Everyone fifteen and under goes to school from ten to three, five days a week, with time in the morning for chores and supervised playtime. The older teenagers get to choose school or work, although if they choose work, we try to tutor them in the evenings or when there's free time. I teach the kindergarteners and grade schoolers, and Nancy takes the high school kids."

She has such pride in her voice.

"You like it. Teaching the kids."

"It was my major in college. I subbed at an elementary school, before. So it made sense."

"You didn't answer my question," I say, pressing her.

"Yeah, I do. I've always liked kids."

I appreciate her humility, among other things. I have not felt this kind of interest in anyone, or anything at all other than getting home, in a long time.

"There are forty rooms, twenty on each side of the hallway, so we're only a couple of rooms short of having to start doubling up. There are two community bathrooms, one at each end of the hall. The showers actually work pretty well, though don't expect anything more than lukewarm water. The boys' bathroom is back down the hallway, the girls' on this end, since that's how the rooms are booked, with the children's rooms in between."

Boys' and girls' bathrooms, shared rooms for married couples, it all seems so…

"Traditional."

"Hmm?"

It takes time for me to realize I had voiced the thoughts in my head.

"Oh. Well, it all seems so…traditional," I repeat. "Appropriate, I guess." I fumble for words that won't offend her. I don't know why I said anything, or why I even care. Separation of the sexes, traditional gender roles…these were typical of the old world just as they are of this new one. Communities build themselves upon the foundations of the old, even if the present bears little resemblance to the past.

"There's nothing wrong with traditional values," she says quietly. "They may seem old-fashioned, but they work for most people, give them something familiar to work from."

Kate studies me. I feel like a psychiatrist's patient, waiting to be diagnosed. Her eyes bore into me, trying to dig out the truth. Finally, her face softens, as if she has found whatever it is she was looking for. And she seems to be happy with what she has found.

"You shouldn't mistake tradition for intolerance, though. What works for some doesn't work for all, and the people here understand that. Everyone on the farm is free to make their own choices, as long as those choices don't hurt anyone. We can all be who we are."

She begins walking again, and this time I force my feet to follow until we reach the end of the hall. Kate turns to the door on the left, the number 39 written neatly in Magic Marker in the upper center of the door. I want to bring her back to our conversation even as I tell myself I don't, but apparently Kate has decided that subject is closed.

"Originally, these weren't numbered, but it became confusing pretty fast."

She twists the worn golden doorknob and leads me inside, reaching overhead and pulling down on a silver chain connected to an uncovered lightbulb at the center of the ceiling. The bulb casts a warm, soft light that doesn't quite push back all the shadows, but still manages to make the room seem cozy.

"After one of the guys, Tony, accidentally walked in on Mrs. Sapple just after her shower, the numbers went up pretty fast." She laughs, shaking her head. "You should have heard the screaming."

I am surprised she is making a joke of such a thing, but only for a moment.

"From Tony, not Mrs. Sapple," Kate rushes on. "She's seventy-two, and I think she kind of liked the idea of a twenty-six-year-old 'strapping lad,' as she calls him, seeing her in her birthday suit."

I laugh despite myself, imagining this spitfire elderly woman in all her glory, while the strapping lad runs shrieking down the hall. Kate smiles at me, as if my laughter delights her. I find myself smiling back. If we were anywhere but here at the end of the world, I might think we were flirting. The thought is too impossible to even consider.

"Anyway, this whole room is yours, at least for now," she says, the moment gone. If it had even been a moment at all.

I take in the small but clean accommodations. Two twin beds line the walls, one to the left and one directly ahead of me, underneath a set of short, sea-foam-green curtains. Wedged in a corner, a rickety wooden chair sits beneath a tiny desk that has seen better days. Kate walks over and draws back the curtains, allowing the indirect rays of the late-day sun to sift into the room.

She is lovely in the filtered sunlight. I tell myself to stop looking.

"All the rooms have windows, so if you're in here during the day, try to keep the light off. We have electricity on the farm, though we try to keep use to a minimum. Buck was a bit ahead of his time. He installed some solar panels about five years ago. That plus a couple of generators, and we have power enough to sustain us, as long as we're careful."

She pulls the cord again, and shadows reclaim what the light had captured.

"Last month we imposed a nine o'clock lights-out curfew for the dormitory, and we have candles if you want to stay up past that. It's a little nineteenth century, but it should help keep the power on for a while. Our water comes from a well, fed by the same underground spring that feeds the creek running through the farm. As for the rest, Buck and his family managed to gather up a whole lot of supplies early on during the plague. When people were cleaning out convenience stores, Buck was making deals with his contractor and supplier friends, stocking up on things like kerosene and lumber, and all the processed food and canned goods they could find. I'm pretty sure he even has a stockpile of beer hidden somewhere."

I slip past her, having decided to make the bed underneath the window my own. As I pass, the faint scent of vanilla reaches out to me, and I know without a doubt it is coming from Kate. My eyes flutter closed as it drifts over me. It is sweet and warm, and I let it wrap me in its embrace.

As I reach the bed the scent fades.

"So where's your room?" The question surprises me as it slips past my lips.

"A few doors down. I'm in 33."

"You have a room to yourself?"

She grins, like she knows a secret she's not planning on sharing. The room suddenly seems a little warmer. "I'm not married, if that's what you mean."

"That's not, I mean, I wasn't. . .I, well. . ."

Oh hell.

She is smiling, but then the smile turns wistful. "My parents died in the plague. I had been living in Indianapolis but went home to take care of them when they got sick. I'm the last of my family. Buck is an old friend of my parents, which is how I ended up here."

I nod, anything I could say seeming insignificant. Maybe if the plague had spared the poets of the world, we would have the words to comfort each other for the loss of everything.

"So, I guess that's about it," she says, shrugging off the melancholy. "Not much of a nickel tour. Maybe a two-cent special."

"No, no, it was fine," I say, trying to sound reassuring. My social skills are rusty from infrequent use. "I appreciate you taking the time."

"It was no trouble," she says quickly.

We stand there for a moment, more than a bit awkward. It's like she's waiting for me to ask her to the prom.

"Well, um," she says, "I guess I should let you get settled."

"Yeah, I guess."

Reluctantly I reach across my chest and lift Mugsy and her holder over my head, setting them on the bed. Kate takes her cue and starts to shuffle toward the door. As I slip the backpack down off my shoulders, I suck in a sharp breath. I had forgotten.

"What is it?" She misses nothing.

"Nothing," I say, willing myself to push down the pain. I fail miserably, wincing as the bag slides down my back.

"Not nothing." Kate decisively removes the bag from my body.

"No, really—"

"Take off your shirt," she says as she lifts its hem.

I open my mouth to protest again, but she catches my gaze with her own, and it is clear she isn't about to take no for an answer. I lift my hands up in the air like a child, wincing again, and let her slide the shirt up and over my head.

"Oh, Taylor." She sighs, her voice full of empathy as she eases my bra strap off my shoulder and out of the way. I know it looks bad without seeing it, know the three-inch gash just below my left shoulder is infected, can feel the swelling and the tightness all around the area.

"It's no big deal." I try to sound convincing.

"Wait here," she says and heads out the door. I want to put my shirt back on. Instead, I stand there and wait, clothed only in my discomfort.

My thoughts are interrupted by her return, antiseptic and bandages in hand. She pulls the light cord. Apparently my wound warrants a little electricity use. I expect her to ask how it happened, but she doesn't. Her hands gently probe and prod my skin, gliding over me with a touch as soft as a whisper.

"This is going to hurt a bit," she says, her voice infinitely gentle. Her words and tone are meant to soothe me. Instead, they make me more uncomfortable. I start to shift back and forth, her compassion making me crazy.

I grit my teeth against the first sting of the antiseptic. The pain quickly grows in its intensity as she works her way methodically down my back.

"Stop fidgeting," she chastises. I do as I am told, stilling my body. My restlessness festers, and I have a hell of a time keeping my mouth from picking up from where my legs leave off. I am almost compelled to tell her the story, but she doesn't need to be faced with the reality of roving bands of thugs and running for your life and rusty fences. The world they have built within the farm's borders is nothing like the one I have often faced outside.

"There."

She steps back, and I sway a little. The pain is beginning to focus my unease into anger. I hate seeming weak in front of her and hate even more that I care.

"How's it look, Doc?" Sarcasm seeps into my words. I am coming apart, overwhelmed by too many conflicting feelings and unable to handle them. I feel like I am under attack, and even though the attack comes from within, I lash out.

"It's not too bad," she says, either missing or choosing to ignore the bite in my tone. "You've had that about four or five days, right?"

I nod, trying to keep myself in check. In a few minutes she will leave, and I will close the curtains and sink into the darkness of my little room. I just need to hold on.

"Seems about right. It's not as deep as I first though, but it's definitely infected, pretty seriously. I'm going to have to see about getting you some antibiotics. My guess is you've been feeling a bit run down the last day or so, maybe a little fever?"

I don't answer her. It annoys me that she knows so much. I don't want her knowing all this stuff about me.

"And we'll need to clean the wound at least twice a day," she says, ignoring the fact that I am ignoring her.

"You volunteering?" I ask with a smirk that borders on a leer. My only defense is to attack, and I am desperate to protect myself.

"Me or someone else," she says evenly, a certain wariness entering her voice. She crosses her arms across her chest. "Whoever's around."

The room begins to close in on me. The air turns to soup in my lungs. I am drowning in a sea of my own making. I must make her go.

"You know, if you wanted my shirt off, all you had to do was ask. You didn't need to invent an excuse to get me naked, sweetheart."

I am acting like the oversexed man-child I used to see on my lunch breaks, belching obscenities and catcalls at women as they walked down the street. I am not this person, this foolish coward who would create a façade and use it to make someone hate me, so I can tell myself it isn't me she hates at all. Except I am exactly this person.

The old me would have just asked her to leave so I could be alone in my discomfort. The old me would have never been uncomfortable in the first place. But that me, apparently, died somewhere on the road to Indiana.

I wait for some kind of reaction, but Kate's face remains neutral. She stands there, and I can't read anything in her eyes that will tell me precisely how disgusted she is.

Finally, without a word or a change in her expression, she turns and walks over to the door. I can't stop my gaze from dropping to the ground or my head from shaking back and forth at what an asshole I am.

I expect to hear the door. I don't expect to hear her voice.

"You know, for the record, you're not naked."

She is leaning against the doorframe, her right thumb casually wrapped around a belt loop. I try to grasp what is happening but come up empty. She was supposed to have fled the room. She was supposed to hate me. She is not supposed to be doing whatever it is she's doing.

"And by the way," she says, her lips sliding into a grin that would have left my knees quivering if I wasn't completely bumfuzzled, "the next time I want your shirt off, I won't have to ask."

And she *really* wasn't supposed to say that.

"Dinner's in an hour."

With that she is gone, and I am left alone to wonder how she turned the tables on me, and why.

CHAPTER SEVEN

Duncan stood outside Taylor's door, his hands shoved deep into the pockets of his most presentable pair of jeans. He had been standing there for quite a few minutes, not really sure what to do next.

He still was unclear as to why Buck had asked him, of all people, to go and fetch Taylor for supper. Not that Duncan minded the chore. Not that it was even a chore, really. It was just that he had not even actually met Taylor yet, not officially, but he was supposed to knock on her door and say...what? "Hi, you don't know me, but Buck sent me to pick you up for dinner?"

Duncan figured he would be lucky if she did not deck him.

Well, maybe he did not really think she would deck him, although he had a strong sense that she could and totally would if properly motivated. After thinking about it for a second, Duncan decided that maybe it really was as simple as telling her Buck had sent him. As for why Buck had picked Duncan, it was not like Buck did not randomly assign duties to everyone, so Duncan supposed it was not really all that unusual. Still...

Oh, quit your chicken-shitting and knock on the damn door already.

And so he knocked.

And he waited.

Nothing. Not even the shuffle of a foot or the squeak of a bedspring.

He knocked again.

And he waited. Again.

Still nothing.

"You looking for something?"

Duncan jumped. Behind him stood Taylor, arms folded across her chest, towel slung across her shoulder, resting up against the wall.

"Shit, you scared me," Duncan said, cursing himself again, this time for cursing.

If the guys could see me now, they'd be laughing at me for sure.

Taylor cocked her head to the side like a dog studying a stranger.

"I'm Taylor," she said finally.

"Duncan," he said, reaching out his hand and gripping hers in return. She shook firmly but not too forcefully. Duncan liked a firm handshake. It reminded him of his daddy. "But you can call me Dunk."

Shit. Now why'd you go and tell her that dumb-ass nickname? She's gonna think you're some stupid kid.

"A lot of people call you that?" she asked, letting go of his hand. There was no hint of mockery in her tone, just curiosity.

"A few," he said as she stepped around him and let herself into her room. "Mostly my parents growing up. My mom thought it was cute, I guess."

She nodded thoughtfully, setting her towel down on the bed.

"I always thought it was kind of stupid," he added, wanting to say it before she could.

"Then why do you use it?" she asked. "If you think it's kind of stupid?"

He thought it over.

"Honestly, I don't know," he said finally. "I guess it's just what I know. Who I am. You know?"

"Well, if it's who you are, then it seems like you should be proud of it."

Duncan thought about that, too. He just did not know how to respond.

"What can I do for you?" Taylor asked, changing the subject. She turned her back on him and started shuffling through the backpack on the bed. Although her voice gave away nothing, Duncan thought he detected discomfort, a certain stiffness in her shoulders that betrayed her seeming nonchalance.

"Uh, well, you see we were all having dinner, and Buck noticed you weren't there, so he sent me to come and get you."

"I thought I'd skip it, thanks," she said, her voice a bit more quiet than it had been. She continued riffling through her bag, and it seemed to Duncan she was not quite looking for something in a fairly obvious attempt to seem occupied, and he wondered why. He knew, though, that asking her outright was not going to get him anywhere he wanted to go.

"Well, you sure are missing out," he said in his most enthusiastic voice. "Tonight we've got barbecue with all the fixings, like potatoes and biscuits and—"

"I get it. There's a lot of food," Taylor said. Duncan thought he heard the faintest hint of a chuckle in her voice. At least, he hoped that was what he was hearing. He pressed on.

"Definitely lots of food, or at least what passes for *lots* these days. One of the benefits of living on a farm, and Franny—that's our resident cook—makes a pretty good meal. She must know fifty things to do with corn. We're usually a little short on meat, which kind of sucks. A lot of the guys are always complaining about that, but Buck says if we slaughter all the cows and chickens, then we lose the milk and eggs, and those go a lot further than meat. Some of them go out hunting every now and then. Most of the time they don't get much beyond a couple of rabbits or birds, but a couple days ago they managed to bring back a deer, hence tonight's barbecue. And that's not the best part."

He felt a little bit like one of those cheesy game show hosts his momma used to watch sometimes, minus the sleaze factor, but it was working. At least it had gotten her attention. She finally stopped messing with the bag and turned to look at him. He swore he could see interest in her eyes, and was that her stomach he heard rumbling?

"No?"

"Oh no. After we've all finished eating, we clear the tables and put on some music and dance until our feet hurt!"

"Sounds very…aerobic," Taylor said, a hint of sarcasm lacing her words. Whether it was a reaction to what he had described or how he had described it, Duncan was not sure, but he knew what it meant. He was losing her, and although he did not know why, he felt compelled to get her to agree to come to the barn.

"No, it's really a lot of fun. Sometimes Buck pulls out his guitar and jams with a few of the other guys, some really great bluegrass stuff."

Something flashed across Taylor's face, but as quickly as it had come it was gone. She turned back to digging in her bag.

"Look, it sounds nice and all, but—"

"It's really not as dumb as it sounds," he rushed on. "I mean, everyone needs a break, right—"

"Duncan—"

"And the food's really good, and everyone's laughing and happy—"

"Duncan—"

"And I can tell you don't really like bluegrass, but there's other kinds of music too and—"

"Duncan—"

"And sometimes Kate sings and you should really come."

Taylor stopped interrupting. Duncan drew in a deep breath, unsure of what her reaction meant. Taylor spoke quietly.

"Kate sings?"

"Yeah," he said excitedly. "She's got a voice like an angel. It's really something." He looked at her curiously, then added, "You know Kate?"

"We've met," she said simply. Taylor looked down at herself, then back up at Duncan. "Am I dressed okay?"

She almost sounded like a kid, Duncan thought.

"Yeah, you're fine. It's all pretty informal," he said, ignoring the fact that he had specifically chosen his nicest jeans and shirt for the evening. He did not want her to feel bad.

Taylor smiled awkwardly, like it had been a long time since she had smiled, so long that she might have almost forgotten how. He filed it away in the growing catalog of things he wondered about Taylor.

"Okay, then," she said, slapping Duncan on the back and opening the door. "Lead on, Dunk."

Duncan smiled. He liked the way she said his name.

Chapter Eight

I should get my head examined. If shrinks were as plentiful now as they had been before the plague, I think I would take the time to seek one out. But just like the poets, the plague seems to have taken all the shrinks. And the soldiers. And the writers and cops and astronomers and clowns. I miss the clowns. Has there ever been a time when we were more in need of clowns? Truth is, I'm sure some of the people who used to fill those roles survived—the plague didn't discriminate based on profession, only by gender. But somehow, I doubt clowns had the skill set or fortitude for survival. Then again, maybe dealing with snotty-faced, screaming children every day gave clowns exactly the survival skills needed to live in a post-plague world.

Last I heard, nearly five billion people are dead. Governments have collapsed, electricity and water are gone, unless you are lucky enough—or smart enough—to have found another way. Buck is one of those people. Between the solar panels and the well that taps into the natural spring beneath the eastern edge of the property, the farm is much better off than so many other places I've been.

Which brings me back to the current state of my sanity. The simple fact that I haven't had a hot meal in weeks should have been enough to quell any other voice in my head. The promise of food other than whatever canned goods I managed to pilfer from abandoned houses or the more-helpful-than-harmful survivors I've sometimes crossed paths with should have made my choice clear.

And yet, before Dunk had shown up, I'd made some half-assed decision to avoid dinner.

I follow Dunk to the mess hall, claim my heaping plate of food, and soothe the rumbling that has been shaking my belly for what seems like forever. I ignore the stares I can feel burning into my skin, choosing instead to keep my head low and focus on what is mine. I stay in my corner with Dunk, responding to his well-meaning attempts at small talk with a well-placed nod or grunt here and there. It isn't as if he is annoying me, or even like I don't appreciate his trying to engage. Truth is, I like the kid, have since I first saw him standing nervously in front of my door, obviously trying to work up the courage to knock.

With nothing left to stare at but an empty plate, I survey my surroundings for the first time. It is a building pretty much like the dorm, albeit without the hallway of doors with those stylish-yet-functional numbers scrawled on them. Folding tables and their accompanying chairs take up one side of the room, set up in a pattern that looks more restaurant than makeshift mess. Red plastic tablecloths that are worn but still serviceable cover every surface, lending an almost festive touch to the room. A couple of eight-foot long, slightly sturdier folding tables serve as a buffet on one of the side walls.

A lot of floor space is left unused in the middle and other side of the room, which makes no sense to me. The far side of the building is not completely barren, however. What is clearly a stage takes up a good chunk of the emptiness.

"So, what do you think?"

Something in Dunk's voice cuts through my mental wandering.

"Um, about what?" I ask absently.

"Was I right, or was I right?" he says. Seeing my confusion, he adds, "About the food?"

"Oh yeah. The food. Best meal I've had in a while."

Dunk's smile has enough wattage to light up the room for a week.

"Now what?"

Dunk's smile brightens further, to the point I am wishing for sunglasses. "Now we party."

Right on cue, the room plunges into darkness, only to be relit a few seconds later. The surprise, however, is that instead of the low-slung, manufacturing-complex fluorescent lights that had been our source of illumination, the room is now aglow in reds and blues and oranges and greens. Multicolored string lights, which I had not previously noticed strung from rafter to rafter, light up the room like Christmas Eve. A few people fill in the dark spots with strategically placed candles, which cast dancing shadows along the walls.

The warmth of memory spreads through me, the kind that comes from a special song or a mental picture long forgotten by your head but still remembered in your heart. Flashes of childhood race along, of Christmas mornings under the tree and cocoa after an afternoon of sledding.

I haven't thought of such things in a long time. I revel in it even as it suffocates me.

The urge to run is overwhelming, and it is all I can do to not jump to my feet and break for the door, to grab my bag and Mugsy and leave this place far, far behind. I have rarely, if ever, felt such panic in the absence of physical violence. That in itself only unnerves me further.

Out of the corner of my eye, I see Dunk sitting there, watching me. He holds only concern in his gaze, and surprisingly, it calms me.

"You okay?" he asks quietly after a moment, as if he doesn't want to draw anyone's attention to my current state of distress. For that, I am grateful.

"Yeah. It's just, um…" I have no idea what to say.

"No worries," Dunk says, shaking his head. "No worries at all."

The first strains of an upbeat 1940s-style dance number float through the air, streaming out of the rather large boom box up near the stage. Immediately, all the kids, who up until now had been sitting in their chairs with swinging legs and fidgeting hands, come running out into the middle of the room, throwing themselves about in time to the music. They are soon followed by the adults, some of whom do fairly good impressions of swing dancers. The rest of the farm's residents gather into smaller clusters on the outskirts of the makeshift dance floor, talking and laughing and watching the dancers do their thing.

I do a quick head count to find that nearly every single person who lives at the farm is in the mess hall. The plague's wrath toward the women of the world is apparent in that moment, as I note only nine females, not including myself, a far cry from the more than thirty males in the room.

Beside me, Dunk rocks on his heels, seemingly caught between wanting to go out and join the others and not wanting to abandon me. Dunk is the honorable kind, it seems. He notices me watching him, and he looks up at me hopefully.

"You wanna dance?" he asks, pitiful as a puppy.

"No, thanks." He is crestfallen. I throw him a bone. "I'm not really much of a dancer."

"Me neither," he covers. "There's only one girl here who doesn't get mad when I step on her toes. But I haven't seen—Kate!"

In the split second it takes for Dunk's mild misery to turn to jubilation, my head snaps around to find the one person I have been dreading and hoping I'd see. She is near the door, chatting with a man and woman I haven't yet met, smiling and laughing. She apparently hears Dunk's somewhat high-pitched squeal of her name, because she turns toward us. Her smile brightens as it falls upon Dunk, and she heads in our direction.

"Hey there, Duncan," she says, wrapping her arms around the boy's shoulders in a warm hug. "I haven't seen you all day."

"Yeah, been busy with the wall," Dunk responds.

"No wonder I haven't seen you. That's definitely a man-sized day of work."

"Yeah," he says, standing up just a little taller, smiling broadly. It is clear how much Kate's opinion means to Dunk, and how fond she is of the boy. They could be brother and sister for the affection they share.

"Taylor," she says with a nod in my direction. Her voice is smooth and rich, and I swear it is slightly deeper than it had been a few seconds earlier.

"Hello, Kate."

I want to apologize for my earlier behavior, but I don't know how. I lost the fine art of the apology long ago.

"Is my favorite dance partner ready to hit the floor with me?" Kate asks Dunk, turning her attention back to him.

"Absolutely," he says. He bows and extends his hand out to her. "If Taylor doesn't mind?"

Kate and Dunk both turn back to me, awaiting my response. While his face is earnest and unassuming, Kate's eyebrow lifts in that way of hers, challenging me, though to what I'm not quite sure. My brain can't handle the possibility.

"Yeah, sure. I'll be fine over here. You guys have fun."

Once again, Dunk's face lights up. Kate smiles as well, although I think I sense the faintest glimmer of disappointment. She covers quickly, taking Dunk's hand and leading him out onto the dance floor.

I watch Dunk swing Kate around merrily to the music, watch Kate drop her head back and let out a throaty laugh, watch the two of them enjoy the night and each other's company. I can't tear my eyes away from them, but especially not from her. There is something so innocent in the way she moves, so unbound by the gravity of the world's destruction, I find myself longing for such weightlessness.

"You having a good time?"

Buck steps up beside me, sipping soda out of a red plastic cup.

"Yes, sir," I say. "The food was excellent."

"I'll be sure to let Franny know. That's my other daughter. You met Margie earlier."

I remember.

"Franny is sort of the head chef around here, though she gets mad when I call her that," he says. "She's got some skill, though, I tell you. Mrs. Sapple, too. She does more of the baking."

Once again, I am engaging in unplanned conversation, despite myself. I can't understand this sudden inability to control my mouth.

"Is that the Mrs. Sapple who forced you all to number the doors?"

"Ah, you heard about that, did you? I don't think Tony's ever been the same."

We lapse into a comfortable silence, just standing there watching folks dance. The party has picked up a bit, with most everyone now out on the dance floor. My eyes once again fall upon Kate, who is still twirling around the room with Dunk. I find myself smiling. I glance over at Buck, who is smiling, too. A warm blanket of contentment washes over me, and I fight the urge to shake it off, choosing to just let myself be, just this once.

The music slows, an old Frank Sinatra tune that begs to be slow danced to coming over the speakers. Kate slides easily into Dunk's arms, and while he keeps a respectful distance, I can't help but feel a twinge of jealousy. Kate looks my way and catches me watching her. Shame creeps up my cheeks, and I feel the intense need to look away, yet I fight that need and keep my eyes locked with hers.

Eventually, Dunk turns and the moment passes. I sneak a glance over to Buck, hoping he missed the whole thing. If he had noticed anything, he doesn't mention it, although for a second I think I see him grin just a little.

That's when I notice them. The three men who had set off alarm bells in my head earlier in the day. They are off in the corner near the stage, surveying the scene. The man I presume to be the leader takes a long pull off his beer bottle, his eyes never stopping their scan of the crowd.

I watch them watch everyone else, flicking from one dancing body to another. They are a pack of wolves silently stalking their unsuspecting prey, sniffing the herd for the weakest one to pick off and devour.

Endless minutes pass with Buck at my side. As one song bleeds into another, the farm's residents—oblivious to the danger I am sure exists—enjoy the night.

I know it all sounds melodramatic, like some movie-of-the-week where the heroine senses the shiftless drifter is up to no good long before the town does, except I am no Valerie Bertinelli. No, here in this barn, *I* am definitely the shiftless drifter. I'm sure I'm overreacting, positive I'm delusional, convinced the intuition I paid too high a price to develop is malfunctioning somehow.

Except I know better.

Still, I try to tell myself it doesn't matter. It is not my concern. Rule Number Three. Yet I keep watching them, every sense I have telling me these three men mean pain.

I notice the leader, who in my sleep-addled brain I have decided to call Sergeant Ratched, has stopped scanning the crowd. He has found his target. He holds out his beer to his comrade on the right, who takes it without a word. I follow Sergeant Ratched's line of sight, which never wavers, across the room. I feel like I'm going to throw up every last bite of dinner. He is staring squarely at Kate.

I stand frozen, my body failing to respond to the *move!* signal my brain is frantically tapping out. I watch Sergeant Ratched take one step, then another, his feet and legs working up to a purposeful stride as he closes in. In an instant, he is upon her, standing ramrod straight next to a still-dancing Kate and Dunk. He says nothing, as if he expects his mere presence at their side will be—should be— enough to demand Kate's attention.

Except it isn't, and it doesn't. From the way she and Dunk keep moving and laughing, it isn't even clear she has noticed the tree trunk of a man staring intently at her from less than a foot away. Or maybe she just doesn't give a damn. If I wasn't focused on the way his eyes narrow the longer he is ignored, I would smile.

His hand is like a sniper's bullet as it shoots out and grabs Dunk's shoulder, spinning him around and away from Kate. Dunk, startled, is still recovering from his sudden forced pirouette as Sergeant Ratched steps between him and Kate. I can't see her face, but I can read the tension in her back. The interruption is unwelcome.

From across the room and over the music, I can't hear a damn thing he says to her, and I am no good at reading lips. Likewise, I can't hear Kate's reply, but the way she crosses her arms and cocks her hip, as well as the grin that appears on Dunk's face from over Sergeant Ratched's shoulder, tells me all I need to know about her response. Equally telling is the snarl that grossly curls Sergeant Ratched's lips as he reaches menacingly for Kate.

Without thought, I step forward, my feet no longer encased in a block of ice. My fists are ready weapons. Only Buck's hand firmly planted on my arm, which hadn't been there a second before, keeps me from charging across the dance floor. I look back at Buck, his steely eyes focused on Kate, Dunk, and Sergeant Ratched.

"Wait," he says, his voice even and calm even as his grip on my arm tightens. "Just wait."

I want to rip my arm away from him and rush in, all fists and fury. Instead, I find myself doing as asked, not knowing why but knowing enough to know I should.

Back on the dance floor, in the few seconds Buck had stolen my attention, the residents of Burninghead Farm have stopped dancing long enough to gather around the unfolding drama. Dunk has managed to step between Kate and Sergeant Ratched in a noble, if ill-matched, attempt to defend her. As Dunk does his best to stand toe-to-toe with him, the other two members of the pack arrive to back up their alpha dog. They look all too eager to drag Dunk outside and give him a thorough ass-kicking. As if reading my mind, Sergeant Ratched gives the slightest of nods toward Dunk, and the two pit bulls advance on the outnumbered boy.

Once again I surge forward, only to be stopped by Kate. She has put herself squarely between Dunk and the two advancing men, and my breath catches. I don't even realize the music has disappeared until I hear Kate's voice fill the room.

"Look, Zeke," she says, her voice steady and sure. "I've told you before, I'm simply not interested in you that way."

"But you're interested in him? This runt?" the man I now know to be Zeke responds, his voice rumbling out of his chest, dripping with disdain.

"It's nothing personal." She keeps her tone calm and gentle, like she genuinely doesn't want to hurt his feelings. "I'm sure you're a very nice person."

"No, he's not your type either, is he?" Zeke asks, snorting as he picks up right where he left off. Kate's well-intentioned words have fallen on deaf ears.

"Why don't we just forget about this whole thing? Go back to enjoying the party?" Kate offers, making one last attempt to defuse the situation. But Zeke will have none of it. He is determined to be a fuckhead.

"He's certainly scrawny enough—*girly* enough—to be your type," Zeke hisses.

"That's enough, Zeke. I've tried being nice—"

"Maybe that's the problem. He's not man enough for you," Zeke interrupts, leering at Kate as he rakes his eyes down her body, lingering far too long on places it is clear he is not welcome to look.

I feel shame, uncomfortably reminded by Zeke's actions of my own actions earlier that day. Except whereas I hadn't meant a single word, Zeke means every one. Not that it makes me feel any better.

I am sure Kate's skin is crawling. Hell, mine is crawling for her. But she doesn't let it show. She refuses to give Zeke the satisfaction.

"What you need," he says, grinning perversely as he leans in to Kate's body, "is a real man. One that'll show you exactly what a woman like you should be wanting from a...*partner*."

"And you're just the man to show me what I've been missing? Is that right, Zeke? You going to show me how to walk the straight and narrow?"

"That's right," Zeke says triumphantly, as if he really thinks Kate is buying into his crap.

"Hmm, I see."

Kate's hand comes up to her chin, the classic thinker's pose, as if she is mulling over Zeke's disgusting offer. Confusion crosses some of the faces in the crowd. Others, like Dunk, are grinning, as if they know something the rest of us don't.

"And what is it, exactly, you think you can show me?" Kate asks, both hands falling to her hips, annoyance and outrage flashing over. "How to be a conceited prick? How a big, strong hunk like you treats a woman like a possession just so he can feel like a man? How I should want to spend my life following you around, picking up after you, cleaning for you, cooking your meals and washing the skid marks out of your underwear and not speaking unless spoken to and making doe eyes at you while being sure to walk at least five paces behind you at all times? And I'm sure you have lots of ideas about how I should service you in bed, right? Tell you what, why don't you drag me back to your room right now and teach me about being unfulfilled in the missionary position? Unless you just want to fuck me right here? But no, you wouldn't want that, because in the three seconds you lasted everyone would know what a teeny, tiny, insignificant little dick you have, isn't that right?"

No one says a word as rage works across Zeke's face. Even his lackeys are left speechless, their mouths agape at the way Kate has dared stand up to him. I swear I can hear Zeke's heart pounding an angry rhythm in the silence. Or maybe it is just my own heart going into overdrive.

Zeke's anger explodes. Like a coiled snake, he strikes, his thick hands reaching for Kate. She doesn't move, doesn't even flinch, standing her ground with steely nerve. I pull forward, feeling Buck's grip give way as he steps in stride, knowing I won't get there in time to prevent whatever happens next.

The group that had formed around Kate, Dunk, and Zeke moves forward as if with a single consciousness, the surging movement halting Zeke and forcing his two comrades backward. The crowd moves behind Kate in an unmistakably protective gesture that leaves no doubt whose side it is on. Dunk, too, moves in, placing his body next to, but not in front of, Kate's. Clearly this is Kate's show.

Zeke's eyes dart around the room. He is now outnumbered, and he knows it. His jaw sets in renewed rage, and I wonder if he is angrier that Kate rejected him, that she embarrassed him, or that everyone else has turned against him. Zeke turns tail and storms out of the barn, his two disciples following closely on his heels.

As the men flee the room, so does the tension. Kate smiles gratefully at her friends, sharing hugs and laughter with some, while Dunk enjoys several hearty handshakes and a few solid pats on the back.

I watch it all unfold, my fists at last unclenching as I blow the remaining stress out of my lungs. Buck walks into the crowd, squeezing a shoulder here and patting a back there. It is as if Buck is a boat gliding across the water, leaving only a gently rocking tranquility in his wake. I can feel the air calming around me, the thickness of fear dissolving like molasses in the hot sun. It only makes me angry all over again.

"Bet this wasn't the kind of entertainment you were expecting tonight," Kate jokes dryly. I had not noticed her approach. I don't respond, too busy trying to rein in the images that have started exploding in my head.

"Taylor?" she asks, her voice softening with concern. I do not look at her. Instead, I try to concentrate on my breathing, on the simple act of inhaling and exhaling which suddenly seems so impossible, like trying to breathe through a straw at 20,000 feet. Images flash in rapid succession, of bruises and blood and tears and pain and fear so real I start shaking.

She places her hand on my arm, and it is enough to break me.

"What in the hell were you thinking, mouthing off to him like that!" I shout.

Kate takes a slight step back, startled by the venom in my voice. Confusion flickers across her face, but it is quickly replaced by understanding. She almost smiles.

"I'm fine," she says, squeezing my arm. "It's all fine."

"What do you mean, *It's all fine*?" I seethe. "That sonofabitch nearly—"

"But he didn't," Kate says, her serenity only enraging me further.

"But he could have—"

"But he didn't," she says, enunciating each word with infuriating precision. I start to repeat my point. In my mind, it is the only point that matters. Kate fixes her gaze on me as if she is willing me to calm down, willing me to concede the point. That pisses me off even more.

"People don't always need rescuing, Taylor."

Those words ignite a firestorm in my mind. I see her lying on the floor, gasping for air. I see Dunk being dragged outside, moaning in the grass while they beat him. Bodies lying broken, women cowering in corners, my bloody reflection in the water, Kate being dragged out of the stall next to mine, screaming…

I am losing my grip, unable to distinguish between reality and memory.

"I could have helped you."

"But you didn't need to—"

"I should have helped you."

"But, Taylor—"

"I should have saved you!" I scream, the desperation in my voice startling me, just as it does everyone else. I can feel the room's gaze upon me, feel the weight pressing down, but I can't meet their eyes. I am in it now, caught up in a past more real than anything in this room.

"Oh, Taylor."

Kate's voice has a quality about it, like walking across hallowed ground, that means she knows. The details don't matter. She knows just the same.

Damn it. Damn it all to hell.

CHAPTER NINE

D uncan stepped up next to Buck, his attention drawn by the shouting. He was not the only one. What had been a spontaneous celebration of their courage had quickly faded, leaving a silent crowd to witness whatever drama was unfolding now.

"Buck?" Duncan asked apprehensively, unsure not only of what was happening between Kate and Taylor, but also about what they should do about it.

Buck stayed silent, his only acknowledgment a swift shake of his head. His eyes were riveted on the new battle being waged on the far side of the barn. He stepped forward, his face drawn with concern. Buck's reaction only unnerved Duncan more.

"I should have saved you!"

Taylor's face was a mask of horror and ashes, her voice strangled and hollow. Her eyes were wild, searching the ground around her, the roof, the walls...for refuge or escape, Duncan was not sure. Taylor was a spooked mare, full of terror and power. Duncan just wished he understood why.

While Taylor's eyes were full of fear, Kate's were brimming with compassion. Duncan saw Kate's lips move but could not make out the words. Whatever she said, though, had an effect. Taylor was backpedaling, turning and stumbling and diving for the door, like she could not get away from Kate fast enough. The heavy wooden door banged shut behind her, plunging the room into an eerie silence that overshadowed the Norah Jones tune flowing from the speakers.

"Buck?" Duncan requested again, still unsure, still uneasy.

Buck said nothing as he started to move, and Duncan followed. They went to Kate, who was still staring at the door after Taylor.

"What happened?" Buck asked, looking back and forth between Kate and the door.

"She has a lot of pain," Kate said after a long moment, turning to face Buck and Duncan.

Buck nodded. A look passed between Kate and Buck, one Duncan could not know but which told him they understood. Duncan, however, was still confused.

"Yeah, but what happened?"

The question was directed at Kate, who looked like she did not want to answer. Buck stepped in.

"It doesn't matter, Duncan."

Duncan did not like the direction this was heading. Had he not just proven himself? And now here they were, Kate and Buck, cutting him off like he was some little boy asking for more ice cream.

"What?" Duncan asked incredulously. "Of course it matters."

"Duncan," Buck said warningly.

"Stop treating me like a kid," he said, his ire rising. "If Taylor's going to be part of this farm—"

"She's not."

That caught Duncan off guard, although whether it was the idea that Taylor would not be staying or the flatness of Kate's tone, he was not sure.

"She's not staying," Kate said to both of them. She seemed sad, but resolved.

"Did she say that?" Buck asked quietly. He seemed sad, too.

"No."

"Then how do you know?" Duncan asked angrily. "Are you reading minds now?"

Buck did not give Kate a chance to answer.

"I know you like her, Duncan," Buck said, placing a firm hand on Duncan's shoulder. Duncan wanted to shrug it off, but he refrained. He knew he was being a brat, living down to the expectations people seemed to have of him. "So do I. But I guess she's got some…things to work through. And I don't know that she can do that here."

"What if we helped her?" Duncan asked, unable to keep the childlike hope from creeping into his voice. Taylor was the first person besides Kate that treated him like an actual person, even if she was a bit standoffish. He glanced over at Kate, noticing the hopeful glow in her eyes.

Guess I'm not the only one who wants her to stay.

He could not help but feel just a little bit jealous.

"It's not our decision to make."

Duncan thought he detected just a bit less conviction in the older man's voice. He decided to push his advantage.

"You're always telling us we have to be there for each other, support each other."

Buck seemed to be considering Duncan's words, and the hint of a smile on Buck's lips told Duncan he was on the right track. He swore he could feel Kate willing him to continue, to succeed.

"Why is it any different with Taylor? Because she's new here? Because maybe she's had a hard time? Seems to me that should mean we make more of an effort, not less."

Duncan felt the pride coming off Buck before he saw it on his face. Kate smiled at him, and Duncan knew he had done right. Just like before with Zeke. It felt good. It made him feel like a man.

"Okay, Duncan. We'll try," he said, squeezing Duncan's shoulder. "But I can't guarantee she'll want our help."

Duncan nodded happily, Kate's smile and Buck's fatherly grin warming him.

"Now," Buck said, eyeing both Kate and Duncan closely, "are you both okay? Nobody's hurt, right?"

It took Duncan a second to register the change in tone and topic.

"We're fine," Kate said reassuringly. "Nothing we couldn't handle. Though I'm sorry—"

"No. No apologies. Not from either of you," Buck said firmly. "Zeke was out of line. It won't happen again."

It was Kate's turn to squeeze Buck's shoulder, telling him it was okay. Duncan nodded his agreement. Zeke had been a bastard since Duncan had arrived on the farm. He and his pals, Billy and Dean, had been there since the beginning, having worked for Buck before the plague. They were therefore close to indispensable to Buck, knowing the farm nearly as well as he did.

They were hard workers and hard drinkers, with hard tempers and hard ideas about what the world owed them. Duncan had heard them grumble about it often enough. But for months they had been getting worse. They barely tolerated anyone, instilling fear through intimidation. They made up their own work detail, never shared a table at meals, slept in the lofts of the main barn instead of the dorm…which was just fine with Duncan. Still, when they were around, the air seemed thicker somehow, more menacing. Duncan heard their half-whispered comments about him, and about others, always insults designed to keep people in their place. Duncan never took the bait, although he always felt a little bit worse about himself for it. But it was the smart thing to do, the right thing to do, to keep the peace.

But tonight that had all changed. Zeke had crossed a line, and he had crossed it with Kate. Everyone knew Zeke had a thing for Kate, that he had since day one. Kate had always rejected him, as nicely as possible but in no uncertain terms. Everyone on the farm knew Kate was gay, in the way that everyone always seemed to know everyone else's business. Not that it mattered. Buck had made it clear to everyone that all were to be treated equally, that biases and prejudices were the only things not welcome on Burninghead Farm. If Duncan was being honest with himself, at first he had wished Kate was straight, if only because he had a bit of a crush when he first arrived. But he mostly saw Kate as a big sister now, so her being gay did not matter to him all that much. Kate was special, warm and caring in a way that made Duncan feel safe and loved. It did not hurt that she was the most beautiful woman he had ever seen.

Zeke, however, did not see Kate the way Duncan saw her. Zeke seemed to view Kate as a piece of meat, and the fact that she did not want him seemed to make him want her all the more. Duncan thought, though, it was Kate not wanting any man that had pushed Zeke over the edge. Tonight, Zeke had tried to force the issue, by whatever means necessary. But Duncan—and everyone else, it turned out—was not about to let that happen.

"So, Taylor wanted to ride to your rescue?" Buck asked with a touch of a wink.

"Buck," Kate said warningly but without menace, a delicate blush gracing her cheeks. Duncan laughed, as did Buck. Kate's raised eyebrow put an end to both men's folly.

The three of them relaxed, watching the party resume its previous swing, enjoying the reality that they were alive, healthy, and for the most part, happy.

CHAPTER TEN

I don't remember leaving the barn, or getting back to room 39, or sinking into the bed. I'm sure I ran, though I hope I waited until I'd gotten out the door to flee in earnest. All I know is I now find myself staring at the moon through the window above my bed, not sure whether the patterns of light filtering in are caused by leaves from the tree outside or the dirt smudged across a wide swath of the glass. I just pray no one follows me. Not that I pray anymore.

When I was a kid, I went to Catholic school. It wasn't like my folks were super religious or anything. My mom was Polish Catholic, meaning that her parents were big with church on Sundays and big with the guilt. Up until my dad married my mom, he was Protestant. That's what his dog tags said, anyway, although his mother once told me he was actually raised Baptist.

As I got older, I started to notice my parents never went to church with me. My grandparents—the Polish ones—always took me. One summer day, I decided that I wanted to go outside and play instead of going to church. My mom said no. I asked her why I had to go every week but she didn't. She told me she didn't go to church because she and God didn't get along too well, and hadn't for a long time. I told her that I didn't get along with God too well, either, and so I shouldn't have to go to church. Seemed like a foolproof plan to me. She smiled at me and said, "Taylor, there is nothing wrong with your relationship with God. Someday there might be, and you can decide for yourself whether you want to keep going to Mass. Until then, you go to church with your grandma and grandpa."

So I went. I didn't really understand her logic—I was still pretty stuck on the whole idea about me having to go even though she didn't—but she was Mom and, therefore, she was right. I went to church and I kept going. Right up until Mom died. I was thirteen. After that, I didn't get along with God too well, either. I decided my presence was no longer required in God's house. My dad agreed.

My issues with God eventually evolved into an issue with all things church-like. For a number of years I considered myself a recovering Catholic, struggling to overcome the church's brainwashing of me during my childhood. Sinners go to Hell. Everyone's a sinner. Everyone's going to Hell, unless of course you do exactly as your friendly neighborhood priest tells you, and you donate at least ten percent of your wages to God. Because God really needed my money.

Whatever problems I had with the church, as an adult I did manage to work on my relationship with God a bit. God still really pissed me off sometimes, and I had no clue what in the hell he was thinking, but I was comforted by the notion that he was there, in my corner, supporting me. I held on to that belief even as the world went fairly literally to Hell and everyone around me started dying.

The first person I knew to get sick was my boss. It was still early then, and we didn't know that the flu that had started to go around was anything more than just another bug. She had been working too hard, was constantly traveling back and forth across the country for meetings, so when she showed up at work one day after a particularly grueling trip, it wasn't a big shock that she was sick. But, trouper that she was, she kept coming in to work. Until one day she didn't. I remember the last e-mail I got from her, joking about how the flu was the best diet ever and how she really didn't mind it so much except that her once-glossy hair was now just a dull, lifeless lump on her head. Two days later, her mom called the office to break the news that she had died.

At first, it was just a few people dying, but within weeks of my boss's death, the death toll was in the hundreds. People started wearing face masks in public, if they came out of their homes at all. Offices started closing, telling their employees to work from home if they were well enough. The federal government ordered all offices closed until what was now being called a pandemic plague had passed. The most powerful city in the most powerful nation in the world became a ghost town.

Somehow, I remained healthy, some kind of natural immunity to the virus. There was no cure. The scientists said it would eventually burn itself out, that we just needed to stay home and wait. But waiting proved impossible. Hundreds of dead turned into thousands. Hospitals were overwhelmed, not only because there were so many patients but because there were hardly any doctors left to treat them. Many of them had gotten sick themselves. The ones who hadn't were home trying to care for their own families. The same was true for the firefighters, the police. The president declared a state of martial law, but it was already too late. There weren't enough soldiers reporting for duty to keep order. Looters ran rampant, stealing everything from baby wipes to televisions on which to watch the horror unfold.

Many people fled the cities, thinking that if they could get out into the country the plague wouldn't find them. They were wrong, of course, but I understood their need to try. I stayed in the city. Everyone I knew had gotten sick by then, colleagues around the city, coworkers from my office, the guys I played pool with on Monday nights. Some had died, and the rest were on their way. I wasn't in a relationship then, having broken up with my last girlfriend two years earlier after catching her in bed with a girl that worked at the coffee shop we went to every morning before work. I suppose I am blessed in that I didn't have to watch someone I was in love with die.

I moved in with my best friend and her husband, mainly because there was safety in numbers. She and I had known each other since college. For a week, the three of us drank wine and played cards and waited for the worst to pass us by. How lucky we were, we thought, that the three of us were immune. Then they got sick, too, and so I stayed to take care of them. I made them soup and wiped the sweat from their brows and emptied their bedpans and read them stories about distant lands and happily ever after. Then they were gone, and I had no reason to remain any longer. I spoke to my parents that night. I could barely hear them over the static, but they begged me to come home. I left the next morning. Three weeks later, a terrorist bomb destroyed what was left of Washington, DC.

But even then, I still believed it would all be okay, that God was still present in the world, that he had not abandoned us. I lost that faith forever on a small farm outside of Pittsburgh.

When I escaped that place I left God behind, along with some good people who didn't deserve what happened to them. Now it is just me and Mugsy against the world, and that's the way I like it. It has kept me alive. It has kept me sane. And now, out of nowhere…

What the fuck are you doing, Taylor?

I slam my fist against the wall beneath the window. In less than twelve hours, I have damn near broken two of the three rules that have saved my life so many times.

Keep to Yourself. Don't Get Involved. Jesus, Taylor, how hard is that?

I've held to those rules for months. Pitiless months of walking and scavenging and surviving, of numbing myself to the bloated bodies and the rotting remains of humanity. Empty months of saying as little as possible, to myself, to others, even to Mugsy, who is the closest thing I have to a friend. Relentless months of keeping moving, of keeping to myself, of not getting involved. The people I meet are just stops along my way, means to accomplish my own personal end. I stay a few days in some places, maybe a week if there's enough food and water to make it worth my while, and then I move on. I don't need anyone, except my family. I don't care about anything, except getting home.

Home.

My whole family lives in Asheville. Dad, stepmom, stepbrother, and stepsister, who I long ago stopped viewing as step-anything. In-laws, niece, nephew…all have great big lives they've built from scratch there, in the place we grew up. I'm the black sheep, the odd woman out who left home to go to college and returned, only to move halfway across the country in an effort to forge some kind of life, something more than I grew up knowing. I moved around, changed jobs, built a career, only to abandon it midstream to go back to school. Through it all, my family supported my choices, accepted my mistakes, and forgave my absences.

In my mind I watch my dad, proud and smiling, cracking jokes at the kitchen table over a cup of coffee and a deck of cards. His whole life he's done for others, spent two-thirds of his life driving an eighteen-wheeler thousands of miles from home, when all he has ever wanted is to be able to see his family every night. My whole life he has loved me, even when he really didn't know me. I know that now. He and I spent a lot of years trying to get to know each other after Mom died, trying to understand each other without anger or defensiveness or recrimination. And when we were finally able to do that, I knew I had the best man I could ever hope to know on my side.

He's what I have spent five months trying to get back to. I owe him that much. Owe him, and the rest of my family. I tell myself they are alive and well and waiting for me, but the truth, the one I have buried beneath layers and layers of lies, is deep in my heart I know they are gone. But the lie sustains me, gives me purpose. The lie is the only thing I have left to live for. The lie is all that matters. Or at least it was. But now…

Now I'm wasting time, breaking the rules, risking everything. For what?

I slam my fist against the wall again, harder this time. I want to scream. I don't know these people. I certainly don't owe them anything. I've been through plenty of places with nice people who needed help way more than anyone here, but I didn't break my rules for any of them. I hadn't even thought about it. I took what I needed, what was offered, and moved on. Like always. That is who I am, who I've become. That is who I need to be. That is how I will get home.

These people don't need me, and I sure as hell don't need them. Then why can't I stop thinking about them? About her?

I turn the previous twelve hours over in my head. What is it that has gotten to me so quickly? What is it that has gotten to me at all?

I swing my legs over the edge of the bed, burying my head in my hands. I am so damn tired. Tired from so many things, not the least of which are these…complications. For the first time in what feels like an eternity, my wall is cracked. Someone has gotten in.

And it isn't just her. It is all of them.

Damn it all to hell.

I spring off the bed, pacing back and forth across the cold, bare floor. I am a tiger in a cage, a mental patient prowling the hallways looking for imaginary exits through steel bars I can't see but can feel tightening around me. Kate is in my head, smiling that sweet little smile, laughing in the sun, talking to me and caring for me and challenging me. I picture myself with her, nestled in the grass watching the children play, relaxed and laughing. Images flare in my mind, of soft words and holding hands and gentle touches and sweet kisses and—

Jesus, Taylor, what are you, a fucking Hallmark commercial? Since when do you want any of this?

I feel the whole damn place crawling under my skin. Dunk and Buck and the kids and even Mrs. Sapple, all making me feel something other than numb.

Just focus on what brought you here. Focus on getting home. That's the only thing that matters. None of these people mean anything.

I stalk back and forth in the moonlit room, hoping the shadows will crawl across the floor and swallow me.

Just do what you always do. Keep moving.

I reach for my backpack, shoving the few possessions I have inside. I grab Mugsy and settle the strap across my chest before the faint light sneaking into the room snaps me back to reality.

It is night, and I am exhausted.

I sink down onto the edge of the bed, my pack slipping out of my hand. I feel every hour of the last five months pressing down on me, trying to drive me into unconsciousness. When was the last time I slept, really? I have never felt safe enough, warm enough, comfortable enough, to let myself go. Not even if it meant an easier road ahead. But tonight I feel the pull of it, the overwhelming need.

With arms of concrete and rubber, I manage to drag Mugsy off my back and myself more fully onto the bed before collapsing down into the soft pillows. I don't remember ever having been this tired. I start to wonder if it has been there all this time, just waiting for an opportunity to sneak in and claim me. I suppose it has. It really has been a long five months. I guess I deserve one night of oblivion.

I will sleep, for once, taking advantage of the opportunity to do so. But in the morning, I will go, and I will not look back. No matter how much I might want to.

As I drift off, I notice a rhythmic tapping at my window. My last thought before I fall unconscious is that Kate was right. It's raining.

Chapter Eleven

The crisp predawn air bites into my skin as I creep along the side of the dorm, Mugsy's comforting weight pressed against my back. I search for signs of anyone who could derail my escape. There are none. In the hazy shadows that fight the dawn's first rays, I am alone.

A chill assaults my skin, last night's rain having chased away the mild air of yesterday. This is the real September making her presence felt, letting me know she is in charge, not me. If she chooses to grace me with her benevolence, I am grateful. If she chooses to rain her wrath down upon me, well, that is her choice. This is her world now, not mine. I am simply a squatter.

I try to ignore the ice forming in my veins as I leave the cover of the two barns and walk the open field toward the footbridge spanning the shallow creek that slices the farm in two. My breath turns to mist as it merges with the morning air, suspended briefly in cotton puffs before dissolving into nothing. I focus on the path before me, on freeing myself of the mess I have gotten myself into. This farm is just a stop along the way home. Nothing here matters. My stepmom's chicken noodle soup, my niece's latest dance routine, my sister's fascination with 1930s gangsters, my dad's hopelessness with anything electronic, those are the things that matter. My determination warms me against the cold.

The farmhouse looms at the top of the hill. I cross the footbridge carefully, hoping the elderly wood won't creak and give me away.

I manage to clear the bridge with little noise, and thank my newly svelte frame for the preservation of my stealthy departure. Fifty pounds ago, that wood would have groaned like a MINI Cooper trying to carry an elephant.

The sun is starting to break over the farm's eastern edge, stealing the cover of night. I quicken my pace. As I near the farmhouse, I know it is the last major hurdle between me and freedom. The house is peacefully dark, every window consumed by a still blackness. Seeing no signs of life, I creep quietly but confidently past the front half of the house.

"Running away so soon?"

Shit.

The morning light has not yet penetrated the recesses of the wraparound porch, and Buck's face is obscured by shadow. His silhouette is clearly visible to me, however, and I curse myself for having been careless. He leans forward in his wicker chair, resting his forearms on his knees as he stares me down. His eyes shine even in the darkness, boring into me.

I straighten up, squaring my shoulders toward him. I'm not about to let him shame me.

"I'm not running. Just getting back to what matters."

Buck comes down the steps, blocking my path. He searches my face, and I fight down a flush of humiliation. We stand that way in silence for quite some time, him refusing to back off, and me refusing to back down. His gaze is unyielding, and I try to match it.

I know I am doing the right thing.

I know.

Finally, he relents. He takes a small step back, sliding his hands into his pockets. I ignore the disappointment he tries to hide.

"If that's what you want, then I guess you should go."

I nod, any words I might say stuck in my throat.

"Might as well at least take some supplies."

Buck turns, heading into the house. I stay where I am, not quite knowing whether I should wait or follow him inside, but lacking the energy to choose either. My indecision becomes its own answer. My feet grow roots in the shallow grass below the porch, and I stare up at the porch, finding solace in the gaps between the wooden slats. Sometimes emptiness is the only safe place you can hide.

I hear the faint clatter and shuffle of Buck working his way through the house, ostensibly gathering things I will need but making no overt haste to complete his task. His delaying tactics might make me laugh, the image of him puttering through the house like some old codger searching for a lightbulb might even make me outright guffaw, if I wasn't in such a hateful mood. Buck, however, isn't what I am hating.

My self-loathing is interrupted by a new sound carried faintly on the breeze that has kicked up without my noticing. I turn to find Zeke and his dog-pound stalking by, packs and duffels slung over their shoulders. They each glare at me as they approach, except for Zeke, whose eyes are trained five feet in front of him.

What should be obvious takes me a few beats to figure out. I can't take my eyes off the set of Zeke's jaw, the muscles twitching there just under the surface as the three men near. I feel the pulse of it in my head, rhythmically pounding a solemn, ferocious song. Somewhere behind me the screen door claps shut, and Buck's boots thump down the aged wood.

He sidles up next to me, silently watching the parade of angry souls. I don't really expect him to explain what is happening, nor do I need him to by now. My addled brain has finally caught up. Buck is sending the boys packing. Last night had been the final straw.

Oh great. Traveling companions. This should be fun.

If they notice my own impending departure, they don't mention it. They don't mention anything at all, a fact for which I am grateful. I just want them to pass without incident, to leave me and Buck and the farm far, far behind. I know it shouldn't matter, but I am relieved they won't be staying on the farm after I leave. Even if that means possibly running into them outside the farm's protective gates.

"Fucking dyke."

Spoke too soon.

Buck tenses beside me, and I feel the answering tension coil in my belly. I really, really hate that word, although I suppose it isn't the word I hate as much as what assholes like these mean by it.

Still, I choose to ignore the slur. What does it matter, anyway? They are leaving, as am I. I feel Buck's gaze upon me. Whether he is waiting for my action or asking me for permission, I don't know. Either way, I give a small shake of my head. It just isn't worth it.

I'm not sure which of the two dogs spewed the words, although I know it didn't come from Zeke. The voice is all wrong. If I had to bet, I would put my money on the shorter of the two, the one with an extra-snide twinkle in his eye just for me. I feel so fucking special.

At least Kate doesn't have to hear this shit anymore.

That thought cheers me, at least a little.

"You boys need anything else?" Buck asks, as if compelled to try and take care of the men even as he banishes them.

Zeke stops, his boys coming to an abrupt halt behind him. His head is slow to turn, but when it does his eyes are full of fire. I can feel flames lick my skin. I have a sudden urge to call for the fire department. Or maybe just make fire-engine noises.

Oh yeah. I'm perfectly sane.

"We're fine." Zeke seethes, staring Buck down.

For the fire in his eyes, his voice is like ice. The contrast shakes me. I can't wait for them to get the hell out of here.

"I'm sorry it had to turn out like this."

Damn it, Buck. Just shut up and let them pass.

I know Buck means well, but all he is doing is stoking the flames. The last person I knew who tried to make peace with the devil paid for it with his life.

Zeke's jaw tightens to the point I think it might explode from the pressure, but he remains silent. His only response is a terse nod. I almost have to give him credit for his self-control. Almost.

"Are you fucking kidding me?" one of the men screeches at Zeke, breaking the implied order of silence.

Zeke turns, glaring at the man, but to no effect. The tall one has decided to join the mutiny.

"We're really just gonna let this shit go down? Let him kick us out over some dyke bitch?"

"That's enough. Zeke, you and your boys best be leaving. Right fucking now."

If Zeke's voice had been ice, Buck's is an Antarctic midnight. From the looks on their faces, I have a feeling they have never, ever, heard the head of Burninghead Farm curse.

Zeke seems less impressed. A barely suppressed rage is brewing, and I wonder if Zeke will be able to control it. Or if he even wants to.

After a moment that verges on extended, Zeke turns back toward the road as if to resume his exit. His brothers follow suit. My exhale of relief is short-lived, however, when Zeke pivots and strides directly up to Buck.

"This is a new world, Buck," he sneers, the words slithering off his tongue like lacerations. "This world belongs to the strong, not the weak. You and your little *family* are never going to make it if you're not prepared to make the hard choices."

"What is that supposed to mean?"

"Look around. The old world is dead. And I say good riddance. There is no room for equivocation, or experimentation, or deviation," Zeke seethes, his venomous gaze now directed at me. I refuse to give in to the chill that sweeps through me. "There's only one way for the new world to survive, and it sure as hell isn't by letting the few women who are left reject their God-given roles."

Something snaps inside. I step forward, invading Zeke's pulpit before my mind officially decides I've had enough. Zeke meets me there, effectively pushing Buck out of the debate.

"What are you gonna do, little girl?" Zeke spits out the words, towering over me with an inhuman glee.

"Come on, Zeke. Just go now. Please."

Zeke ignores Buck's plea, as do I. My blood rages with the memory of death and violation.

"A few months back I met some guys like you, Zeke," I say, my voice a mixture of icy calm and molten will.

I will not back down. I am done with backing down.

"They thought they knew what was best. Especially for the women. Sow the seeds and inherit the earth, right Zeke?"

He doesn't respond verbally, but I see it. He knows exactly what I am talking about. He leans in, his breath heavy on my face.

Heat rises in my cheeks, anger spinning in my head, making me dizzy with its force. But I hold my ground, unwilling to do anything less.

"One day," he breathes, "one day you're going to get exactly what's coming to you."

"Been there, done that, Zeke. But if you want to try, bring it on."

I don't know why Zeke doesn't take a swing at me, but the blow doesn't come. I push for it. Maybe even want it. And he and his friends certainly could take me. Maybe they are afraid of Buck. Maybe they are afraid of what the rest of the farm will do when they find out.

Zeke turns, finally, after I've seen what little is left of my life flash before me at least twice, and storms off down the road that leads away from Burninghead Farm. After a couple of stutter steps, the other two follow.

I watch them go, watch the shadows their retreating forms cast in the early morning sunlight lengthen and fade in the dust, watch their bodies dissolve into a hazy apparition and then disappear altogether.

My breathing slows. At first I think I am just releasing the fuel that was driving the fire beneath my skin. I turn to Buck, whose face is lit up with pride and a little bit of awe. I have to admit, I am pretty proud, myself. I stood up to Zeke, and I feel good. And whole. And extremely nauseated.

And then, the world goes black.

Chapter Twelve

L ight has this way, every now and then, of slipping into your consciousness without revealing where or when it began. It brushes your skin and you feel the weight of it, wrapping you in its warmth. The glow surrounds you, indistinct yet focused, a guiding hand out of the shadows. The last thing you sense, before the light reveals its true identity, is the sudden absence of darkness. And then you know.

I feel it, the light. Holding me. Comforting me. I am self-aware, but only in the vaguest sense. Where there had been cold, there is heat. Where there had been absence, there is presence. Where there had been darkness, there is the light.

My eyes flutter open slowly, adjusting to the change from nothing to something. I blink once, then again, over and over in search of some sort of clarity. Greasy streaks mar my vision, fighting to keep me blind to the light. The remnants of shadow.

The tears come, doing what they do, washing away the last of the darkness. The room around me is bright, white and blue with cheerful daisies peeking out from behind curtains of gold. My arms are heavy, even trapped, and a slight panic sets in before my sluggish brain recognizes my prison for what it is. A blanket. A big, fluffy blue blanket. A big, fluffy blue blanket that was not on my bed last night. And I am surrounded by walls covered in flowers that definitely do not adorn the walls of room 39. Which leaves me with a question, or maybe two.

Who in the hell's bed am I in, and how did I get here?

I try sitting up but quickly discover it is a very bad idea. If the quivering masses of gelatin my arm and leg muscles have become are not a rather obvious clue, the sudden and overwhelming dizziness fairly well confirms it. I am on a rickety old rollercoaster doing nauseating loop de loops, and I need it to stop moving. Right now.

The creak of hinges sounds faintly in my head, but I am too preoccupied with my alcohol-free hangover to care.

"You're awake."

She is a vision gliding into the room, an angel in blue jeans, complete with halo, although that is more likely a remnant of my… collapse? coma? abduction by aliens? than an angelic aureole. She smiles that smile at me, the one that would make me weak in the knees if I wasn't already horizontal. She rounds the bed and comes to rest at my side. Her fingers are cool against my forehead, and my eyes flutter closed involuntarily at the gentleness of her touch.

My mouth is chalky and sour, my throat scratched and burned, and every time I think of speaking my stomach does another round of somersaults. I assume speaking is going to be a bit of a challenge, and decide to go slow.

"What happened?" I scratch out, my voice a tangle of grit and glass. I swallow thickly and try to clear the sediment from my throat. It stings even worse than I thought it would, but I try to ignore it.

"You passed out," she says gently, patting my arm.

"How long?"

"How long were you out?"

I nod. The throbbing in my head from moving is a bit easier to take than the fire in my throat from speaking.

"Two days."

I feel relatively rested, more than I have been in quite some time, and yet weaker than I can ever remember feeling. It's pretty odd, really.

"We were worried about you."

Maybe it is my near delirium, but it seems to me her voice carries a world of emotion, far more than such a simple statement would imply. Her fingers brush my cheek as she searches my face, and I swear I can feel the stroke of her hand against my heart.

The door creaks again. "You're awake." It's Buck this time, though I barely notice. I am too focused on the tilt of her head and how her eyes crinkle at the corners as she locks her gaze with mine.

"Fever's down," she tells Buck. She checks my forehead again, as if she wants to be sure. Then her hand falls away from my face, and I mourn the loss.

"Good, good," he says, stepping up to the bed. He looks down at me kindly. "You had us worried there. That was a nasty infection you had. I wasn't sure you were going to wake up. Kate was though. She took really good care of you."

"You took care of me?" I croak, cursing the vulnerability in my voice. I am just too damn weak to hide my insecurity. I need to know that she cares, need to feel her compassion directed at me and me alone, need to have that something between us wrap itself around me and hold me close.

"She sure did. Barely left your side, as a matter of fact."

She drops her gaze, her cheeks flushing. "It's not a big deal."

"Sure it is," Buck continues, either not noticing her embarrassment or not caring. Hearing the pride in his voice, I figure it is the former. He turns to Kate. "I thought we were going to have to hit you over the head just to force you to get some sleep."

She meets my eyes hesitantly, as if she is afraid I will somehow reject her for having cared. But I don't. How can I? Buck's words are music to my ears, her actions a peaceful quiet in the raging storm.

I curve my lips into the best smile I can manage, which given my state probably resembles a goofy-toothed snarl more than a grin. Still, her face lights up, and I feel as giddy as a schoolgirl at her first high school dance.

Her hand slides along the blanket and slips over mine. I feel each millimeter of progression, a glorious torture against my flesh. Her skin is velvet, soft and warm and heavenly to touch. She searches for confirmation, for acceptance, for desire of this. She is reaching out to me, offering herself in a way I have no right to expect or even want. But I do want. So much.

I edge my fingers out, sliding them between hers, finding a home beneath her palm. She grins shyly even as her eyes sparkle with confidence. The contrast nearly makes my heart stop.

I hear the distant sound of a shuffling foot, followed by a throat being cleared. Clearly, Buck is trying, in his delicate way, to let us know he is still in the room. Kate's expression tells me she caught the not-so-subtle gesture as well.

"So, I guess you'll be staying a little while longer then? No more sneaking off before dawn?"

It is like a blindfold being removed.

Damn.

It all comes rushing back. The plague, my parents, the barn, Zeke, my journey...I'd been so caught up in Kate I'd nearly forgotten.

I'd decided to leave.

I'd been trying to leave.

I need to leave.

Damn it.

I find regret in Buck's expression. He misread things, and he knows it. He thought I'd made a choice, but I hadn't. I'd just forgotten the last one I had made.

I can't look back at Kate. I release her hand, slipping my fingers out of hers as I start to slip my wall back into place. I have a mission. I have someplace to be. I can't...won't...stay.

"Well, I've got things to do. I'm glad you're awake. You should be well enough in a few days."

Her words hang in the air. Our moment is gone, and I wish with everything I have that I could get it back, even as I push it away. I stare down at the blanket covering me, focusing on the worn threads poking out here and there. They are a distraction. A cruel but necessary distraction.

Coward.

I know she is gone before I hear the door close. I can feel her absence in every corner, screaming at me to fix it. A banshee in the silence.

My eyes meet Buck's. He sighs, but I do not see the disappointment I expect to find, only compassion. I am as relieved as I am resentful.

I want him to hate me.

I want him to fix me.

"You should get some rest," he says gently.

"That's all I've been doing for two days, it seems."

"I suppose so."

"What I need is a drink."

My words are full of the venom I hold for myself.

"I think I can accommodate you there. Feel up for a walk?"

CHAPTER THIRTEEN

I'm not sure you could call what I am doing walking. I shuffle, trip, flop, and fluster my way along after Buck as my legs reacquaint themselves with solid ground. We make our way down the hallways and, to my horror, stairs of Buck's home, where I have apparently been since my collapse two days ago. Buck is patient, respecting my need to make it on my own but hovering close enough I know he will catch me if I fall, my pride be damned. I don't tell him how it frustrates me to think of myself lying there, helpless and drooling—in my nightmare-image of my mini-coma, I drooled all over the place—but I don't seem to have to. Buck is no fool, and I am certainly no enigma.

The house is small but comfortable, cozy in an antiquated sort of way. My legs grow more stable as we wander the first floor, but my exhaustion digs in deeper with each step. Buck chatters on about the house, about his daughters, about life before the plague, and quite possibly leprechauns and rainbows for all the attention I am paying him. It's not that I don't want to hear it, or even that I'm not interested. In truth, I kind of am interested, but his words just bounce around in my head, never quite landing in a coherent sentence.

The first floor is quiet, unexpectedly so, although I swear I can hear the faint echoes of family conversation and smell the distinctive aroma of the meatloaf and mashed potatoes of my childhood. Probably just my delirium.

A light breeze slips in through the open screen door, carrying with it the soft clinking of wind chimes from the front porch. Buck leads me through the living room, past walls decorated with children's drawings of Mr. Sun and Mrs. Moon. Priceless artwork, indeed.

"Through there is my office," Buck says, pointing down a short hallway to the left. "We'll get to that in a minute. But first…" He opens the door at the back of the room and ushers me inside.

"—kinds of nastiness coming through." A young man with sandy brown hair waves at Buck and me before turning back to his conversation. "You guys are okay, though. Right?"

"Yeah, we're fine," comes a disembodied voice from the metal box in front of the man. "A little more on guard these days, but fine."

The man presses down on a large button at the front of the microphone on the desk. "Well, you guys be careful."

"Will do. Say hi to Buck and everyone for us. Oh, and would you ask Franny if maybe she could whip up some of them oatmeal raisin cookies of hers?"

"You got it. Talk to you tomorrow. Burninghead Farm out."

"Milton Station out."

With the conversation apparently over, the sandy haired man turns his full attention toward Buck and me.

"They having trouble?" Buck asks.

"Not them. Over in Templeton. Walt heard reports from Midland about some marauders coming through Templeton and causing trouble," he says, frowning.

Buck nods thoughtfully. His concern is palpable.

The sandy haired man looks at me with interest.

"You must be Taylor. I've heard so…well…I've heard about you, anyway."

I bristle. I assume an accusation in his words, but his earnest eyes belay my paranoia. At least for the moment.

"Oh, I'm sorry. Yeah, Emmett, this is Taylor. Taylor, Emmett."

"Pleased to meet you," he says with a friendly nod. He seems sincere enough. I nod back.

"He asking for cookies again?" Buck asks, chuckling.

"Yeah," Emmett says, shaking his head with a laugh. He explains. "Franny's oatmeal cookies are kind of famous around these parts, although Walt's never had 'em. Annie, Walt's wife, can't cook worth a spit, God bless her. But he'd never tell Annie that, no ma'am. I think asking for cookies is Walt's way of letting us know he's had tuna casserole one too many times lately."

Buck chuckles a bit harder, and I can't help but smile.

"We good for the day?"

"Yep. Spoke to Milo at Ferrybrook this morning. All's quiet there."

"Okay, shut her down for the night."

"You got it, boss."

I mutter a quick good-bye to Emmett before following Buck out of the radio room and down the hallway into his office. He ushers me in, pointing me to one of the worn but deliciously comfortable-looking leather chairs near the window. I sink down gratefully into the soft, scarred leather, my limbs groaning their approval. I feel like I've just finished running a marathon only to be dipped in oil and torched by an angry mob.

I think I must have fallen asleep, because the next thing I know I am startled by a strong smell emanating from a short glass of amber liquid Buck is holding under my nose.

"Bourbon?" I ask, taking the glass and tentatively sniffing the contents. I may not be sure what it is, but I know damn well it is going to burn on the way down.

"Close. Irish whiskey. Smarter than bourbon, less pretentious than Scotch."

I down half the glass with an ungraceful gulp. The alcohol splashing the back of my throat makes me wince. I was right. It burns. Soon, though, the sting settles into more of a warm tingle, soothing and not entirely uncomfortable. Still, I decide to sip the rest of my drink.

"Better?"

Buck is watching me. Waiting. He always seems to be waiting for something, especially from me.

I nod. He takes a slow sip of his own drink, holding the liquid in his mouth for a moment before letting it roll down his throat. He settles back into his chair.

We sit that way for a while, sipping in silence. I am wiped out, my body aches, and sitting here snuggled into this leather chair with a half-full glass of whiskey feels like a little piece of heaven.

I glance around the room, taking note of the grandfather clock in the corner, its soft ticking filling the quiet. I see a worn guitar on a stand at the opposite corner of the room. I recognize it immediately, and despite having thought I was beyond such things, my heart speeds up.

"You play?"

"What?" I say, my attention still on the old Martin in the corner. "Oh, I used to. Is that a D-18?"

"Good eye," Buck says approvingly. "You want—"

"No," I say, firmly shaking my head. Just the thought of holding it in my hands is too much. "No."

"It was my father's. He bought it in a little pawn shop after the war. Used to play for my sisters and me every night after supper. He gave it to me on my sixteenth birthday. They made that guitar in 1937, and it still sounds as clear and true as I remember it sounding as a kid."

I am in awe. I have never actually seen a pre-war Martin in person. The wood is dark, the grain deep and rich. The varnish is worn off in broad swaths, and the face is nicked and chipped in a number of places. It reminds me of an old, wild palomino. It is truly a thing of beauty.

"Someone offered to buy it once. Would have given me more money than I knew what to do with. But even in the worst of times, I couldn't bear to part with it."

"Of course," I say knowingly.

"Are you sure?" he says, gesturing toward the guitar.

"Yeah. But thanks."

We lapse back into comfortable silence for a while, each lost in our own thoughts. Eventually, I notice Buck staring out the window to his left.

"Sometimes I watch them play," Buck says, his words slow, deliberate. "I watch them play, so free and easy, and I marvel at their innocence."

"Children are resilient," I say, following his line of sight to the kids playing outside and thinking I understand Buck's point.

"Yes, they are," he responds with a weak smile. "But at some point, don't they get pushed too far? Can't they lose so much they lose that innocence as well?"

The despondency in his words nearly rips the glass from my hand. It seems unnatural, nearly inhuman, coming from him.

"We've all lost too much," I say. He keeps looking out the window, and I keep talking. "But kids…kids always have this way of bouncing back. They always bounce back. Always."

There is a desperation in my voice, and I'm not sure if it is caused by a need to convince Buck that what I am saying is true or to convince myself. I find myself leaning forward in my chair, despite my exhaustion, willing Buck to look at me. If he would only look at me, it would all be okay.

Seconds tick by like eons as I wait. And wait. And wait.

"Always?" he says, almost childlike in his insecurity.

"Always." I am firm in my conviction.

He smiles again, but this time it reaches high enough I am able to relax back into my chair. Later, I will spend hours contemplating Buck's seemingly sudden lack of faith in all that he has built, as well as my own need to restore it. But in this moment, I am content to simply take another sip of my drink.

"Emmett mans the ham radio twice a day, two hours at a time," Buck says after a while. The change in topic has my head spinning again.

"We've got a little network of communities out there, up in Michigan, over in Illinois and Iowa and farther. Each station talks to two others every day at set times. It keeps things organized. Keeps information flowing."

The word *Illinois* echoes in my head. I wonder if Buck knows anything about Asheville, but I decide not to ask. There is nothing they could tell me that I do not already know, even if I pretend not to know it.

"It's been a pretty good system for us. All of us, I think. We can help each other out with supplies and food and such, and warn each other if something bad is coming. That system is the reason we're putting in the wall."

I wonder why Buck is telling me all this, and reject the idea that he is simply making conversation. Buck isn't one to waste words on idle chitchat. With Buck, it is often the unspoken words in between the ones he actually says out loud that make the difference.

"Something bad is coming?" I supply.

"Could be," he says. He looks down into his whiskey like he's reading tea leaves. "My dad fought in World War II. Helped liberate Buchenwald in '45. When I was older, I finally asked him about it. He told me about the camp, about all the people that had been murdered by the Nazis, and about the people his guys saved. Then he said, 'The world is what we make of it, son. It either reflects the worst of us, or the best of us. But we do have some say in the matter.'"

"So is that what you're trying to do? Make the world reflect the best of us?" I ask. I can't help the bit of sarcasm that slips into my question.

"Maybe not the best. But we can make it a bit better."

"The world is full of bastards who get off on inflicting pain. Always has been, always will be."

"Everyone is capable of doing bad things, Taylor. But if we give them the chance to do good, then maybe they'll take it."

"And if they don't take that chance? If they choose instead to try and take what they want by force?"

"Then we fight," Buck says simply. "And we build walls to protect the kind of life we've chosen to make for ourselves."

"And what kind of life is that?"

"Hopefully, a happy one."

"That's a bit hokey," I say, willing my cynicism away. Buck doesn't deserve it. "But I can respect that."

He smiles.

"Still," I continue, unable to help myself, "I don't know if that kind of life is possible anymore."

"I have to believe it's possible."

"Why?"

"Because a world without hope isn't a world I want to live in."

I find myself wanting to believe him. I want to believe his version of the future is possible, that the world can be the way he sees it. But the past and present both scream their warnings at me. Danger is everywhere, from Zeke and the countless others I've met who act just like him, who think they own the whole damned world and everybody left in it. Those men are the reason Buck's future isn't possible. Those men, who plunder and pillage their way across the wasteland of America, who can kill without remorse and who take what they want and leave you broken and bloody on a cold, dirt floor. I find myself growing angry, because of his naïveté or my own hopelessness, I'm not sure.

"Hope is a lie. It's a lie that only causes pain."

I see the disappointment. It is a look I am coming to know well. I polish off my drink.

"What happened to make you so cynical?" he asks, and I can tell he thinks there is a chance I will tell him. He is wrong.

"Life. Death. People like Zeke. Take your pick."

Later, after Buck helps me back upstairs into bed and Margie checks on me to make sure I am comfortable, sleep doesn't come easily. I go back over my conversation with Buck, trying to understand it all. Since arriving on the farm, I have been a mess of contradictions. I know I care too much, know it is only going to bring me pain, and yet I can't help myself. I have found something good, something worth believing in. But I can't allow myself to believe.

I glance over at the pile of clothes stacked on top of the dresser in the corner of the room. They aren't mine, but they have been left for me. Kate brought them over at some point, or so I was told. She didn't come up to the room. She had "other things to attend to," according to Margie. Margie has become my new nursemaid, and I curse myself for noticing the difference. I hadn't even been awake while Kate had taken care of me, but still…I miss her.

I have spent months not letting anyone in. I am damn good at it. And before Burninghead Farm, I hadn't hurt anyone in the course of doing it. I had worn a big Do Not Disturb sign around my neck, and everyone had gotten the message. I came, took what I needed—what was offered—and left. No strings, no regrets, and no pain. I knew where I was headed, knew that was what mattered, and knew it was enough.

And I can tell myself that is still the case, except it isn't.

Not anymore.

I want more. Damn it all to hell, but I need more. And it is going to kill me.

I feel like pacing but know my legs won't carry me. Instead, I just stare at the ceiling, balling the sheets in my fists, praying that sleep will come so I won't have to think about how the defenses I have built inside are crumbling all around me.

CHAPTER FOURTEEN

Morning came early on Burninghead Farm, well before the sun rose over the eastern slope. There was simply too much to do for it to be any different. Duncan supposed it had always been that way here, even before the plague and all the extra mouths to feed. And now...well, now there was just always more work to be done.

Except this morning, it seemed. His crew had finished planting the posts for the wall early the day before and had spent the rest of the day shoring up all the posts with an extra layer of cement, which they needed to let set at least another twelve hours before beginning on the crossbeams. They would have to wait until tomorrow, which left Duncan with only the list of daily jobs to sign up for. It was not that he minded the little jobs. Duncan knew mucking out the stalls or milking the cows or, Lord help him, even cleaning the chicken coop could make him just as sweaty and satisfied as working with a crew on one of the bigger jobs. Still, he would much rather have been working on that wall.

Like most days when Duncan only had smaller chores to keep him occupied, he found himself with more free time than he knew what to do with. Duncan rose early, earlier than the roosters and the sunshine, even earlier than Franny and her breakfast crew. This morning had been no different, and consequently, he had already finished half the horse stalls before Kate had arrived just before dawn. Kate worked the stalls each morning before school started. She did not have to since she had a full time job on the farm, but she did it anyway. She loved horses, had loved them since her momma had read her *Black Beauty* when she was four, or so she had said. Kate went riding as often as she could, usually after school but before dinner, or for longer rides on the weekend. Duncan had been out with her a few times, though he did not have the same passion for it as Kate. He had grown up around horses, but the truth was he was a bit scared of them, with their enormous heads and giant teeth and their tendency to have minds of their own. Of course, Duncan would never admit he was scared. Men were not afraid of such things. They were strong and worked hard and did what was asked of them and defended the people they loved. They were certainly not afraid of horses.

Duncan heard Kate's arrival, heard the soft *hello* as she settled into an easy rhythm beside him. Duncan frowned. Kate had been unusually quiet at dinner the night before, brushing off Duncan's attempts first at conversation, then at discovery. This morning she seemed even more in her head, lost somewhere she apparently did not want to be found. Duncan thought about trying again, but then thought better of it. He figured he knew the cause anyway, and talking to Kate about it was not going to solve anything.

Which was how he found himself leaning back against the steps of Buck's farmhouse later, watching the sun spread its golden glow across the farm. If he was going to find out what was going on with Kate, he needed to seek out what he assumed was the source of her silence.

"Well, good morning."

Duncan turned. Margie stood just inside the screen door, steam rising from the coffee cup clenched in her hand. She blew across the cup's surface before taking a sip.

"Morning, ma'am."

"Don't you *ma'am* me, Duncan," Margie said, frowning. "I'm not that old yet."

"No, ma'—I mean, no Margie," Duncan replied, shaking his head.

"That's better," she said, giving Duncan a bright smile. "What brings you up here this fine morning? You planning to join the music class later?"

Duncan brightened. He had nearly forgotten it was Wednesday. He usually missed music class because he was out working, but every now and again he found himself with no big job to do, like today.

"If that would be all right?" he asked hopefully.

Margie dismissed Duncan's insecurity with a wave of her hand. "Pfft. You know you're always welcome. You're one of Dad's favorite students."

Duncan beamed, both pride and joy settling into his cheeks in equal measure.

"Taylor's awake, if you wanna go up and see her."

Duncan nodded. It wasn't the first time he had visited since Taylor's collapse, but it would be the first time she was awake for it. It was the whole reason he was there.

Margie held open the screen door for Duncan as he slipped past her and made his way up the stairs. He knocked lightly on the door, just in case she was not as awake as Margie had said. A muffled response from inside the room indicated she was.

Duncan eased himself into the room. Taylor was propped up in the bed, watching him. He noticed the flicker of disappointment, which was quickly replaced by a slight smile.

"Hey, Dunk."

"Hey," he responded, stopping near the edge of the bed. "How are you feeling?"

"Okay," Taylor said quickly. "Better than yesterday."

Duncan sensed a restlessness in Taylor, not that it was anything new. She had seemed restless since she had first arrived. But this seemed different somehow, deeper and more consuming. He wondered how much was caused by her current condition, and how much stemmed from something—or someone—else.

"Well, you'll have to take it easy for a few days, get your strength back."

"So everyone keeps telling me," Taylor said, clearly not happy with the plan.

"You had some people worried," Duncan said. He thought about elaborating, but held his tongue. Instead, he added, "You look better."

"Better than what?"

"Better than before."

Taylor eyed him. Duncan scuffed his foot against the carpet.

"You visited me."

It was more a statement than a question, and it made Duncan a bit uncomfortable. Still, he held his ground. He returned her gaze.

"Yeah. That's what friends do."

It was presumptuous of him. He knew that, and yet it felt right somehow, both the idea and the voicing of it. He wanted them to be friends. He watched her closely, waiting for her reaction. Finally, Taylor nodded her acceptance.

"Thanks for that," she said, with no trace of insincerity or condemnation. Duncan rocked on his heels. He felt happier than he could recall feeling in a long time.

"Dunk?"

"Yeah?"

"Sit," she commanded, although her smile belied the authoritative way in which she said it. "You're making me nervous."

Duncan smiled. He grabbed a chair and slid it up next to the bed, straddling it backward, resting his forearms across the back. They sat quietly for a while, Taylor not seeming to have anything pressing on her mind, while Duncan tried to figure out how to ask what he wanted to know. Despite her seeming acceptance of his offer of friendship, and his existing friendship with Kate, he was not sure if it was his place to interfere. In fact, he was pretty sure it was most definitely not his place. He disliked meddlers, and he had come to see Taylor with the intention of meddling, which bothered him. But Kate was clearly upset, and it was not too hard, at least not to anyone paying even the slightest bit of attention, to figure out the reason probably rested with Taylor.

"Spit it out, Dunk."

"Huh?" he said, startled.

"You obviously have something on your mind."

"I...well...I'm not sure..." Duncan sputtered, internally cursing his inability to articulate anything at all.

"I'm not going to bite," she said, her voice holding an unexpected kindness. Not that she was unkind.

He smiled nervously. "Well, it's just that...I was wondering why...I mean..."

Duncan paused, letting out a deep breath.

Focus, Duncan. Just say what you mean.

Taylor sat there, patiently waiting. He was grateful for that, and it gave him the confidence he needed.

"I know you haven't been here all that long," he began, trying to put his question into some kind of coherent context, "but it's pretty clear, or it seems pretty clear, to me anyway, that there's something going on. Between you and Kate."

Taylor sucked in a breath, but she stayed quiet.

"I mean, not that there's anything wrong with that, 'cause there's not. Nothing at all. It's totally fine, in fact. Everyone here knows Kate's gay, and Buck made it clear that it was a non-issue on the farm. Not that anyone would have an issue. I definitely don't."

Duncan knew he was rambling, but he could not seem to help it. He had developed the worst case of verbal diarrhea he had ever had, but he knew if he didn't keep going he would never finish.

"I'm saying this all wrong," he continued, shaking his head. "I'm just wondering, I guess, if...if you have feelings. For her."

Taylor let out a deep breath and examined the fibers of the blanket. Duncan waited for her to respond, to say something. Anything at all.

"Why are you asking me this?" she finally said. She picked at the blanket covering the bed, keeping her eyes averted.

Duncan thought of Kate, of what she meant to him, and it filled him with a confidence he had only occasionally felt before. The same confidence he had held within himself that night with Zeke.

"Like I said, she's like a sister to me," Duncan responded. He had lost his hesitation. "And I don't want to see her get hurt. She doesn't deserve that."

"No, she doesn't," Taylor agreed sadly.

"But last night at dinner, and this morning, she was quiet. See, Kate's normally like this force of nature. She can make you happy just by walking into a room. She cares about everyone."

"I know."

"Look, I don't know what happened between you two, but I came here to ask you because Kate won't talk about it. But the truth is, I don't need to know. All I really need to know is whether you care about her, or whether the pain she's feeling is pointless."

"I don't want to hurt her."

It was a simple statement, but to Duncan, it spoke volumes.

"Then don't," Duncan answered. It was clear she was struggling. He wanted to put an arm around her and would have if he did not think she would reject it.

"It's not that simple," Taylor said sadly.

"Sure it is. Look, I may not be the brightest guy around, and I know I'm young, but I do know a few things. One of them is that a person always has a choice, even if it's a hard one. And this situation? This thing between you two? If you care about her, it doesn't seem all that hard."

"What if I don't know how?"

Her voice was small, fragile. She seemed almost helpless.

"Know how to what? How to not hurt her?"

"How to care."

They were such little words, but they left Duncan reeling. Taylor's desolation was overwhelming. Even when the plague had come and stopped the world cold, even when his parents had died, stealing away everything Duncan had ever known, even when he was scared and alone in the dead of night, with nowhere to go and no one to go to, he had never lost himself.

Taylor, apparently, had not been so lucky.

"It's all a choice," Duncan said. "You have to choose to care, and the how will follow."

Taylor nodded, but Duncan was not convinced she had truly understood him. He struggled to figure out what he could say that would break through the hardened bricks of misery that had become her world. He started to speak, but Taylor beat him to it.

"What's going on down there?"

It took Duncan a moment to catch up. He smiled as the excited voices of the farm's youngest residents filtered into the room.

"It's Wednesday," he said, his own excitement rising. "Time for music class."

"You're kidding," Taylor said, her face a mask of incredulity. Duncan thought she could not have looked more surprised if a UFO had just landed on the front lawn.

"Nope," he said, standing up. He had an idea, and he was not about to take no for an answer. "Get dressed."

"I'm sorry?"

"Come on," he said, grabbing a shirt and a pair of jeans from the top of the dresser and tossing them onto the bed. "Time's a wastin'."

Taylor's eyes widened. "Oh no. I'm not going down there."

"Why? You got something better to do today?"

Taylor crossed her arms across her chest, as if that ended the conversation. But Duncan was not about to let it. He crossed his own arms, a mocking reflection of Taylor's pose. She frowned.

"Dunk," she said warningly, but he stood firm. If she was ever going to allow herself to be happy, she needed to be reminded of what happiness was. Even if he had to force it down her throat and hold her mouth closed while she swallowed.

"Tay-lor," he responded in the sing-song whine he had mastered as a child, frustrating Taylor even more. Her frown slid into a scowl.

"No."

Duncan just kept smiling at her with his arms folded.

"Du-unk," she said, her voice taking on its own whine. "I'm still not feeling all that well. I need to rest."

"What you need," Duncan corrected as he flipped the blanket and sheets off Taylor's lap and down toward the bottom of the bed, "is to get out of this bed and live a little."

Taylor's expression was caught somewhere between a pout and an indignant scowl. Duncan decided to really push her buttons.

"What's the matter? Is big, bad Taylor scared of a bunch of kids?"

Taylor growled at him, making Duncan jump back half a step. If Taylor had been feeling better, Duncan would have turned tail and run out the door. He knew full well she could kick his ass all the way to the cow pasture.

He laughed a little nervously as she swiped up the pants from the bottom of the bed, shooting large, pointy daggers at him with her eyes all the while.

"I'll just give you a little privacy," he said, shuffling toward the door. "I'll be right outside the door."

He could not quite make out the words she was muttering under her breath, but he caught enough to know she was not going to offer to buy him a thank-you dinner anytime soon. Not that there were any restaurants to take him to, anyway. He shut the door behind him and leaned against the hallway wall, waiting.

CHAPTER FIFTEEN

I finish dressing in my borrowed clothes, thinking about the satisfying thwack my palm will make against Dunk's skull when I get into the hallway. I surprise myself, and probably him, by not smacking him upside his smug, little head. Maybe I am growing as a person. Then again, I let him bait me into following him downstairs to join the weekly music class, so maybe I am just as petty and ridiculous as I have always been.

The scene on the porch is like *Romper Room* on Red Bull. Three of the children are sitting on the floor, bouncing up and down as if they are suspended by rubber bands. A couple of the teenage supervisors stand chatting amidst the chaos, seemingly oblivious but following the action out of the corners of their eyes. Two more kids are chasing each other around the porch, weaving in and out of the human obstacles. Next to them, a little girl sits combing her Barbie's hair, giving what appears to be a very serious lecture to her doll on proper hair maintenance. And there is Buck in the middle of it all, perched on an armless rocking chair, watching the scene before him, that beautiful old Martin resting gently across his lap. A couple of other adults I don't recognize are crowding in at the edges of the porch, and I notice a few more lurking a little farther out in the yard, like they are embarrassed to be here but unwilling to miss anything. I notice, of course, that Kate is nowhere to be found. The disappointment I feel at her absence is as unsurprising to me as having woken up this morning with both a left and a right foot.

Dunk yanks on my shirt sleeve and heads for the center of the porch, plopping himself down dead center of the action. I stay rooted to the floor, just in front of the house's screen door. He beckons me with a nod of his head and pats a space on the floor beside him, and I will my feet to move. But they don't.

I feel like an outsider, an intruder of the first order, an interloper with no right to the two square feet of space next to Dunk. I shake my head and sidestep to my left, finding that my legs are willing to obey my commands as long as the direction is away from the group. I lean up against the wall of the house, my arms locked in that familiar place across my chest. I am as inconspicuous as a moose in a ballet recital. Something bumps my leg. It's Rusty, angling for a head scratch. I give him a little rub, and he settles down on the floor beside me with a contented sigh and begins snoring.

Buck clears his throat, and all attention turns toward him. He flips the guitar upright on his lap, settles his left hand onto the fret board, and begins to play. His first selection is a rousing rendition of "Old MacDonald."

What have I gotten myself into?

He sings in a rich baritone, each verse in perfect pitch. He is quickly joined by the less than perfect voices of the children and adults gathered around him, but Buck doesn't seem to mind. Although they sing off-key, they sing—and in some cases, shout—with enthusiasm. I want to be glib and signal how above it all I am with a roll of my eyes or a sigh, but instead my foot betrays me, tapping out its approval in time to the music.

I am pathetic.

"Now, who can tell me what chords I was playing?" Buck asks, his song finished. Eager hands shoot into the air, and a few more eager voices call out a random assortment of answers. The most insistent of those voices is Dunk's, much to the group's amusement. He looks around sheepishly once he realizes he has less restraint than the seven-year-old sitting beside him. Buck smiles, though, and congratulates Dunk on being right. Dunk's embarrassment quickly turns into pride.

"Okay, what shall we sing next?"

A chorus of voices shouts out their opinions, ranging from "Pop Goes the Weasel" to "Freebird." Finally, Buck settles on one he likes and begins to play again.

And so it goes for the next hour, with Buck playing a song and everyone singing along, followed by Buck asking a series of questions about music and music history. His repertoire extends, thankfully, beyond children's songs. He is definitely a child of the 60's, not that anyone seems to mind. I certainly don't. But Buck also plays a variety of other songs of differing genres, including one song from *The Sound of Music* that has me doubled over with laughter. By the time he gets around to "Row, Row, Row Your Boat," I am singing along under my breath.

After one last Dylan song, Buck lays the guitar back down on his lap, eyeing the group.

"Time for me to hang up the old pick. Now, who's going to take over for me?"

Five hands immediately go up, including one belonging to a little boy sitting next to Margie, who is no bigger than the guitar. Buck makes a show of selecting his successor, studying each of the wannabes carefully. Finally, Buck chooses one of the teenage boys, who hoots and pumps his fist with all the exuberance someone his age should have. I worry his enthusiasm might lead to carelessness that could endanger the priceless instrument he is about to play, but I needn't bother. He takes the proffered guitar with the care and gentleness of a father picking up his newborn daughter for the first time. Clearly, Buck's music lessons have included teaching respect for the Martin.

"What are you going to play for us, Sam?" Buck asks, leaning back into the rocker.

"Well, sir, I thought I'd play one of my sister's favorites. If that's all right?"

"Go ahead, son," Buck says, patting Sam's shoulder. "Show us what you've got."

Sam nods and looks to the sky, his silent prayer obvious. He closes his eyes for a moment and lets out a long breath. Then he begins to play.

I can't name the song right away, although the strum pattern and notes tickle some kind of memory in the basement of my brain. Sam's playing is nearly perfect. The strings resonate smoothly, each tone crisp and bright.

I know I recognize the song, but I still can't place it. A concert, maybe? Sam's voice is different than I expect, higher pitched than his speaking voice yet gravelly and soulful, but still managing to hold a measure of youthful innocence. He sings softly, his voice contrasting beautifully with the lower octaves of the guitar.

I know the tune is right, know Sam is singing on key, know the lyrics as they fall from his mouth. I am definitely remembering a concert of some sort. In college.

Sam plays gently at first, letting the music lead him into a progressively stronger and sharper rhythm. The next line comes, and it acts like a balloon being rubbed against my head, the static electricity causing my mental hairs to stand on end. I am increasingly sure that not only do I know this song, but I need to remember what it is very quickly for some reason I have yet to identify. I glance over at Buck, who similarly seems to be trying to puzzle it out.

I was in college, and a whole bunch of us crammed into my tiny Geo Metro and drove three hours to see this concert. I didn't really want to go, but I had the biggest crush on this girl who was going, so I offered to drive. Of course, the whole night she was mooning over some guy in her world literature class who had blown her off the night before, so that didn't go anywhere. And I kind of thought she was being a bit of a bitch...

Oh, wait, I do know this! Cool, that...Uh-oh.

It's like watching a movie and recognizing the star even though you can't think of her name or anything else she's been in, and it nags at you throughout the movie and bothers you long after you've finished your popcorn and soda and have had your after-dinner cocktail, until finally you're in a meeting the next day with several colleagues and your boss, and they're all in the middle of a conversation when you suddenly yell out, "Helena Bonham Carter!" as it explodes in your head, and you find yourself beaming with pride at everyone around you until you notice the quizzical looks on their faces, and your pride quickly dissolves into horror.

"I'm a—"

"Sam!" Buck and I shout in unison, both of us lunging forward, having recognized the impending train wreck at the same time. Sam freezes mid-strum, his eyes darting back and forth between me and Buck. I, of course, having no idea what to say, just stand there like a deer in the aforementioned train's headlamps. Buck, thankfully, is as cool as usual.

"That was great, Sam. Good work. Maybe we'll have you play the song again Saturday night. Late. After the children are asleep?"

Buck puts a little added emphasis on that last bit, which, combined with the interruption, finally gets through to Sam. His cheeks redden, and he quickly hands the guitar back over to Buck. Thankfully, the kids seem to be oblivious to the subtleties of the conversation. The murmuring and muffled laughter among the rest of the group says that if they hadn't understood before Sam stopped playing the song, they do now.

"You did play it well, Sam," Buck adds, a mixture of reassurance and relief that Sam won't be finishing his performance of "Bitch."

"So, who's next?"

Several hands wave excitedly in the air. Once again, Buck's eyes track over the group, glancing at each volunteer in turn. I ease back against the wall, reclaiming my position as head wall-holder-upper, willing my heart back into a steady rhythm.

Dunk is, if possible, even more excited than the last time. He reminds me of one of those boy band groupies just before the inevitable fainting. I chuckle at the image of Dunk in the front row, swooning as the boys on stage, in all their glittery glory, blow kisses to their twenty thousand number-one fans.

"How 'bout you, Taylor?"

All chattering ceases in an instant, and the focus falls on me like I'm Captain von Trapp about to sing "Edelweiss" for the first time. The weight of those stares is enough to punch me through the wall. If it were nighttime, you'd be able to hear crickets chirping from a mile away for all the silence. There is no escape, no place to hide. And Buck knows that, the sneaky little bastard.

"Uh, no. Thanks," I say shakily, hoping my mildly polite decline will be enough, even though I know better. Buck's hazel-hued laser beams have me pinned to the wall.

"Do you know how to play?"

Buck's voice grins at me even as his face does its best impression of the clueless but encouraging grandfather who just wants little Johnny to join in the fun.

Damn it, Buck.

He's trying to trap me. If I say yes, he can keep pestering me to play. If I say no, I am a big fat liar.

Buck's eyes twinkle. He is most definitely pleased with himself.

"I used to," I grind out through clenched teeth. I give him my nastiest glare, which only entertains him further. He damn near breaks his unassuming-old-coot façade by laughing.

"Well, come on then," he says, holding the guitar out to me. "Don't be shy."

He is working me for all I am worth. Blood colors my cheeks, though I'm not sure whether it is more from being supremely pissed off or from being terribly embarrassed.

I take the guitar from Buck's outstretched hands and proceed to just stand there, staring at it dumbly. A soft chuckle from Buck breaks me out of my stupor. He moves over onto the love seat next to Margie, sliding the little boy onto his lap. I take the hint and settle onto the now open chair. Rusty ambles over and takes up residence at my feet and is quickly snoring again.

The long-faded scent of the mahogany wafts up to my nose, and I breathe it in deeply, knowing full well I have to be imagining it. My fingers find the fret board, and I slide them along the strings, testing their tension. I wrap my right arm over the body, pulling it in so the back bumps against my chest. It feels familiar, comfortable.

I slip the pick out from between the strings and set it down. I've never liked picks. They always feel unnatural between my fingers, and they have this annoying habit of flying out of my hand when I play. I always just use the side of my thumb, liking the feel of the strings vibrating against my skin as I strum. I know I can't unleash the full power or beauty of the Martin by playing this way, but I don't care. It feels better to me somehow. More personal.

The audience, my audience now, quietly awaits my performance. Butterflies begin fluttering in my stomach. Of course, the fluttering feels more like angry jackhammers, and I'm pretty sure the butterflies are of the Jurassic persuasion, probably the size of Tonka trucks. I'm not really nervous about playing, or even playing for people. I have played in public before, at a little coffee house on the town square near my college, with a girl who loved Ani DiFranco. We did two songs together, and at least five people told us we sounded like the Indigo Girls, which I thought was the coolest thing ever. No, my nerves now are caused by something other than playing in public.

"What are you going to play?"

Dunk's voice forges across the silence. He looks up at me expectantly, supportively, urging me forward.

I rack my brain trying to remember something I know how to play, or at least something I can fake, and come up empty. I cannot for the life of me remember a single song, let alone the opening notes to one. I half expect people to start shouting out suggestions like they did with Buck, but they don't. After a minute or two, people start shifting uncomfortably, but still they say nothing.

"It doesn't have to be anything we know. Just play from your heart."

Play from my heart?

Sometimes Buck is too cheesy for his own good. I start to give him a look to tell him exactly what I think about his play-from-your-heart philosophy, but stop.

Sonofabitch.

My left hand finds my favorite chord, the G. My friends used to laugh about how all my songs started with a G. It is my home chord, my safe place.

I have written four songs in my life, three of which were so unmemorable I forgot them mere days after having written them and probably couldn't remember even a single word if I was administered truth serum or put under hypnosis. But as my fingers find their home, there is one song I do remember.

My right hand floats over the strings. My left hand switches chords instinctively. I close my eyes, giving myself over to a melody I haven't played in a long time. The guitar sings beautifully. I only hope my own voice can match it.

Oh well. In for a penny...

I am surprised at how steady my voice is as I begin to sing. I expected it to be shaky, to fade in and out while I stumbled and stuttered out the lyrics. But the words fall smoothly from my lips as I work my way through the first verse. I keep my eyes closed. I am partly afraid of seeing people writhing on the floor, clutching their ears in agony. Of course, that wouldn't be the guitar's fault.

The music leads me, and I allow myself to be led. My lips pass the words without thought, my fingers craft the chords without intention. I am lost to the music, and to the moment. For the first time in a long time, I feel free of the burden of life after the plague.

I wind my way through the chorus and second verse, my voice and my playing growing stronger. I can hear nothing save the music I am creating. It fills my ears and flows through my body. It is like the ocean crashing against my skin, overwhelming every part of me.

As I leave the bridge and enter the third verse, I finally trade the darkness behind my eyelids for the light of the front porch.

I don't know how long she's been here, or how much she has heard of my pitiful excuse of a song, but it doesn't matter. She is here, her eyes upon me, speaking to me, shining for me. There are tears there, yes, but they do not fall. They don't need to.

It all feels easy, simple...normal. Sitting here, playing this guitar, singing for a bunch of mostly strangers, it feels like the world isn't a wasteland, like I didn't watch people die or Washington crumble or spend months struggling to survive as I crawled across America. It feels familiar and surprisingly good. It almost feels like maybe there can be more to life after the end of the world than just surviving it. Maybe it's not pointless to dream of a future. Maybe I can dare to believe I can love and be loved, here on a tiny farm in the middle of nowhere, with a woman who captivated me from the moment I saw her.

A few weeks ago, or a few days ago, or even a few hours ago, I would have rejected such a notion instinctively, purging the idea that anything could ever be normal again. The world had changed too much. I had changed too much. Everywhere I have been since leaving DC has been steeped in misery. Even the places where I have briefly found refuge along the way, places with people willing to provide food and shelter for a night or two, have been awash in sorrow, steeped in a desperation so palpable it simply mirrored my own. Children cry through the night in those places, their tears falling thick as rain in a summer storm for a world they are barely old enough to remember. Then there are the other places, where people take what they want and want more than you have to give. In those places, places like Pittsburgh, tears only provoke the infliction of more agony.

Until now, my life has been about my journey home. I have given no thought to what happens after I keep my promise to my father, no consideration to what will happen when I have to face the truth of whether they are alive or dead. But things are different now, and I know I want them to be. I must still go home, for myself and for my family, but maybe that does not have to be the end of my story. Maybe it's time to look beyond Asheville, to what happens after. Here, in this place, I feel safe for the first time in five months, and people who care about me are offering me a place to belong. Sitting here with this guitar in my lap, staring into Kate's eyes, I allow myself to feel something other than pain or sorrow. I allow myself to care. And for the first time in forever, I dare to allow myself to just be.

CHAPTER SIXTEEN

The next few days pass as days should, as they used to before...well, just before. I spend one more night in the farmhouse, just to be on the safe side, Buck says, but then I am deemed well enough to move back to the dorm. I have supervision, of course. Buck comes by to check on me, as does Margie. Dunk spends most of his free time lurking about, chatting up a storm. Then there are the others, people I have barely met or don't know at all, knocking on my door and poking their heads in just to say hello. It seems like everyone has a vested interest in my well-being, and while part of me wants to be annoyed by all the attention, I can't really say I mind it all that much.

They used to talk about paradigm shifts when I was in college, though to be honest, I never paid much attention. I had a bad habit of skipping classes and spending my days experiencing the non-academic parts of college life, going on road trips for no good reason, playing Frisbee in the quad, hanging out with friends in coffee shops and talking about all the things we would fix when we were finally running the world. Not that it really matters now, except that I have been wondering a lot about paradigm shifts over the last few days, and wishing just a little that I had paid more attention in school. The one thing I know is something has changed, both inside me and in the world around me. Something significant.

Among the parade of nursemaids and well-wishers is Kate. She left quickly after my performance on the porch, without a word but not without a smile. That smile had been a beginning. Kate is waiting when I return to room 39. Buck hands me off and excuses himself. I say nothing at first, unable to find anything close to the right words. Kate, too, is quiet, settling me into the bed, fluffing my pillow, putting away my extra clothes, tucking me in. I had forgotten what it feels like, being taken care of in such a way, and the devil inside screams at me to fight it, to shout that I am not a child needing to be taken care of. But there is this other voice, one which sounds strangled but vaguely familiar, telling me to just shut up and melt into the bed and soak up the gentle care that is being offered. I listen to that second voice, leaving the demon to fume and pout in his corner. Paradigm shift.

Once Kate is finished making me comfortable and has tucked me in just a little tighter, she drags the chair from beneath the desk over to the side of my bed. Out of a backpack I hadn't noticed, she slides out a pile of paperback novels, setting them on the nightstand. The spines face her, and I can't make out the titles. She studies them for a while, her head tilted in contemplation. My curiosity is muted by the fact that as she studies the books, she scrunches up her nose and purses her lips in the most adorable way. With a triumphant grunt and a nod of her head, she slips one of the books out of the stack and onto her lap.

Kate begins to read, and I burst out laughing before she finishes the first sentence. She has managed to pick one of my favorite books, Douglas Adams's *The Hitchhiker's Guide to the Galaxy*. I choose not to consider the astronomical odds of her picking that particular book for fear of making my head explode from the math. She pauses, her eyebrow raised at me, questioning my interruption. I promise her I won't panic. She grins and starts again.

She spends the rest of the afternoon and evening reading to me. It is surreal on many levels, not the least of which is she is reading to me, and I am letting her, and it seems perfectly normal to both of us.

She has a radio voice, mocha rich and marble smooth. It is hypnotizing, her voice. It cradles me, rocking me to sleep and then wrapping me in its care when I awake. I have no sense of time and no concern for the lack of it. Sometime that night, we finish the book and start another, the first story blending into the second like some wonderful dream from which you never want to wake.

Eventually, my napping gives way to real slumber. In the morning, when the light streaming in through the window finally grows harsh enough to light my world through my curtained eyes, I wake to find her still sitting in that rickety old chair. Her stocking feet are propped up on the edge of my bed, her only seeming concession to her own comfort the act of having taken her shoes off at some point in the night. Her head hangs down low on her chest, rising and falling in a deep rhythm, her neck bent forward in a way that makes me cringe in sympathy for the stiffness I know she will feel when she wakes up.

I want to make her breakfast in bed like they used to on TV, to carry back a tray laden with pancakes and syrup and juice and bacon, with a small flower, maybe a tulip, carefully arranged in a bud vase in the center. It is a ridiculous notion, and yet the urge is strong. I begin to slowly shift under the covers, trying to inch my way out of the bed so as not to wake her, despite the inherent clumsiness that has taken up residence in my still-recovering body. I choose to ignore the fact that I am acting like we aren't on a farm in the middle of nowhere with an encampment full of survivors, where meals are prepared by the pound instead of for two. And that I can't cook. And that breakfast in bed is far too intimate of a gesture for our situation, regardless of the peculiar intimacy we already seem to share.

"What do you think you're doing?"

Her eyebrow is raised at me, as I know it will be. I shrink back down into the mattress and pull the blanket up under my chin.

"Stretching?" I reply lamely.

"Uh-huh." The eyebrow ticks higher. "Wanna try again?"

I decide to see how far into her hairline I can make that eyebrow go.

"Okay, fine. You caught me," I say, my words laced with defeat. "I was going jogging."

She stifles a laugh.

"Really," she replies, more statement than question. She is apparently up for our little game.

"No, not jogging. Rock climbing."

"Mm-hmm."

"Water skiing?"

She almost breaks with that one.

"Because there's that big lake out back."

"Okay, scratch the water skiing. I was making that up."

"Really."

"Yeah," I say shyly. I hang my head a little. "I was covering."

"Covering for what?" she says with a note of concern.

Nervously, I say, "For what I really wanted to do."

I search her eyes, which have grown wide.

"You can tell me."

I look away for a moment, gathering my courage.

She leans forward expectantly.

"What I really want?" I say, scooting up in the bed, my eyes once again taking hers. She leans even closer.

"Yes?"

"To go to clown school."

Both eyebrows hit her hairline. She looks like an owl. I think she might hoot.

I let out an easy grin, savoring my victory. She knows she's been had. I wait for her to retaliate. Instead, she laughs.

"I can see it now. You. Polka dot tie. Big red nose. Jumbo-sized shoes."

"Don't forget the suspenders."

"I bet you'd wear the hell out of a pair of suspenders."

I start to chuckle, but it dies in my throat. Her tone has changed. I feel a flush creep up my cheeks. She looks up at me through her eyelashes, all innocence and seduction. I swallow hard. My blood stirs. There is no longer any question about how I feel about her, and she knows it.

So she gets up and reaches for the door, leaving me sputtering on the bed.

"You're leaving?"

She turns back to me, giving me most charming grin I have ever seen.

Damn.

"I'll be back later."

Then, with a wink, she is gone, leaving me alone with the knowledge that I am simply no match for her. But I like a challenge.

I shake my head, deciding to get up and test my legs in the privacy of my…well, privacy. Turns out they are stronger than I thought they would be. All of me feels stronger, actually. If I didn't know better, I might actually think I had never been sick.

I get dressed, deciding to take my newfound strength out for a spin. A cautious, non-exertive spin—I'm not entirely crazy—but a spin nonetheless. I know I'm not yet well enough to resume my journey to Asheville. I try to ignore the guilt I feel over being relieved that I do not have to leave just yet.

I go down to the mess, thankful to discover I haven't slept past breakfast. I gratefully gobble down a bowl of oatmeal, swirled generously with brown sugar and cinnamon. The few stragglers in the dining hall all wave or say hi before heading out for their daily chores and responsibilities. I feel a bit like some D-list celebrity, back when we still had those.

After breakfast I walk. I have no destination, no sense of purpose. I have forgotten what it is like to walk without need. It is exhilarating, albeit tiring. I ramble along, watch men and women working at the boundaries of the land, watch others tend to livestock and work crops, hear the children laughing under Kate and the other teachers' loving guidance, feel the breeze touch my skin and simply enjoy the sensation, instead of trying to decipher what the air holds next for me.

I find a small cluster of trees and nestle in, watching the day slip by without me. Clouds billow and drift apart, like some unseen hand is playing with giant balls of cotton. I try to see patterns in the sky, dragons riding the wind before melting into bunnies and castles and ice cream cones. As a child I spent hours upon hours staring up at the sky, lying in the grass, seeing worlds of wonder in the clouds. It came easily to me then. It comes easily no longer. This sky is devoid of dragons.

"UFOs or signs of rain?"

Dunk really is a strange boy.

"What?"

He kicks at a stray stone in the grass, shoving his hands into the depths of his jean pockets.

"Around here, someone spends that much time staring up at the sky, they're either trying to figure out when it's gonna rain or they've recently had a close encounter with some little green men and are waiting for the mother ship to return."

He slumps down beside me. The sky is beginning to trade its bright blue majesty for the golds and grays of early evening.

"You've been watching me, have you?"

I feel him studying me, trying to determine whether or not I am mad. I'm not, but I let him wonder.

"Just keeping an eye," he says with deliberate vagueness. "You've been gone all day. Folks started to worry."

"Folks?"

He shrugs. That means Kate or Buck, or both. Maybe my fan club. He is studying me again, now trying to figure out whether I'll be mad they sent him. I'm not, but this time I tell him so. He seems happy about that.

"Did you get any work done today? Other than stalking me, I mean?" I banter.

"Hey, I'm no stalker. I was tracking. Totally different thing."

"Really."

"Yes, really. It involves skill and stealth and it's, uh…much more manly."

"Manly, eh?"

"Sure," Dunk says, apparently missing my sarcasm. "See, it's about reading the land and opening yourself up to the world. You look for things other people don't see and listen for things other people can't hear. My daddy started teaching me when I was young, like his daddy taught him, and his daddy before that."

He pauses, studying some thought in his mind, or maybe just remembering something he had forgotten he knew. He grins and shakes his head.

"I wasn't good at it when I was younger. Daddy always said, though, that my time would come once I was older, when I was man enough to focus on what wasn't there."

"Well, you seem pretty good at it now. I guess you must be man enough."

I think Dunk might actually burst. Clearly the idea of being a man is important to him. I can relate, if not to the gender then to the concept. I spent my whole life younger than most of the kids, and later adults, around me. My first-grade teacher was concerned because I was unengaged in the classroom, refusing to work on my reading with the other kids. Kids like that usually get shipped off to a remedial class somewhere, but thankfully I had a cussing and smoking nun for a principal who wasn't content to assume I was incapable of success. She asked me why I wasn't living up to my potential. I told her I was bored, that the work we were doing was way too easy. I was a precocious five-year-old. Within a year they had moved me up a grade. They thought about promoting me two years ahead, but decided it would be hard enough for me socially to move up one year. They were right. My new classmates never let me forget I was an outsider. From that moment on, I always had something to prove.

I know Duncan lost both of his parents to the plague. He doesn't talk about it, at least not to me, but it is clear it still hurts. Of course it does. It is bad enough to have lost people you loved, but on top of everything else, Dunk was just a kid when his whole world was stripped away.

"I think your mom and dad would be proud of you, Dunk."

He looks up at me, startled for a moment. Tears threaten to flow, and he works hard to hold them back. He seems to be fighting with himself, the need to be a man warring with the need to express his grief. I will him to let it go.

Whether he wins or loses his internal battle, I don't know, but once the dam is breached there is no turning back. He sinks into my arms, sobbing for all that he has lost. I stroke his back and hold on tight, fighting back my own tears as his pain soaks into my shirt. It just won't do for us both to be bawling messes up on this hill.

After a while, his choking sobs ease into softer sniffles, and he withdraws to sit beside me. He avoids my eyes, I am sure out of some sense of manly embarrassment. The notion that boys don't cry, shouldn't cry, is as stupid as it is destructive. Yet another psychological disaster for which we have football and beer commercials to thank.

"There's nothing wrong with crying," I say, taking care to keep my tone neutral. "But just so you know, no one else needs to know."

He swipes away the last of his tears.

"You won't tell anyone?"

"Nope. It's just between us."

"Promise?"

"Promise. And I don't break promises to friends."

I'm not sure what compels me to add that last part, although both the statement and the sentiment are true. I guess somewhere along the way, although I didn't mean for it to happen or even know that it had, I started thinking of Dunk as my friend.

Dunk, for his part, does not miss the classification, and the dazzling smile that lights up his face makes his delight plain. It is my turn to be embarrassed, but I shake it off. Then I punch him in the shoulder.

"Ow. What was that for?"

I laugh and stand up, stretching my back.

"We should probably head back. I'm getting hungry."

"Dinner!" he shouts, jumping up to his feet and setting a brisk pace back toward the barn. He might have manlike tendencies, but in the best ways, he is still a boy.

We arrive back at the dorm with just enough time to wash up before dinner. I meet up with Dunk in the dining hall and settle in for the best bowl of homemade chicken noodle soup I have ever had outside of my stepmother's. The tables fill up quickly, and soon the barn is full of chatter and laughter.

"Hey there, you two."

Just the sound of her voice makes me smile. I'm not the only one.

"Kate!" Dunk says excitedly, giving her a one-handed hug with his spoon still in hand. As excited as he is to see Kate, he is even more excited about his soup and quickly dives back into his bowl.

Kate sits down next to Dunk with her own bowl. Funny how I have suddenly lost interest in my dinner. I idly push my spoon around the bowl while stealing glances at her from across the table.

"Where were you guys all day?" she asks absently, although her eyes are directed at me from above her bowl as she swallows her first spoonful.

Dunk tenses, glancing up at me nervously. I shoot him a quick look.

Trust me.

"I decided to go for a walk."

Kate's spoon pauses in mid-air. "All day?"

"I know. Not one of my brighter ideas. But thankfully Dunk was there to bail me out. He nearly had to carry me back to the dorm."

Dunk's surprise is clear as he looks back and forth between me and Kate.

"He did?"

His mouth opens and he starts to sputter, but I cut him off.

"Absolutely. There I was up on this hill, practically in a coma, when Dunk spotted me. He pretty much saved me."

I'm laying it on a little thick, but I figure the white lie won't really hurt anyone. Dunk's mouth hangs open, and I am sure he is going to blow the whole thing.

Kate looks between us skeptically, but finally seems to decide to accept the story. She pats Dunk's shoulder. "Good job, Duncan."

Dunk looks back to me, and I nod, trying to convince him to just let it drop.

"Uh, thanks?" he says weakly before returning to his neglected soup.

I feel slightly smug about my deft handling of the situation. Of course, that illusion is quickly shattered upon my next glance at Kate, who is discretely giving me that eyebrow of hers. She hasn't bought a second of it, but she doesn't let on for the sake of Dunk's pride.

"So, Taylor," Kate says, changing the subject much to my relief, "I was thinking you might want to join me for a ride tomorrow."

Although I can't be sure, I have a dreadful suspicion I'm not going to like whatever she's talking about.

"Ride?"

"Horses," Dunk says helpfully, having once again found his voice.

"Horses?"

My voice shifts about an octave higher than normal. No one seems to notice.

"Kate goes out for a ride every weekend. You don't have to go for a long ride though, right Kate?"

"No. I suppose I could take it easy on Taylor, seeing as how she's still weak and all."

Somewhere I am vaguely aware that Dunk and Kate are still talking, that Kate is teasing me, but words have lost all meaning. All I can do is repeat them. That tends to happen when I'm petrified.

"Weak," I say, nodding.

"How about it?" she asks. I force my eyes to regain their focus and look up at her, and see understanding dawn on her face. "Oh."

"What?" Dunk asks, not comprehending. He looks at Kate, then at me, still not getting it. "You should really go, Taylor. It's fun. Kate will go easy."

"She doesn't have to go, Duncan," Kate says, trying to give me an easy out. She smiles to tell me it is okay, but I see the glimmer of disappointment.

"Sure she does! What else is she going to do all day?" Dunk presses.

"Duncan—" Kate starts to warn.

"No, it's okay," I interrupt, making up my mind as I speak. "Yeah, sure. Riding. Sounds...fun."

Dunk nods triumphantly, pleased with his powers of persuasion. Kate smiles at me, concerned yet obviously happy with my decision. I smile weakly at both of them and wonder how I am going to convince myself to get out of bed in the morning, let alone ride a horse.

CHAPTER SEVENTEEN

The last memory I have of riding a horse is the blurry view from the ground after being thrown off. I was ten. I don't know if it was more the tears or the minor concussion that turned practically everything around me into undulating lava lamp globules. I wasn't so much thrown off as spun off, the result of a saddle that decided to slide down the galloping horse's side with me still in it. One minute I was riding the wind, the next I was eating dirt. The thing I remember most isn't the suddenness of the fall or the pain in my head, but how there on the ground, amidst the churning acid trip my vision had become, there was one thing I could see with perfect clarity. The horse, towering over me, all legs and chest and bottomless, soul-sucking eyes.

Despite the mind-numbing fear that accompanies that childhood nightmare, I somehow end up standing in the barn doorway Saturday morning, thinking the unthinkable as I watch Kate brush down a chestnut mare. Kate is oblivious to my presence, but the horse notices, pinning me with those hellish, obsidian eyes.

"She's not going to bite your arm off."

Okay, not so oblivious after all.

"Well, maybe a little nibble, but only if you don't give her enough carrots."

The horse snorts her agreement. I shudder. Apparently, the compassionate Kate of the night before, who seemed to understand my fear of horses, has been replaced by tease-me-mercilessly Kate.

"You just going to stand there all day, or are you going to give me a hand?"

Kate strides toward me, her ponytail swinging in time with her hips. It is a nice distraction from the arm-chewing monster behind her.

"Hey," she says, her voice softening a touch. I glance at her momentarily before shifting my attention back to the mare over her shoulder. "Are you okay?"

"Uh-huh," I mumble, my brain unable to focus on things in the room that are not the horse.

Kate moves in closer, blocking the animal from view. Her face is less than a foot from mine, demanding my attention.

"You don't have to do this, you know."

Her voice carries no judgment, her face carries no condemnation. I can stay or I can go, my choice. I search her face for some hint of what she wants from me but find nothing other than patience and concern.

That makes it seem silly, this fear of mine. Heaven knows I've seen a lot scarier things than a stupid horse, and I have lived through much worse pain than any horse could bring me. So I could fall off. Big freakin' deal. What's the worst that could happen? A broken arm? Maybe a leg? And I have to be taken care of a little while longer? By Kate?

That thought sparks a naughty nurse fantasy that has me ready to become a professional rodeo rider. If Kate notices my eyes glazing over while I let the fantasy play out in my head, she doesn't mention it.

"I'm fine. Just a little nervous."

"There's nothing to be nervous about. I promise."

Her smile chases away the last of my doubts. I follow her through the barn and out the back to where two gigantic behemoths stand saddled and waiting.

"The dark brown one is Goldie. This one is Stormchaser. Stu for short."

Goldie is the color of melted chocolate, except for a white patch extending from between her ears down to the top of her nose. Stu is pure black, like the deepest, darkest moonless night imaginable. Goldie nuzzles Kate's hand, happily accepting a scratch between her eyes. Stu, on the other hand, just stares at me.

"Goldie sort of adopted me when I first got here. She's been mine ever since. You'll be riding Stu."

I eye the horse warily, wondering if he is as thrilled with the idea of me riding him as I am. He snorts and stomps his front hoof in the dirt. It isn't a good sign.

"So, is that for me or the horse?" she asks, glancing at the bat peeking at her from above my shoulder as she tightens the saddles on Stu, then Goldie.

"I don't know. You planning on making trouble?"

Her eyebrow answers my question.

"Mugsy's my don't-leave-home-without-it. Like American Express used to be."

"You like being prepared, don't you?"

"It makes things easier. You have everything you need, whenever you need it. You're never left wanting. You're never left wishing for something you don't already have."

"Sounds kind of sad."

I bristle slightly. "How's that?"

She shrugs. "It's the wanting more that drives us, keeps our lives from being ordinary. Everything we've achieved in the course of history came from wanting something we didn't have. Fire, the lightbulb, airplanes…they all came from wanting something more, something better."

Here I was just making light conversation, and she goes all psychoanalyst on me. Okay, my light conversation had gone a little Zen, but still.

"Tell that to the millions of people Hitler exterminated. He wanted something better, too."

I have grown defensive. Old habits die a slow, painful death, if they ever die at all.

"Yes, but Hitler was a paranoid xenophobic masochist with delusions of grandeur. Not everyone's like that."

"More than you think."

Kate starts to object, so I press on. "It's a biological imperative to take as much as you can as often as you can, and to protect all that you have taken. It's survival of the fittest. He who has the most has the best chance of surviving. But unlike the rest of the animal kingdom, man eventually evolved past all that. Through tools and technology, we learned how to make and grow and gather enough of what we needed until survival was no longer our primary concern. Suddenly we had free time. It was the beginning of the end."

"Technology didn't cause the plague, Taylor."

"Didn't it? How do we know that damn virus wasn't created in a lab somewhere? That some scientist didn't create it in a petri dish one day, just to see if he could? Or test it out on some unsuspecting mental patient somewhere, and then it got loose?"

"You don't know that."

"True. But it's not like it hasn't happened before. Remember Tuskegee? Or what about those Guatemalans in the '40s? Man gets dangerous when he gets bored."

"Well, we're not bored now. We're too busy trying to survive again."

"Which just means we're back to killing each other over the basics."

"You always see the worst side of everything, don't you?"

"You see the glass half full. I'm a half-empty kind of girl."

"No, you see the glass as cracked and laced with arsenic."

I would laugh if she wasn't serious.

She cocks her head, as if she has had some new insight into my psyche. "What's wrong with seeing the world as it could be instead of as it is? What's wrong with choosing hope instead of fear?"

"Nothing. Other than it's a waste of time."

"I don't believe it's a waste of time to believe in what might be instead of dwelling on all we've lost. My parents are dead, my friends, my neighbors, the first girl I ever kissed. They're all gone, either killed by the plague or God-knows-where now. I grieve for them and for myself. Every night I pray for them, pray the ones who died are someplace better and tomorrow will be better than today for the ones still living. And then I go to sleep and dream about building a new life from the ashes of the old."

I have a hundred pithy responses to that. Instead, I find myself speaking in titles from the *Cinderella* songbook.

"'A Dream is a Wish Your Heart Makes'?"

She smiles shyly. "Something like that. There has to be something more to life than just surviving it, Taylor. Otherwise, what's the point?"

"I don't know," I say. And I really don't know anything other than that I have lost the will to argue. "I guess we'll just have to agree to disagree."

"I guess," she says. "For now."

She is damn near as obstinate as I am. I like that about her.

"So, are we ready?" I ask.

"Just about," she says, handing me the reins to both Goldie and Stu, which makes me return my attention to the momentarily forgotten horses and the fear they inspire. Goldie happily munches on some tall grass at her feet. Stu is staring at me again.

Kate returns from the barn carrying a rather ominous looking shotgun.

"I'm just going to assume that's for me and not the horses."

"What can I say?" she says, smiling as she slides the gun into the holster I had failed to notice attached to Goldie's saddle. "You're not the only one who likes being prepared."

With that, she sets her foot into the stirrup and mounts Goldie in one fluid, graceful motion. If Grace Kelly had ever mounted a horse on the silver screen, this is what she would have looked like doing it. I, unfortunately, have none of Kate's grace, and I'm sure I look more like Jerry Lewis as I haul myself up and plop down into Stu's saddle with a less than delicate thump.

Kate guides Goldie out of the corral with practiced ease and without looking back. Clearly Stu and I are meant to follow their lead, but Stu isn't having it. He doesn't even shuffle a hoof in their direction.

"All right, Stu." I lean down toward the horse's ear, which he flips at me with an indignant flutter. "You and I need to have a little chat. It's not like I like this any more than you do. But here we are, and there they go, and it seems to me we can just stand here all day being annoyed with each other, or we can agree to disagree, too."

Stu snorts. But I take it as a good sign that he hasn't bucked me yet. At least he is listening.

"Let's make a deal, you and I. You don't bite my arm off, I'll play the happy passenger, and after today you'll never have to see me again."

Stu shuffles forward a couple of steps but then stops again. His head levers back toward me, and he eyes me with that big, black hole of his. I lift my hands up in the universal sign of surrender. He's in charge, and he knows it.

"It's your show, Stu. You can stand here glaring at me, or we can spend the day following the ladies."

His large head turns away from me and toward where Kate and Goldie are sauntering off into the day. Stu whinnies lightly. I think he has a bit of a crush, which leaves me with one last card to play.

"Wouldn't you rather spend the day staring at the view than sitting here all alone?"

Stu kicks at the dirt and snorts his assent, and takes off after Kate and Goldie.

Figures. Stu's an ass-man.

We catch up quickly, much more quickly than I am comfortable with. For the first half mile, I have a death grip on the reins, bouncing up and down in the saddle with such force my tailbone is scratching the top of my head, which I think amuses Stu to no end. Eventually, we settle into a rhythm, and I ease back enough to notice we have left the farm.

Stu keeps us a few horse-lengths behind Kate and Goldie for a while, enjoying his own view while I take in the world around us. Barren fields lead one into the next, surrounded by rolling hills as green as emeralds. These are the ruins the plague has wrought. With no one left to tend them, the crops waste away, sagging in the fields, picked apart by birds and animals. Yet all around them life flourishes, the trees and grass man so arrogantly tamed now growing free. It is as if the earth has chosen to let the remains of man die while she nourishes the natural world, reclaiming the ground we spent lifetimes taking as our own. The world is hers now, and she is using it as she sees fit. We are no longer her master, but instead, her lowly tenant.

Eventually, Stu sidles us up next to Goldie, and the four of us stroll on in companionable silence. It is peaceful, this silence, only broken by the muted sounds of the horses' cantering and the wind riffling through the trees. I imagine this must be what it sounded like to the earliest settlers, back before the trains and cars and cell phones. This kind of quiet is a foreign thing, even though it has been accompanying me for months. It is amazing how quiet the world has gotten since the fall of man. I wonder if the animals are relieved to finally have an end to all that racket.

At some point I notice I am growing tired, so I can only imagine how the horses feel. The noonday sun signals we have been at it for hours, and I am about to suggest a break when Kate reads my mind.

"See that group of trees up ahead?" she asks, pointing off toward a small cluster just below the horizon. After hours of silence, her voice is like a song. "It's not as much a group as it is the edge of a small forest. Might be a good place to take a break."

It is nearly another half hour before we reach what turns out to be much more than a small forest. The trees offer needed relief from the cloudless sky, and the temperature drops noticeably as we weave in and out of their shade. We arrive at a small stream, and Kate dismounts as if she hasn't become unbearably stiff from the long ride. I, on the other hand, find I have even less grace getting off my horse than I had getting on and would have landed flat on my ass but for Kate, who catches me with surprisingly strong arms. I grin shakily up at her, a bit unnerved by our sudden proximity, but she just steadies me before retreating to tie up the horses.

Stu, for his part, pays me little notice before nuzzling up next to Goldie. I guess he has his priorities, although I swear that horse is laughing at what a smooth operator I am. While I stretch and try to regain the feeling in the lower half of my body, Kate unpacks some sandwiches and water and a small blanket. We might be picnickers in some lovely park.

"Thanks," I mumble as I sit down beside Kate, a bit ashamed that I have nothing to offer in return. I feel like the prom date who forgot the corsage. Not that this is a date. From what I remember of my last one, there should be wine and flowers and candlelight. I let my friends fix me up a few months after I found my girlfriend cheating on me. Bad idea. I knocked over the candle trying to pour more wine to numb myself against my date's incessant nattering. Interesting how effectively catching a tablecloth on fire can end a bad date.

"No problem," she says, offering me a sandwich before digging in to her own. I eat greedily, surprised at how hungry the trip has made me. Goldie and Stu chew on the grass at their feet, occasionally nudging each other with their noses. It seems very much like flirting to me.

Kate finishes her sandwich and leans back on one elbow, watching me finish my lunch. It makes me nervous, and I feel compelled to say something, anything, even though I seem to have lost the art of making light conversation. Not that I have ever been good at that.

"So, you come here often?" I ask, nearly laughing at the ridiculously cheesy line as it leaves my mouth. Kate does laugh, putting me at ease.

"I've been here a few times."

"It's beautiful."

She looks around, as if taking it in for the first time.

"Yes, it really is."

I struggle for something else to say but come up empty. I am entirely distracted by a ray of sunlight that has pierced the canopy and is playing with the highlights in Kate's hair. It is pathetic, but I am completely smitten.

"What do you miss most?"

And the fly ball into left field award goes to...

"Um...huh?"

She laughs again. If I could do nothing else for the rest of my life, making her laugh would be enough.

"From before? What do you miss most about the world?"

It is a serious question, and yet it feels as light as the breeze rustling the grass around us. I choose to follow the wind's lead.

"Starbucks."

"Starbucks?" she chuckles. "Of all the things in the world... Starbucks?"

"If you'd ever had an iced mocha you wouldn't be asking me that."

"I was more of a green tea Frappuccino girl myself."

Of course she is. I smile.

"Seriously, though. Iced mochas, Wi-Fi, those exclusive CDs? And they really were on every corner in DC. What's not to miss?"

"I see your point."

"What about you?" I lean back, settling in against the base of a large tree, my arms propped on my knees like I don't have a care in the world.

"Hmm, many things." She shifts on the blanket, propping her head in her hand, her other hand idly plucking at imaginary pieces of lint. "I think I miss music on the radio. How you'd be driving along in the car, switching stations, until you'd stumble on a song you hadn't heard in forever. Then you'd be singing along to words you could barely remember but somehow still knew. I miss that."

I remember the last time I had that feeling. A whisper of a nondescript memory washes over me, and although I can't remember the song or the road or when it was, I remember the feel of it. "I miss that, too."

"What else?" Kate prompts.

"Movies."

"We still have those. Well, we have Buck's three John Wayne DVDs, anyway."

"Yeah, but I'm talking about real movies. In theaters. With surround sound and popcorn."

"With butter."

"Of course with butter."

"I miss baseball," Kate says wistfully.

"Oh, me too. Favorite team?"

"Well, my dad was a Cardinals fan."

I think the scowl on my face tells her all she needs to know. The hissing sound I make seals the deal.

"Oh boy. Cubs?"

I nod. "You know what this means?"

"Of course. Thankfully, I said *my dad* was a Cards fan. I never much cared for them."

"That was close. I really didn't want to have to bludgeon you to death."

"Well, no, that would have been bad," she says gravely even as she smiles broadly. "I liked the Padres."

"Respectable choice."

"I'm so glad you approve. Your turn."

"Airplanes."

"But not airplane food."

"God, no."

"Bumper cars."

"Bumper stickers."

"Barnes & Noble."

"Comic books."

"Captain America?"

She couldn't delight me more if she was wearing an "I Heart Geeks" T-shirt.

"Captain America. And the Flash."

"Wally West?"

The girl knows her comic books. Now I am impressed as well as delighted.

"Okay. But Barry was always my Flash."

"I can respect that," she says.

"I miss ice cream cones."

"Ben & Jerry's."

"Nah. Too much…stuff. Give me a scoop of mint chocolate chip melting on a cone any day."

"Because it's better when it's melting?"

"Of course," I say. I get lost in a memory, of better times that don't seem so far away despite their distance. Kate remains silent, as if she senses the memory rattling around in my head.

"I have this memory," I begin distantly, like I am telling a fairytale instead of a story from my life. "I couldn't have been more than five or six. I was with my dad one Saturday, which was unusual because my dad wasn't home much. He was a trucker, and he was on the road more than he was home, especially on weekends."

A wistful smile tugs at my mouth as I flash through a dozen other memories of my father. Watching him shave, getting to blow the horn of his truck, the sweetness of finally beating him at Sorry because he refused to ever let me win, watching him watch a Bears game on the rare Sunday he was home...

"Anyway, he had taken me out for the afternoon on his motorcycle, first to the park, then for ice cream. Mint chocolate chip on a cone. We decided to bring some ice cream back for my mom, so we got on his motorcycle and headed home. I still had the cone in my hand, and it was a pretty hot day..."

"Oh no..." Kate says, laughing already at the inevitability of it all.

"Oh yes. Not the smartest move, granted. So there I was, holding my cone, watching this stream of green flying past me and directly onto the windshield of the car behind us." We are both laughing now, and I can barely get the words out. "Nice old couple in that car. Reminded me of my grandparents. I could see them smiling at me from behind their windshield wipers."

Kate sits up, wiping away tears of laughter. My stomach clenches from laughing, and I rub the knot away. I can't believe I just told her that. Yet instead of wanting to take it back, I only want to tell her more. I want to tell her everything.

We lapse into silence again, enjoying the day. I glance over at Kate and find her watching me. She has grown thoughtful. I can tell by the way her head is cocked to the side she is gearing up to start a conversation I won't necessarily be happy about. She isn't hard to read that way.

"Your dad, is he...?"

And there it is. The $64,000 question, which adjusted for inflation is more expensive than I can ever hope to afford.

I have two choices, sitting on this blanket in this not-so-small forest with this person I barely know and yet feel I know deeply. I can fall back on my usual cynicism and use sarcasm to deflect the question, or I can actually act like a human being who has something left to offer the world.

To run or not to run. That is the question.

"I don't know," I say, the words catching in my throat.

Putting voice to these thoughts is like bathing in acid. It burns everywhere, tearing at my flesh and my heart. I am speaking words I have not used in more than five months, and they taste like copper pennies on my tongue.

"I haven't spoken to my parents since…" I have to work to remember when that last conversation happened. It's hard to place even though the call is etched in my mind, the words half shouted between bursts of static, desperately begging me to leave the city. "It was a few weeks before the bomb. They were still okay then. Neither one was sick. The line was so garbled with static I couldn't hear a lot of what my dad said. I don't know whether my brother or sister or their families were sick. I kept feeling like there was more he wasn't telling me, like maybe…He sounded okay, like he was healthy, but maybe he wasn't. Or maybe someone else was sick. Dad never liked to give me bad news over the phone, so who knows?"

I make light of it, trying to keep the countless *what if*s at bay. I have spent countless hours imagining who had caught the disease.

Kate is sitting up now, her arms wrapped around her knees, listening. Her eyes hold a world of grief, for me, but also for herself. She has lost people, too. Everyone has.

"I just remember how desperate he was for me to leave the city. He kept begging me to come home. For weeks I had stayed, watched everyone I knew get sick. The people I worked with, my neighbors, my friends. I moved in with my best friend and her husband. They had managed to not get sick for so long, we thought they were immune. We were wrong."

I refuse to cry. I deny the tears even as they well up. If I start crying now, I know I will never stop. I shake my head, forcing it all back down.

"I knew that woman for fifteen years. We met in college. I always thought we were sort of the odd couple. She was all athletic and confident and straight, and I was this introvert nerd just starting to figure out I was gay. But somehow it worked. When we both ended up in DC years after college, it seemed like the craziest, most wonderful coincidence in the world. And then the plague came, and I held my best friend while she died."

I blow all the air out of my lungs, releasing that particular ghost. I did what I could for her. I stayed, and I held her, and I buried her and her husband out in the backyard, beneath the fire pit where we spent countless fall evenings talking and making s'mores and laughing like those were the things that truly mattered in life.

"After that, there was nothing left to stay for. The call with my dad just confirmed what I already knew—that it was time to go home. The last thing my dad said was to make me promise to come home. Then the line went dead. I tried calling them back, but I couldn't get a call through. So the next morning, I got in my car and started for Asheville. I went as far as I could with the little gas I had left. I'm still trying to get there. I have to get there."

I stop talking. That is only the beginning of the story, but it is too much to continue on with right now.

"You have to know."

It is said simply but with perfect understanding. I give a terse nod, still trying to fight back the emotion threatening to overwhelm me. I can't tell her what I fear I already know, for if I speak the words aloud, it will make them real. And if they are real, then I truly will have nothing left. As long as I am going home, I have something. The mission sustains me. The lie is my life.

There is more to say, and she knows it, but for now what I have said is enough, for both of us.

"We should probably start heading back," she says reluctantly. Already the day's light has started to angle through the trees, and it won't be long before the shadows begin stretching toward nightfall.

We make quick work of our picnic, content in the peace that comes from two people who have just shared what we have. Kate brings the horses over, and they both seem more subdued than before. I chalk it up to boredom on their parts, but as I take Stu's reins, I notice him eyeing me with an understanding that had been missing from our earlier encounter. I know I am being ridiculous, thinking somehow the horse understood our conversation, yet it makes me less anxious about the ride back.

I am in the midst of ungracefully mounting my horse when Goldie screams. I turn, only to find the horse rearing up on her two hind legs and Kate plunging toward the earth.

I barely hear myself shout Kate's name as I jump to the ground and run to her. She is clutching her head in agony. "Stupid snake," she mutters as I drop down to her side.

"What happened?" I am panicking. I pry her hand away from her head. A purple lump is already forming beneath the blood running out of a deep gash.

"Goldie got spooked, and I hit my head on a rock," she says, wincing as I probe the cut. I strip off my overshirt and dab away the blood.

"Sorry. I have to put pressure on this," I say, pressing the shirt against the wound.

"It's okay," she says weakly, grinding her teeth. "Goldie's not easily spooked, but it was a pretty big snake."

I glance around nervously. That's all we need, for the snake to come investigating while we are on the ground, defenseless.

"It's gone. I think Goldie scared it just as much as it scared Goldie."

I remove the shirt and take another look at the cut. It isn't as deep as I feared. The blood is already slowing. Still, it is going to leave a nasty bruise, and I'm not convinced Kate doesn't have a concussion. I return the shirt to her head, wanting to make sure I stop the bleeding.

"I told you next time I wouldn't have to ask."

"What?" I ask absently.

"Next time I wanted your shirt off."

It takes me a minute to focus on anything besides the gash on her head and the panic I feel. I look down to find Kate grinning up at me, and I relax.

"Are you flirting with me?"

"Yes?" she says a bit hesitantly, losing some of her bravado.

"Good," I respond, smiling broadly. My heart thunders in my chest, and it is no longer from worry. "Now let's get you up and back to the farm, where someone more qualified than me can take a look at that hard head of yours."

CHAPTER EIGHTEEN

The ride back to the farm is agonizingly slow, the wait outside the makeshift hospital room in the farmhouse where I woke up earlier in the week even slower. I pace outside the door after having been practically shoved out by Margie, who had deemed my presence in the room distracting.

"She didn't have to kick me out," I mutter as I prowl the hallway. My lack of control over the situation is making me cranky. But more than that, I am worried. It's not like we have an X-ray machine or CT scanner lying around.

Buck chuckles behind me, but I choose to ignore him. Dunk, on the other hand, who arrived out of breath just in time for my ejection from the room, is harder to ignore.

"Well, you did kind of get in the way."

I pause in my pacing to glare at him. I might have growled.

"You threatened to shove the needle where the sun don't shine if Margie didn't back off," Buck says, responding to Dunk's silent plea for a little help.

"Yeah, well…" I realize that threatening Buck's daughter hadn't been one of my brightest ideas. "But did you see the size of that needle?"

I really had acted like an idiot. Am still acting like one.

"Sorry," I say with a groan, sinking back against the wall.

"We're not the ones you should apologize to," Buck says with a laugh. He settles his hand on my shoulder. "She'll be fine."

I search his face for reassurance as the bedroom door finally opens.

"The patient will see you now," Margie says sweetly to no one in particular. I shove off the wall and surge toward the open doorway, only to be stopped by a resolute Margie blocking my path. She crosses her arms in a clear challenge.

"Sorry about before," I squeak out.

She nods her acceptance of my apology and steps out of my way. Kate is sitting on the bed, her legs dangling over the edge. She greets me with a warm smile. I can breathe again. She is going to be okay.

A large bandage is taped to her forehead. My fingers reach out and skim the edge before slipping down the side of her face. She nuzzles her cheek into my hand.

"Ahem."

Buck's throat-clearing startles me. I had forgotten there was anyone else left on the planet, let alone in the hallway waiting to come into the room. I start to pull my hand away, more than a little embarrassed, but Kate's own hand snags mine and holds it in place for a moment longer. She is telling me that this, too, is okay. Then she withdraws, and my hand falls limply to my side, having lost its home.

"She going to be okay, Doc?" Buck asks his daughter. Dunk hovers in the doorway, his baseball cap clenched in his hands.

"I'm fine," Kate says dismissively. "It's just a bump."

"Pretty big bump," Margie responds, her voice stern. "And you'd do well to remember that. No riding for at least a few days, and take it easy, will you?"

"Pfft."

Kate's bravado, combined with Margie's lecture, is making me more than a bit nervous.

"We were worried about you, kiddo."

Buck's concern seems to deflate Kate's defiance.

"But she is going to be all right, right?" Dunk asks quietly, taking a hesitant step farther into the room.

"She'll be fine," Margie says, recognizing the true distress behind Dunk's words. "She just needs to take it easy for a bit, despite what she may think."

Kate holds up her hands, surrendering to the will of the group. "I promise. No marathons for me." Dunk still fidgets nervously in the corner. Kate looks him in the eye. "Promise."

Dunk finally relaxes.

"Feel up to some dinner?" Buck asks, helping Kate to her feet. I stand dumbly at the side of the bed, wanting to reach out but too insecure to make a move. Kate slips her hand around my arm. For balance, I tell myself.

"Sounds good," she tells Buck, squeezing his arm before letting go and wrapping her free hand around the other nestled in the crook of my arm. "Lead the way?" she asks me softly. My stomach flutters.

We take our time walking to the north barn, me and Kate, Buck, Dunk, and Margie. Along the way, we are stopped at least half a dozen times by the farm's residents, who fuss and fret over Kate's injury. It seems everyone has heard about our little misadventure with the horses. Kate is gracious, making time to chat with each well-wisher and always making sure they are okay, as if *they* were the ones who had somehow bashed their heads on a rock, but her kindness is taking its toll. The pressure on my arm increases steadily, and I can see the fatigue in her eyes. It takes everything I have not to lift Kate up into my arms and carry her the rest of the way, knocking down anyone who gets in my way. I know that's not what she would want, and I rein it in and support her the best I can. Thankfully, Buck reads the situation and intervenes, keeping us moving and leading folks away from Kate so we can continue our way up to the barn.

"Thank you," she sighs as I finally ease her down at one of the dining tables in the hall. I hover protectively over her until I am sure she is settled and then sink down beside her. Dunk immediately races off to get Kate a plate of food and is back barely after having left.

"Thanks," she says. The boy nods, grinning like a fool, before heading back to get a plate of his own.

"Aren't you going to eat anything?" she asks me. I think about saying no, but my rumbling belly betrays my intentions.

"Will you be okay? Just for a minute?"

"I'll be fine. You are quite the knight in shining armor, aren't you?"

I wonder if I have gone too far, if maybe my actions have been read as some kind of inappropriate possessiveness. I am acting on instinct, and for all I know maybe I have stepped over some invisible boundary. But her voice holds no recrimination, and I realize she is telling me I am doing right by her.

I feel myself blushing.

Not wanting to embarrass me further, she pats my arm and says, "Go. I'll be right here."

I nod, my voice having left me, and leave to retrieve my supper. When I return, Buck, Dunk, Margie, and a few others have wedged themselves into every open space at the table. I notice, however, that my seat remains conspicuously empty. I grin at that.

I tuck into my dinner, keeping an eye on Kate with regular glances. She is tired but less fatigued than before, seeming to get her second wind from her food and the conversation at the table. I eat silently, content to just listen to the chatter around me, which jumps from farm talk to favorite films to, strangely enough, a lively discussion of the benefits of capitalism versus those of socialism. The purpose of such a debate in our present circumstances is lost on me, but it is familiar and vaguely comforting in an odd way.

Soon enough, the plates are cleared, and the Saturday-night party is in full swing. The music, which begins by featuring the greatest hits of disco, weaves its way through the room. I sit beside Kate, watching the citizens of Burninghead Farm do their thing, watching Buck lead Margie around the room in a mismatched waltz, and I am content. Kate's attention is focused on Dunk's attempts to dance with a nine-year-old little girl by the name of Rachel, which has ended in a mutual decision to just let Rachel stand on Dunk's feet as he shuffles around the floor.

I take a stolen moment to study Kate in the soft glow of the Christmas lights, watch the play of emotions cross her face as she watches her friends, the way the candlelight from the table dances across her skin, the way the corner of her eyes crinkle as she smiles, and I feel myself falling. I turn away just as she turns toward me. I pretend to be watching the crowd but risk a quick glance back at her only to find her grinning in such a way that I know I have been busted. Somehow, I don't mind.

We stay that way for a while, just the two of us, enjoying the joy around us. Eventually, the frenzied up-tempo tunes give way to softer fare, and the dancers settle into a new, more subdued rhythm.

"Dance with me?"

Her voice is a whisper. She is still looking ahead, watching the dancers in the center of the barn, and I wonder if I am hearing things. Then she turns to me.

"Dance with me?" she asks again, her voice still petal soft, but this time I see her lips move. She holds out her hand to me, palm up, both an invitation and an offering. How can I refuse?

I stand, slipping my hand into hers and offering her my other one, which she accepts with a shy smile. I help her up and slowly lead her out onto the dance floor, careful to pick a spot that is not too crowded. We stand that way, facing each other, our hands locked together, until I tug her gently into my arms. She slides her arms up around my neck. My hands find her waist and settle there. I am caught between wanting to pull her closer and not daring to make such a bold move. She makes up my mind for me.

She steps into me without pretense, molding her body against mine and tightening her arms around my neck. All I know is how good she feels in my arms, how warm her breath is against my neck, how soft her hair is against my cheek, and how I want this dance to go on forever.

I am not, nor have I ever been, a good dancer, and while I might wish for the dapper feet of Fred Astaire, I am much more like Mister Ed on the dance floor, even if my partner is Ginger Rogers reincarnated. Still, somehow, I find my way without inflicting grievous bodily injury. We move as one, neither leading nor following. One step simply leads to the next without thought or plan, and we move so easily I would not be surprised to look down to find that we are floating.

Her cheek slides against my own as she pulls her head back, her eyes finding mine in the muted light. The hum of her skin tickles my nose. My hands tighten around her waist both in anticipation and uncertainty, and my gaze falls to her lips without thinking. They part softly, and the inevitability of it all overwhelms me. There is no denying what is about to happen, what I know beyond reason we both want to happen.

I don't know who moves first, or if our mouths simply fall toward each other, no longer able to withstand the pull of gravity. Her kiss is soft and unbearably sweet, cocoa smooth and velvet rich. Her lips feel weightless, brushing over mine once and then again, infinite with the promise of things to come. My eyes close, my brain unable to withstand the sensory overload of both the kiss and her beauty. I feel a hunger I have never known, which is tempered by the knowledge that we have all the time in the world.

The kiss seems to go on forever, until it finally ends, and I press my cheek against hers, unable to bear the separation of our lips. I have to remember how to breathe. I feel her smiling. I pull back to look at her, my mind unable to fully comprehend the magnitude of what I am feeling. Her hand brushes my skin, her fingers dancing in the fine hairs at the base of my neck, and I feel like I am home.

Hazily, I become aware of the music around us, which has regained its upbeat tempo once more. Somewhere along the way we have become the focus of everyone's attention. I begin to feel the blood rushing to my face. Kate notices the attention, too, but doesn't pull away. Her courage bolsters my own, and I decide I have no reason to be anything but proud. I slide my arm around her shoulders and face the room.

I needn't have bothered. Smiles light up all around us, and I half expect someone to start clapping. Thankfully, no one does. Soon people are talking again, going back to whatever it was they were doing before our little show. I turn back to Kate.

"Would you like something to drink?" I ask, stroking my thumb along the side of her face.

She nods.

"Want to sit back down?"

She shakes her head, and I think about pressing the issue but see Dunk hovering at the edge of the dance floor. I know that as soon as I leave he will rush in, and that is good enough for me.

I head over to the other end of the room. When I reach the drinks table it occurs to me that I have no idea what Kate likes to drink, which seems funny to me in some bizarre way considering our intimacy. There is so much I still don't know about her, but I am looking forward to learning.

"Go with the lemonade," I hear Buck say. He steps up next to me and hands me a plastic cup. He must be reading my mind.

"Thanks," I say, accepting the cup and grabbing one of the two-liters on the table.

I grow nervous, wondering if Buck is going to disapprove in some way, but he says nothing about the kiss. At least not directly.

"So," he says, pouring his own cup of soda, "you still planning on leaving us soon?"

I look over at him, the hope in his eyes contradicting the phrasing of his question.

"I know you have to find out what happened to your family. But you have family here, too. This is your home now, Taylor, if you want it to be."

I look across the room at Kate, and at Dunk, and at the rest of the people of Burninghead Farm, and I know Buck's words to be true. I have known it for days, since I played guitar on the porch and was struck by the first glimmer of hope I have felt since leaving DC. I just hadn't been ready to fully embrace it until now. Leaving the farm does not have to mean the end. The promise I made to my father is not the only thing I have to live for. I have journeyed toward one home only to find another, one that will be here for me regardless of what I find in Illinois.

"I'll go to Asheville, and then—"

My words die in my throat as Buck's face falls.

"Did you say Asheville?"

His voice is strained, his skin ashen.

Please. No.

"A few days ago. We heard a couple of boys had wandered into Milton Station, scared, practically starving. There was a raiding party, they said. It had come to the boys' town. There were about twenty survivors still living there, mostly men, a few women, children. The raiding party came, about a dozen men, heavily armed, demanding food, supplies. The survivors offered to share, but it wasn't enough. The raiders demanded everything they had, and they couldn't let that happen."

Buck doesn't have to finish the story for me to know what happens next. I can feel it in my blood, know it in my bones, and still I want to scream at him to continue, to hurry up and tell me everything is going to turn out okay. But I can't. I just stare at him. He doesn't look me in the eye.

"A few of the men from the town pulled out guns, just trying to scare off the raiders. Then one of the guns went off. The boys didn't know who shot first. They ran and hid. After a while, when they were sure the raiders were gone, they came out. Everyone was dead."

Buck's voice shakes with the horror of it. I do not feel it. I have gone numb.

"Milton Station took the boys in. They're only fifteen."

"Which town?" My voice sounds dead to my own ears.

"What?"

"Which town?" My voice is harsher now, but just as dead.

"Taylor…" The sorrow on his face nearly kills me. I already know the answer, but I am going to make him say it. I need him to say it. It is all I have left.

"What was the name of the town, Buck?"

"It was Asheville."

CHAPTER NINETEEN

Duncan did not understand how the world could change so quickly. It should not have surprised him, he supposed. After all, one day the plague had been only an interesting puzzle on some scientist's shelf, and the next it had been the beginning of the end.

The world had changed all over again on Saturday night, at least for Taylor. Taylor's family, it appeared, was dead. If they had managed to survive the plague, they had not survived the raiding party that had come to Asheville.

That had been a week ago. Duncan had wanted to follow her that night, to try and calm her down and tell her everything was going to be okay. He had lost his parents, too, as had Kate, and they were both okay. But Kate had stopped him. If he was honest about it, he was still kind of mad at her for that.

"How can you not want to help her?" he demanded as she *grabbed his arm to keep him from following Taylor.*

"You think I don't?" Kate asked, visibly shaking. *"You think my heart isn't breaking right now?"*

"Then why don't you?"

"Because that's not what she needs right now."

"How do you know?" His sorrow was thick in his throat.

Kate shook her head, slumping down onto one of the benches outside the dining hall. "I don't know. Not for sure."

"*Then why—*"

"*The world just ended all over again for her. She's going to need time to deal with that, and nothing we say is going to make that any better for her.*"

"*But she's alone,*" Duncan said, sinking down next to Kate. He stared off toward the dorm, feeling like his insides had been turned inside out. Duncan just could not understand. Taylor was his friend. You did not just let your friends suffer alone.

"*I know.*"

"*Will she be okay?*" he finally asked, defeated.

"*She has to be,*" Kate said. She nodded to herself. "*We'll make sure of it. We just have to give her some time.*"

Which is exactly what they had done. Duncan had not seen Taylor for the first few days. They had let her be, alone, locked within her room. She did not touch the trays of food Duncan and others brought and left outside her door every morning, noon, and evening. After two days, they had begun to worry in earnest, but Taylor would not let anyone in, would not answer the knocking on her door or the voices on the other side of it. No one could get through to her, not even Kate.

The only reason they even knew she was still alive was the sound of her sobbing every night. The sound haunted him well after he left his spot in front of her door in the hallway each night to try and get a few hours of shuteye.

Finally, on the third day, they had decided to intervene, to break down the door if they had to. Turned out it was not necessary. Duncan, Kate, and Buck arrived at Taylor's door to find the tray half empty of its lunch.

It was a start.

For two more days Taylor stayed in her room, still refusing to talk to anyone or come outside, but she was eating. For that, Duncan was grateful, as he was that she had stopped crying all night. He wondered if the pain was easing, or if she had just run out of tears.

Finally, on the sixth day, Taylor emerged. Emmett reported seeing her walking along the eastern edge of the farm, far away from any of the work details or any of the farm's other daily activities. Clearly, she still wanted to be alone, which saddened Duncan more than he could say. He wanted to talk to her, to try and offer some comfort, but one look at Kate told him it still was not time.

On day seven, Taylor once again left her room before dawn and spent the day far out on the property's edge, only to return well after dusk. That night's dinner was subdued at best. It seemed that everyone was worried about Taylor, though no one talked about it. After dinner someone turned on the music just like every Saturday night, but no one seemed to have an appetite for celebrating. The party, if you could even call it that, ended early for the first time that anyone could remember. After everyone had gone to bed, Buck came to Duncan and asked him if he would mind being taken off the wall crew for a few days and given a new assignment. Duncan was more than happy to oblige.

Sunday morning began to break across the horizon, but Duncan was already awake and dressed and lurking around the side of the north barn. He did not have to wait long before he saw her, a ghost in the October breeze. He waited next to the barn, not hiding exactly but being sure to keep to the shadows. She headed out and away from both barns toward the southwest, where the darkness was still deep and quiet. He waited until she began to disappear into the gloom before setting out, confident enough in his tracking skills that he knew he would be able to find her even if he lost sight of her.

He did not want to spook her, he told himself. The truth was a little more complicated than that.

He followed her for more than an hour, until the sun finally began to show itself. Their pace was slow, set by Taylor. She plodded along, her hands shoved deep into her pockets, her head always pointed toward the earth. Flames of crimson and gold licked the morning sky, a rich contrast to the rapidly deepening hue of blue that served as a backdrop. It was going to be a stunning day. Duncan wondered if Taylor had even noticed the sunrise, or if the only color she could see was the sluggish green of the autumn grass dying beneath her feet.

She began to slow, and Duncan had to practically crawl so as not to catch up to her. A small cluster of rocks lined the base of a gentle hill that edged the property line, like a mini-Stonehenge looking out over a good deal of the farm. The hill served as a natural windbreak to the west, but this part of the farm was slightly elevated over the rest, providing an excellent vantage point. Duncan had been here before, enjoying a bonfire and a couple of beers with his crew after a long day of work. He had always thought about coming back on his own. It was a nice spot to be alone.

Duncan watched Taylor ease herself down onto a small boulder between two larger ones, feeling even more like an intruder than before. He inched closer, scanning the area for someplace to be inconspicuous but finding none. Hiding between the rocks, she would be invisible to anyone looking up toward the hill from another part of the farm, but *she* could certainly see *them*. She could see him, too, Duncan quickly discovered.

"You might as well have a seat."

She spoke quietly, without any hint of emotion, and yet her words carried clearly along the crisp morning air as if she were shouting. He did not move at first, unsure of what to do. He wanted to go to his friend, even as the concept seemed daunting, and yet he had been given strict instructions by Buck, which he had already failed to follow.

Taylor said nothing more, and Duncan wondered if he had just wished she had spoken. But the flatness of her tone echoed in his head, propelling him forward. He picked out one of the stones along the outer edge of the natural rock garden and sat, perching on the edge, ready to take flight with the slightest provocation. Taylor remained silent, neither acknowledging his acceptance of her invitation or even his presence any further. She had apparently said all she was going to, at least for now.

The sun rose higher in the sapphire sky, announcing the passage of the day. Duncan shifted in the dirt, trying to find a more comfortable part of the boulder against which to rest his back, having slipped to the ground early on after realizing just how tiring it was to perch on a rock. Birds spent their whole lives perched on things, although maybe that was why they were always flitting about.

He was starting to grow hungry, and thirsty for that matter. He cursed himself for having left this morning without even thinking about bringing any supplies. No tracker worth his salt would have done something that stupid. His daddy had taught him better than that.

Once he started thinking about food and water, especially water, he could not seem to stop. He might as well have been wandering the desert for how dry his mouth felt, how harshly the sun seemed to be beating down on him, leaching what little water he had in his body. Taylor, however, seemed immune to such concerns, still sitting in exactly the same position in which she had settled hours earlier. He wondered how she could be so still. Maybe it was some sort of Zen thing, some Buddhist trick of the mind far outside his Christian upbringing. When he was a boy, his daddy had told him stories of the warriors and chiefs of early American tribes who would spend hours or even days fasting in sweat lodges, without food or water, communing with spirits, purifying themselves to some unknown but perfect point of clarity. Duncan wondered if that was what Taylor was doing, consciously or not.

She stared out upon the farm, unblinking. But Duncan didn't really think she was seeing anything in the here and now. He thought if he stood up and stepped before her and looked into her eyes, he would see images flickering upon them, movie screens playing some private film just for Taylor.

"When I left Washington, I thought it would only take a few days to get home. I was so naïve."

Taylor spoke quietly, leaving Duncan again to wonder whether he had simply imagined that she had spoken.

"I thought I'd have enough gas to make it to Pittsburgh. I hit empty southeast of the city, in the mountains. The stations were all out of gas by then, but the emergency broadcast on the radio said the National Guard was trucking more into the area, so I waited. I waited for nearly a week, but no trucks came. There were maybe a dozen of us camped out in this town, just waiting and hoping. Eventually, we realized we were on our own."

Her voice was monotone, like she was reciting a book report she had memorized for school.

"We'd pretty well run through the food at the gas station by then. Some folks decided to start walking to wherever it was they had been headed, but I was scared. I didn't think I could make that kind of journey on my own. I wasn't the only one. But there was this boy, Tim. Not a boy, really, probably about nineteen. He had been heading home from college and said his family lived only about twenty miles from where we were, and he was sure we'd all be welcome there. It seemed like the best option, so I followed Tim home."

Duncan leaned forward, mesmerized by both the tale Taylor was weaving and the fact that she was telling it at all. Especially now. He assumed there was a reason she was telling him this, but he could not understand yet what that reason was.

Taylor had not looked at him, was speaking as much to the rocks around her as she was to him. All he could do was keep listening.

"Three of us followed Tim. Me, Claire, and Claire's husband John. He'd wanted to head out with the others, to keep going, but Claire was scared they couldn't make it. Better to wait for help, she said. So we went with Tim, too frightened to go on to more unknown. It took us two days to reach Tim's home, and we were all exhausted when we finally got there. I felt bad for the kid. He had never considered that his family might not have made it. His parents were gone, along with his grandmother and younger sister. But Tim's brother, Jacob, had survived."

Although her voice barely wavered, there was something in the way Taylor said Jacob's name that made Duncan shudder. He studied her, trying to figure out where this story was heading. Taylor kept her eyes straight ahead, still watching that movie of hers in her mind.

"Jacob had opened their parents' farm to other survivors, and before we arrived there were already about twenty camped out on the property. A few women, but mostly men, from teens to maybe midforties. They had been scavenging for weeks and had built up a pretty good supply of canned food and bottled water, but I worried it wouldn't be long before things were stretched to their limits, especially with four new mouths to feed. Tim reassured me that we would make do, that we were all welcome. He was a sweet kid.

"Jacob welcomed us all in, said we would be safe there on that farm. He said they'd heard a military convoy was moving through the area, distributing gas and supplies to folks who were stranded, and they should arrive in a few days, maybe a week. I didn't question how he knew that. None of us did. We were just relieved that we would all be okay. The army was coming. The government hadn't abandoned us. It was all going to be all right."

It took a moment for Taylor to continue, and Duncan wondered whether he should move closer. His gut told him to stay put, to give her the space to finish her tale as much as he wanted to sit beside her and put an arm around her shoulder.

"Things were fine for a while. Days stretched into a week, then two, but Jacob just kept telling us the convoy was coming, that we would be saved. But soon our supplies started to run low and tensions began to flare. The men who went out scavenging for supplies had to go farther and farther out, and soon there was nothing left within walking distance to find. We began to ration what we had, and it seemed like we had solved our problem, at least for a while. What we didn't realize was the lack of supplies wasn't our real concern.

"It was the little things at first. A comment here, a look there, things that we were used to ignoring in the old world but that here, where the women were surrounded and outnumbered by men, seemed more threatening, somehow. We had all been sleeping in our own tents, but soon we started pairing up, then tripling up, afraid of something of which we had not spoken but understood all the same. Except for Claire. She stayed with her husband in their tent. You could tell, though, that John was nervous, too.

"We started to talk at night, whispering with each other so the men wouldn't know. It felt like they were watching us all the time. I could feel their eyes on us even as they kept their distance, and it started to feel like any minute something was going to give. It wasn't all of them, of course, but it was enough. And Jacob...he was the worst because he was the most quiet. He never said a thing, but you could see it, and it was like the others were feeding off it."

Taylor shook slightly, just for a moment. The knot in Duncan's stomach tightened and grew.

"We finally started talking about leaving, but we knew we needed supplies, which we couldn't get access to because Jacob had ordered they be guarded. Just a precaution, he had said. It wasn't until it was too late that we started wondering what threat he was taking precautions against. But I knew we could trust Tim, and we agreed I would ask for his help. Just a few things to get us through a couple days until we could find more supplies. Tim told me we were being paranoid, that his brother and the others wouldn't hurt us, that they just wanted to help. He said we should just tell Jacob we wanted to leave. He didn't understand why we were trying to be secretive. I begged him not to say anything, told him we would just go and to not worry about the supplies. He said he would keep it to himself."

Taylor grew quiet again. Duncan waited for her to continue, but she remained silent. He knew there was more, knew this was not even close to the end of the story, but as the seconds stretched to minutes in the stillness, Duncan realized Taylor was done talking. And that, Duncan knew, was a problem. Not only because he wanted to know what happened next even as he dreaded hearing it, but also because his bones and blood understood in a way that his mind never could that this tale needed to be told. That Taylor had started talking for a reason, even if she did not consciously understand it, and she needed to finish. She needed to get it out. She needed to let it go.

"But he didn't," Duncan finally said. His voice, though soft as a whisper, startled Taylor. She turned her head slightly, as if truly seeing him for the first time. Her eyes were wide, but they were focused entirely on Duncan. She reminded him of a doe caught in the open, ready to run but too frightened to move. "He said something."

She continued staring at him until finally, almost imperceptibly, she nodded. Taylor breathed in deeply, as if she was trying to inhale the will to continue.

"We went to bed with the intention of sleeping a few hours, just until we were sure the others were asleep, and then leaving in the middle of the night," she said, looking away from Duncan once again.

"The screaming woke me. Then there were hands grabbing my clothes and dragging me out of my tent. I didn't know what was happening. They lined us up, tied our hands behind our backs. We were crying, and they were shouting at us to shut up, to quit our fucking crying. John was arguing with one of the men, pleading with him. Jacob walked up then, right up to John, and told him there was no room for thieves on this farm. Then Jacob…"

Taylor's voice caught, and she choked back a sob, forcing herself to go on.

"Jacob pulled a revolver out of his coat pocket and shot John in the head. He just shot him down, right in front of us, in front of his wife. Claire fell to the ground, clutching John's body, screaming. I couldn't scream, couldn't cry. I just stood there, numb. The other men…well, I think Jacob had surprised all of them, because for a moment they looked as scared as the rest of us. Then Jacob was barking out orders, and we were being dragged off to the horse stable.

"They locked us into the empty stalls and left us there, told us to stay quiet. Morning came and we were still there. Any time we tried to talk to each other through the stalls, one of the men came and beat on the stall doors. We got the message. Day turned into night again, then another day. I don't think they knew what to do with us, not really. I heard some of them arguing outside sometimes, but I could never tell what they were fighting about. Eventually, there was no more arguing.

"Three days went by, just locked into those stalls. They brought us food, water to drink and wash with. I started to wonder if maybe this was all just a big mistake, if Jacob had really just misunderstood what we had been planning and was trying to protect the rest of the people on the farm. But then, that night…"

She took another deep breath, another attempt to find the strength to continue. Duncan's heart broke for her. For all of them.

"Their footsteps pounded as they came. Two or three of them, I don't know. Then there were shouts. Someone, I think it was Liz, started screaming, 'No, no, please no.' One of them slapped her and she cried out. I could hear her being dragged out of the stall. She screamed the whole time. She was gone for hours. Everyone was crying while she was gone, sobbing to themselves. We were all too afraid to speak. Then I heard them bring her back. She was moaning.

They threw her back into her cell. I heard her body thud against the floor. Once they had left, I tried calling out to her, but she didn't answer. She just kept moaning. I might have thought she was dead but for the moaning.

"A few nights later they came again. I don't know if it was the same guys or if they were taking turns. They took Melanie that night. Another few days went by, and it was someone else. For nearly three weeks all we would hear were footsteps and dragging and screaming, then them bringing whoever it was back and throwing her in her cell. Every time it happened it was worse than the time before. I can still hear them laughing as they brought someone back.

"Then one night they took someone, but they didn't bring her back. It was Claire."

Duncan's heart pounded with the horror of it. In his most terrible nightmare he could never have envisioned such things. The urge to scream, to beat something into bloody oblivion, was overwhelming. But he remained silent, knowing there was more to tell.

"After Claire, it became every night instead of every few nights. I guess they really had developed a taste for it then."

She paused again, and Duncan could not help himself.

"Did they…?"

Taylor let out a long, slow breath. Her voice lost all trace of emotion.

"Not they. Jacob. Just Jacob."

Duncan shut his eyes, trying to block out the truth. But it was no use. The images came rushing in, and he could do nothing to stop the onslaught.

"The first time, he came into my stall, all quiet and calm. He knelt down before me, talking softly, cooing words of apology and reassurance. I was terrified, but I couldn't help myself. I spit in his face, told him to go to hell. He decked me, sent me flying back into the wall. My head was spinning. He grabbed me by the neck and hauled me to my feet. His hand was like a vise. He punched me in the face, over and over. I was starting to lose consciousness, from the blows or from his hand squeezing my throat, I'm not sure. Finally he threw me to the ground. But that was just the beginning."

Taylor's body shuddered and shook, but her face remained an impassive mask. Then she turned to Duncan.

"He didn't come back for several days. I had almost convinced myself it was over, but…then he was there. He came in the same way, oozing concern and compassion. He liked playing that game, acting like this was somehow all okay, like it wasn't his fault. Like he thought I would actually buy his lies. I stood up, my fists clenched, ready to die before I would let him rape me again. He noticed my hands and clucked his tongue, shaking his head like I was a five-year-old who just wouldn't learn. He was on me before I could move. He slammed my head into the wall. This time I did pass out."

Taylor idly traced the scar under her eye, and it broke Duncan's heart a little further.

"None of the other men ever came for me. I guess Jacob had marked me as his." She snorted derisively. "Maybe I should be grateful for that."

Duncan started to protest, but the words died on his lips as Taylor turned her eyes back to him once more.

"Jacob wanted to break me. And by the end"—she swallowed hard, tears sliding down her cheeks—"I stopped fighting him. I know I should have fought, should have…but I…"

She broke off, sobbing now, unable to dam the flood. Duncan wanted to say something, tell her it was okay, tell her she had just done what she needed to survive. He wanted to scream that it was not her fault, to shake her until she understood she had done nothing wrong, to absolve her of the shame she felt but did not deserve, but he knew anything he said now would sound hollow to Taylor's ears.

He watched as, slowly, her sobbing eased, and the impassive mask that protected Taylor from the horrible reality of her past slipped back into place.

"Finally, one night, after they were done with one of the women, I heard footsteps again. What little was left of me, that could feel anything but numb, was terrified. I knew one of us was going to die. I heard the lock on my door crack open, and I knew the one dying was going to be me. I looked up through the eye that wasn't swollen shut and found Tim there, staring down at me.

"He was crying. He raced over to me and untied my hands, asked me if I could walk. I didn't understand what was happening. He helped me up, told me I had to be quiet. He led me out of my cell, leaned me up against the wall, and told me to wait. I watched him go to the other doors and, one by one, repeat the process with the rest of the women. He led each one out and propped them up next to me while he went for the next. They all stood there silently, hollow and broken, just like me. He came back with Liz and said, 'Follow me. Quietly.' Melanie wasn't with us. I cleared my head enough to ask where she was, and Tim just looked at me sadly. He said she didn't make it. Then he was leading us out into the night.

"We stumbled along blindly, following Tim past the barn, away from the tents. We rounded another building, and he stopped us. I watched him creep over to some high shrubs and pull out two packs. 'Food, water, flashlights,' he said. 'It's everything I could get my hands on.' He handed me one, I guess since I was the most coherent of us, and hiked the other over his shoulders. It was so dark, but we couldn't turn on the flashlights for fear of being caught.

"Turns out, the flashlights didn't matter. It wasn't long before we heard shouts coming from the darkness behind us, then flashlight beams piercing the night. Tim screamed at us to run, and we did. Some of us, anyway. Liz just stood there, frozen. They caught her first. One by one the others fell away, until soon it was just Tim and me crashing through the trees."

Taylor's voice hardened, her words growing sharp and dangerous.

"They caught us near a small creek. Or rather, Jacob caught us. He yelled at us to stop, but Tim pushed me forward and told me to keep running. Then I heard the gunshot. I turned back to Tim. His eyes were wide, and he was already falling. I caught him as he fell. He was crying, couldn't breathe. Blood was trickling out of his mouth, and all he kept saying was *sorry, sorry, sorry*, over and over. I told him it was okay, that everything was going to be all right. And then he was gone.

"I looked up. Jacob was standing over me, his gun pointed in my face. He glanced down at his brother and then back at me. There was no sadness on his face, no remorse. Only anger. And hate. He pulled back the hammer and fired. Nothing happened. He fired again, and still nothing. It was empty. I knew this was my only chance. I felt around in the dirt, and by some miracle my fingers closed around a large branch. I clenched it in my fist and swung with all my might. Jacob went down and I ran. I left Tim lying dead in the dirt and I ran."

"You couldn't have done anything else," Duncan said softly. Taylor did not acknowledge him.

"I ran and I ran until I finally dropped from exhaustion, my legs just buckling beneath me. I crawled into some bushes and prayed no one would find me. They never did. The next morning, I started moving again. After two days, I found an abandoned house to hole up in. It wasn't abandoned, exactly. An old woman lay rotting in her bed, forgotten by the world that died around her. I buried her out back underneath a large tree. I thought she might like it there.

"I stayed a couple of weeks, building up strength, pilfering from the other houses nearby for food and such. Eventually, I recovered enough to move on. I couldn't stay. The world was dead, and for all I cared the people who hadn't died could go straight to hell. All I had left was to go home. So I started walking."

She lapsed into silence again, still looking at Duncan. He drew in a deep breath, buying himself a moment to figure out what to say. Then he realized there was really nothing he could say. He hated what she had been through, hated Jacob and those men for what they had done to her, to all of those poor people. Even more, he hated that she had gone through all that, had not only lived through it but past it, all for the simple hope that one day she would find her family. Now that hope was gone, and everything she had survived meant nothing.

"I'm sorry," he choked out, tears threatening to overwhelm him. They had all been through so much, but this, what Taylor had been through, was more than any human should have to endure.

Even after his parents had died, Duncan had still seen the beauty in the world. He had heard the stories, knew that desperation and hopelessness had caused some people to do horrible things. He was not entirely stupid. Duncan knew how terrible man could be, had been, even before the plague. Animals could be just as vicious. Duncan's high school biology teacher had taught them all about survival of the fittest, and how animals were capable of fierce, even cruel, aggression in order to secure food, water, territory, and even mating rights. But where the animals did these things on instinct, man's inhumanity to man was caused by something far worse.

Thought. Logic. Reason.

These powers might separate man from the animals, but Duncan knew they certainly did not make man any better. Butterflies did not feed Christians to lions. Sparrows did not give Native Americans gifts of disease-ridden blankets. Whales did not try to exterminate the Jews. Monkeys did not build the atomic bomb.

Or maybe they did.

Yet even after the plague, Duncan had thought mankind would overcome its own worst instincts. It seemed so much smarter to work together, like they did at Burninghead Farm, than to struggle separately, fighting for scraps. Everyone had lost family and friends, jobs and homes. Duncan figured people had seen enough death and destruction for one lifetime, and eventually, those who survived would somehow rise above the terrible things men were capable of doing to each other.

Stupid, Duncan. You were so stupid.

Clearly, Duncan had been wrong. Maybe Taylor was right. Maybe they should all just go to hell.

Maybe the earth was right to take the world back from us and kill us all.

"You remind me of Tim."

The words shot through him like a bullet. She could not have hurt him more if she had ripped out his heart, which is exactly what it felt like to hear that she equated him with the boy who had caused her so much pain.

"But he betrayed you," Duncan turned toward Taylor, seething.

Taylor reached out to him. "Duncan—"

"No!" he shouted, brushing off her outstretched hand. "He took you to that place, left you to Jacob, and didn't do a damn thing to help you!"

"He was a good kid," Taylor said, reaching out once again.

"He was a sonofabitch. He never should have left you there. I wouldn't have left you there."

"He tried, Duncan," she said softly. "He did the best he could."

"He should have stopped them." Duncan's shoulders sagged, his head dropping just a little. He wondered if he would have been able to do anything differently than Tim had. That thought wounded him even further.

"He did," Taylor said, forcing Duncan to meet her gaze. "In the end, he did."

"He should have done something sooner," Duncan said halfheartedly. He was angry with this boy he had never met, even as he was grateful for what he had been able to do.

"His heart was in the right place, Duncan. And in the end, that's all that matters."

Duncan nodded, finally understanding what Taylor was driving at. Maybe there was still a chance the world could right itself. Maybe there was still hope for a better future. And maybe, just maybe, that future included Taylor. If Taylor could find her way back to the world.

"I won't say anything," Duncan said quietly. "About what you told me? Not if you don't want me to."

Something flashed in Taylor's eyes, a spark of something Duncan could not quite understand but that caused him to hold his breath just the same. Her expression hardened, as if she was realizing for the first time just what she had done. Duncan began to worry he had said the wrong thing, but her eyes, formerly so hollow, deepened. She said nothing, but she patted his shoulder and started to walk back down toward the farm.

Duncan let out a slow breath. He did not know exactly what it all meant, but he knew it was a beginning.

Chapter Twenty

I can't sleep. The day keeps replaying in my head, refusing to let me rest. My mind circles around something I can't quite understand, yet I know is important. And so, like a dream from which you have just awoken, I keep trying to grasp the meaning, only to find it slipping through my fingers.

I don't know why I told Duncan about Pennsylvania. I have kept it close for so long. It has been more than three months since I escaped Pittsburgh, but today it feels as horrifyingly real as if it were yesterday. But maybe it's like a dam pushed to its limits by a swollen, raging river. Eventually, it just has to break, no matter how soundly it's constructed.

Something broke in me upon learning that Asheville, my home, is no more. I have spent months spinning lie upon lie, telling myself I knew they were dead while pretending I thought they were alive, when the truth was infinitely more complicated.

Over and over again as I made my way toward home, I tried to convince myself that hope was irrelevant, that deep down I already knew my family was dead, and I was simply on a fool's errand to find an answer I already had. And that was okay with me. The lie kept me going. But I knew once I reached Asheville and saw for myself what I already knew to be true, then I could finally stop. Whether I killed myself or simply stopped living would be of no consequence. Turns out, that's only what I thought I knew. The ultimate, frightening, and unspeakable truth beneath the web of lies I constructed was that somewhere deep down I had hoped. I had believed that somehow, someway, they were still alive and waiting for me. If I hadn't, then I would have just let myself die in that field in Pennsylvania.

I thought when the end came, when I finally faced the reality that my family was gone and there really was nothing left, I would be relieved, it would somehow be comforting to know my journey was done and I would have to fight no longer. I would be able to rest at last. But now, facing the reality of their deaths, I feel no such things. I feel only anguish. And grief. And guilt.

I have failed my family. I have wasted my survival, bought and paid for by the lives of others. The nearly two months of torture in Pennsylvania were for nothing. The last three months crawling and scavenging my way home were for nothing. The hope that sustained me through it all, that kept me alive and forced me forward even when I didn't consciously know it existed, has been for nothing. Even worse, the shattering of that hope has torn a gaping hole in my heart with the force of its destruction.

I thought I had already lost everything, that no more pain could be inflicted upon me. I was wrong.

If I had only been faster, stronger, smarter, *more*, I could have made it to Asheville before those murderers had slaughtered what was left of my town. Instead, I paused. I lost sight of my goal. I allowed myself to be subdued by this place, these people. I allowed myself to dream again, whether I knew it or not, and that had cost me everything.

It would be simpler if I just felt like dying. I certainly want the pain to end, the grief, the guilt, the shame, all of it. Everything I have lived for these past months is gone, and even though to continue in this world means having to live through the pain I feel in every cell and synapse, every ounce of blood and bone, and even though I just want it all to be over, for some reason I cannot reconcile dying. Despite myself, and despite the guilt, the last few weeks on the farm have snuck through my defenses and shown me that maybe, just maybe, there is something left worth living for after all.

Now I am on a precipice, caught in the hairsbreadth between falling and stepping back, and I don't know which way I want it all to go.

And yet, it seems that some part of me has already made a choice. Call it my subconscious, call it whatever is left of my soul, but I opened myself to Dunk despite my tangled mind. I took a step back from the ledge before I even consciously recognized I was standing on it, and while it unnerves me, it also feels remarkably like peace. A peace I don't deserve yet crave just the same.

The thought of peace naturally conjures up an image of Kate. I have not spoken to her since that night in the barn. I want nothing more than to wrap myself in her arms and lose myself in her gentle care, and yet I can't. I do not deserve such respite. I do not deserve anything but the weight of the guilt that is pressing down upon me.

My guilt burns into anger, and I do nothing to prevent the fire from raging. My guilt demands punishment. My failure demands justice. My selfishness demands that my life serve as penance. And my anger demands that I deny myself anything resembling happiness.

I have to keep living so I can properly pay for my sins. I have to pay. I need to pay. And in that moment I know my decision is made. I will begin again, here on Burninghead Farm, and spend the rest of my miserable life making amends. And I will start tomorrow.

Chapter Twenty-one

D uncan stretched his arms high above his head, trying to wring out the last of the hold sleep still had on his body. Today he would be out with the boys working on the wall again. He liked working the wall. It was an important job, critical to the farm's future, Buck had said. For a while that had been reason enough, and Duncan had tried not to think about the need behind building the wall. It did not matter why, he told himself. Buck had said it was so, and that was enough. Or it had been, until his conversation with Taylor the day before. Now, Duncan could not help but think about all the reasons they needed to build that wall, and build it right.

He dressed quickly and plowed through a quick bowl of oatmeal, then headed down to the equipment shed where they would load all their gear into the pickup for the day's work. It was early enough that the crickets were still chirping out their night songs, and he expected to be the first to reach the truck. He figured he would be able to get the pickup loaded with their tools for the day before any of the others arrived, for which he knew they would be grateful. Most of the guys were not early risers like Duncan. He did not mind. It was just another opportunity to be helpful.

The dark outline of the pickup materialized in the distance, and Duncan's pace quickened, his feet as eager as the rest of him to work. His eagerness quickly morphed into surprise as two shadowy figures emerged from the darkness next to the pickup. He could not imagine who in his crew was awake yet, let alone who could have beaten him to the shed. In another twenty steps, Duncan had his answer, which surprised him even further.

"Mornin', Duncan." Buck sipped his morning coffee, steam rising from the mug, *World's Greatest Dad* emblazoned on the side.

"Morning, sir." Duncan's voice cracked as his vocal cords adjusted to the damp morning air. "Taylor," he added, a seeming afterthought even as her presence was at the forefront of his mind. She acknowledged his greeting with a nod.

"Coffee?" Before Duncan could answer, Buck was pouring coffee from a thermos into a mug he had retrieved from a canvas bag at his feet. He held out the coffee cup to Duncan, who was not about to deny the offer despite really disliking coffee, at least without a large helping of cream and sugar.

Duncan blew across the top of the mug, delaying having to drink any of the bitter brew. His eyes moved back and forth between Buck and Taylor. They must have had some purpose to being at the shed this early, Duncan thought. Yet there they stood, silently sipping their coffee, content to just watch the day begin to melt away the lingering night, casting shadows where only moments before the world had been shrouded in a single shade of black. It was starting to bug Duncan.

"So..." Duncan began, hoping one of them would pick up and explain what was going on. Neither one took the bait, forcing Duncan to just come out with it. "What are you guys doing here?"

"Just enjoying our morning coffee," Buck said, infuriatingly deadpan. Duncan knew there had to be more to it than that. Buck did not work a detail and had more important things to do than hang out with Duncan sipping coffee next to the equipment shed.

Then there was Taylor, who had still not uttered a word. Her presence truly confused him, if for no other reason than it was the first time she had willingly put herself in another person's company since the night she had found out about Asheville. Their conversation the day before had only happened because Duncan had been following her, not because she had sought him out. Or maybe she had, at least in the sense that she had spoken to him first. As hard as hearing her story had been, Duncan hoped maybe it had helped Taylor in some way to tell it. His momma had always felt better when she let something out after holding it in. Still, Duncan was surprised to find her there, drinking her coffee, seeming almost normal.

Except she was not normal. He searched her eyes, trying to find the truth behind them, and could only find resignation and a barely concealed despair that seemed to Duncan far worse than anything he had felt from her the day before.

Duncan opened his mouth to ask the question again, but Buck stopped him.

"All in good time, son. Just enjoy your coffee."

Something in Buck's voice told Duncan eventually he would have his answer. He supposed he could wait a little longer, as frustrating as it was. He did as he was told, taking a swig of his coffee before remembering that he hated the stuff. For some reason it was not as bitter as he remembered. He grudgingly took another sip, watching Taylor out of the corner of his eye, trying to wrap his head around whatever it was he was sensing from her.

It was not long before they were joined by the rest of Duncan's work detail, who greeted them warmly but whose eyes were full of the obvious question, which Buck quickly put to rest.

"Taylor here's going to be joining you boys today. She's on your detail until further notice." Although Buck's tone was pleasant, there was an undercurrent that brooked no argument. Even though the demands of this new world had a way of shredding antiquated notions about the sexes, and Buck had made a point of treating everyone equally on the farm, sometimes old notions died a hard death. Still, as Duncan surveyed his crew, he was pleased to see no open hostility toward Taylor. Not that Duncan would have expected any real objection to having a woman on board this crew, anyway. Bottom line with these guys, as Duncan had well learned, was if you pulled your weight, then you were all right, and Duncan had no question as to whether Taylor would pull her weight.

"Well, let's get going, then," Tony said. They quickly loaded up the tools into the pickup and headed off.

They had managed to finish hoisting the crossbeams on Friday, and another detail would spend the next week circling back around and checking the stability of the beams and shoring up any weak sections. Duncan's team was tasked with beginning the second phase of the project, which was to set the heavy sheet metal panels along the outside of the posts and crossbeams. But first, they would have to ready the ground for the panels, and that meant more digging.

They would dig a deep but narrow trench into the earth, just enough room for the metal sheets and a thick bed of cement to seal them into the ground. The other detail, the one checking the crossbeams that week, would follow along about a week behind, laying the cement while a third crew would sink the sheets and attach them to the existing support structure. They would likely be fighting the snow, but with three details working full time, they all believed they could get the job done before winter fully set in.

They knew the wall would not be enough to keep out someone determined to get in, and phase three would involve putting a six-foot trench around the entire property. Not a moat, exactly, but certainly a hole deep enough to swallow a man. There was talk of a fourth phase that would involve building guard towers, but Duncan had always thought that was a little extreme. He was not sure anymore.

The day was cool, but their work had them all stripped down to shirtsleeves within minutes. They worked in teams of two, digging a trench four feet down and only as wide as a man. It was tough, backbreaking work, but to Duncan it felt good. He liked the pain of his muscles straining, the sweat as it rolled down his face and arms, the calluses on his palms.

The soil was fairly dry, which made for easier digging, but it also meant the wind blew it around at will. The deeper they dug the lower they sank, until they were nearly chest deep in the earth. This put them face level with the wind-driven dirt. The fine grains stung Duncan's face, and he had to keep turning his head away every time he dropped another shovelful onto the ground.

Taylor, for her part, seemed immune to the sandstorm they were creating. She kept her shoulders squared, facing down the grating dirt head on, refusing to let it slow her down. Duncan admired her unflinching determination even as he worried about what was behind it. Taylor had been a machine all morning, digging out one shovelful of dirt after another without a moment's pause. She was setting a brisk pace, and Duncan struggled to keep up. Not that this was a race, but Duncan was not used to anyone working harder than him, and he liked the challenge of trying to maintain the pace she was setting. Still, he had begun to worry that if Taylor did not take a break soon, she was going to be forced to by virtue of passing out.

He leaned his shovel up against the wall of their trench and grabbed his canteen of water. "Drink?"

He half expected Taylor to ignore him, or at least turn him down, but she did not. She took the canteen from him with a nod of thanks and took a good, long swig, so long that she was out of breath when she finished. Duncan wondered if she had even realized she was thirsty, or if she had simply been ignoring her thirst and would have kept on ignoring it without his intervention.

"Thanks," she said, handing him back the canteen. She leaned on her shovel and surveyed their work. It was a nonchalant move, but Duncan could tell it was anything but. She looked as if she was about to fall over if not for the support of the shovel. "I think we're about done here."

Duncan looked around and realized they had reached their depth. "Looks like."

"Well then, let's start on the next one."

Duncan started to object, wanted to tell her they should take a short break, get their strength up, but Taylor was already pulling herself out of the hole. They had decided to take the trench in sections rather than try and continue on from within the trench. Digging was much easier from above than below. Once they had two sections completed, they could attack the foot of earth between to connect them. Before he could lift himself back up to ground level, Taylor had sunk her shovel into the ground above and behind him for round two.

❖

Dinnertime, when it came, was a much welcome relief to Duncan. He could not remember having been hungrier than he found himself that night, or more tired. They had dug enough of the trench to lay sixteen sections of the wall, far more than any of them had anticipated, thanks mostly to Taylor. Duncan had not been the only one who wanted to keep up with her. By noon, the rest of the crew had doubled their pace, leaving them all exhausted. Duncan was proud of how much they had accomplished, and by the smiles on everyone's tired and grimy faces, he thought the others were, too.

Duncan quickly found Kate in the dining hall and settled in beside her. He barely had the energy to mumble a brief hello, let alone lift his fork to his mouth, but somehow he managed.

"Long day?" Kate asked with a chuckle. Duncan grunted his response. They lapsed into companionable silence, letting the muffled conversations going on around them fill up the empty spaces. Despite his exhaustion, it did not take long for Duncan to finish his dinner and settle back to relax.

"We made good progress today," Duncan said after a while. The food and the opportunity to rest a bit had restored some of his energy, enough to make him feel like talking. "At this rate we might be able to double back and help lay the wall."

"That's great," Kate said, giving Duncan's shoulder a light squeeze.

"Taylor went out with us today."

The words hung in the air as Duncan watched Kate from the corner of his eye, waiting to see what effect the statement might have. Kate's expression did not change, but she started shuffling the food on her plate around with her fork.

"I know," she said quietly. "Buck told me."

"She worked really hard," Duncan said quickly, not quite knowing why but feeling like he needed to defend Taylor somehow.

"That's good," Kate said absently. She was making mountains with her mashed potatoes. It reminded Duncan of when he was a child, playing with his food in some lame attempt at avoidance. Usually the thing he was trying to avoid was being in trouble for some stupid thing he had done, but he did not think that was behind Kate's homage to *Close Encounters of the Third Kind*.

"She seems...better."

The word sounded wrong even to Duncan's own ears, and it did not go unnoticed by Kate. She looked up at him questioningly.

"Well, sort of better. I mean, she did ask to work the detail instead of going off by herself again. At least she was with people."

Kate nodded slightly, but she seemed unconvinced. Truth was, so was Duncan.

"She worked hard. Real hard."

Kate was no fool. She could read between the lines.

"Too hard?" she asked.

"I dunno. Maybe." Duncan felt guilty, like he was betraying Taylor somehow. But he was also her friend, and he decided his concern was far more important than loyalty. "She just kept pushing. Never stopped to take a break unless I forced her to. It was like..."

Duncan shook his head, not quite sure of what he was trying to say and also not wanting to infer something that was not there.

"Like what?" Kate finally pushed. Duncan looked at Kate long and hard, wishing he had some kind of telepathic ability and could just project his memories of the day into Kate's mind, so she could see for herself and make her own judgments. But absent such ability, he had to just do his best to explain what was troubling him.

"It was like she was possessed. Or obsessed or something. I swear she would have worked 'til she dropped if we'd have let her, and I'm not sure she would have even noticed."

Kate nodded. Duncan's assessment was clearly as troubling to Kate as it was to him. He looked around the barn and realized Taylor had not come to supper. It should not have surprised him, he supposed. He could not expect that suddenly everything would be fine and she would rejoin the human race, or their little part of it anyway, all at once, regardless of how much he might want her to do just that. And besides, everything was not fine. If it was, he and Kate would not even be having this conversation.

All Duncan knew was Taylor simply could not continue to push the way she had today, especially if she was not taking care of herself.

"You could drop a tray by her room later." Once again, Kate was reading Duncan's thoughts. Duncan, however, was more interested in why Kate had not offered to do it herself.

"Or you could?" Duncan suggested hopefully. He hated that Kate and Taylor were avoiding each other when clearly that was not what either of them wanted, or needed. Or at least it was not what Kate wanted. Duncan was not stupid. He could see it on her face, the sorrow that crept into her eyes every time Taylor's name came up.

Kate shook her head at Duncan, which only frustrated him. He could not understand why, if Kate had such feelings for Taylor, which she clearly did, she did not just go and bang down Taylor's door and force Taylor to face her. That was what they did in the movies. That is what Duncan would do if he were Kate.

That's a load of bull and you know it.

And he did know it, because he had no real experience with such things and had no idea what he would do if it were him. Maybe Kate was right not to rush Taylor. She was like a spooked mare. If rushed, she might be scared off for good. Then again, if they did nothing, they might lose her just the same.

"You haven't seen her in a week," Duncan said, his need to do something overriding everything else. "Maybe you should take her some dinner. Try to talk to her?"

Kate looked away, but not before Duncan saw the tears forming. It hurt him to see her like this. So sad, so lost. She was normally radiant, like the North Star guiding the way even through the blackest night. But now her light was muted, unable to penetrate a cloud-laden sky. Duncan did not know what to say next, and he simply put a hand on Kate's shoulder, trying to offer some form of comfort. She looked back at him then, forcing a smile and wiping the moisture from her eyes.

"She'll talk to me when she's ready."

Duncan nodded, not wanting to upset Kate any further. He tamped down the guilt that began to stir within him. He did not know why Taylor had chosen to open up to him and not Kate, but he would never betray her confidence by telling Kate what he knew. He felt burdened by his knowledge and Kate's lack of it, like he had betrayed Kate somehow by being the one that Taylor had talked to. It was not his fault, he knew, that Taylor had chosen him, and he therefore knew logically that he had nothing to feel ashamed of, yet that truth did nothing to assuage his guilt.

"Just keep an eye on her? Will you do that for me?"

To Duncan, it was a sacred task. It was something he could do for Kate, and for Taylor, when he felt like he could not do much else.

He did not really understand why it was important to him that Taylor and Kate find their way to each other. Just a few weeks ago, days really, he might have been threatened by it, that thing that hung in the air between them, like the entire universe was holding its breath in anticipation. Duncan might have been jealous over the kiss he had witnessed in the barn that night, the way Taylor and Kate had been lost in each other, as if within each other's arms they had found everything they had ever wanted. But Duncan was neither threatened nor jealous, and felt only the intense desire to ensure they made it, whatever it took. For if the hope he held for Kate and Taylor, that in this terrible world of loss and grief these two people could build something beautiful together, if that hope could be realized, then maybe there was hope for them all. Maybe, someday, Duncan too would find love, build a life with someone, maybe even have a family. And maybe, just maybe, a better tomorrow lay ahead for everyone.

Chapter Twenty-two

The weeks fly by faster than any I can remember. The days grow shorter, beginning their descent into winter. They have been for a while, though the change was imperceptible at first. But now the October sun seems lazier somehow, like a teenager hitting the snooze button for longer and longer intervals now that the novelty of the first days of school has worn off. Old Man Winter looms large on the horizon, and the sun seems to recognize the inevitability of it all. Not that it makes the workday any shorter. The only acknowledgment any of us make to the shrinking of the day is to start loading kerosene lanterns into the truck along with our shovels and picks. Once again, I marvel at Buck's resourcefulness. He has managed to stockpile a little bit of everything, including kerosene. It won't last forever, but it's good enough for now.

We have made tremendous progress in our digging, at least according to Dunk. I don't talk to him much at first, just wanting to focus on the work, but he chats me up anyway, either ignoring my lack of response or simply not caring. The kid is completely mule headed. And yet it isn't all that long before I am chatting back to him, at least as far as the occasional grunt or clipped sentence can be considered a form of speech. That doesn't last long, either, and pretty soon we are talking, really talking, mostly about stupid things like whether Joan Baez's version of "Blowin' In the Wind" is better than Dylan's, and who would take an imaginary World Series between my beloved Cubbies and the White Sox. I still have a hard time wrapping my head around Dunk being a White Sox fan. Even the dastardly Cardinals would be better.

I don't know whether it is exhaustion or something else, but with each passing day, each turn of the shovel, I burn off a little more of my anger. My guilt and the fire it had sparked within me are not gone but have lessened some, fading into white noise that drowns out what is driving me. I sink into the work, into just trying to contribute toward building something better. I don't let myself think about who I am trying to build that something better for, or whether that includes myself. I'm not ready to think about such things.

By the fifth day, I am taking my lunches with the rest of the crew instead of going off on my own. I don't say much, but they seem to respect that and let me be. I think Dunk wishes I would join in their camaraderie, but I'm not ready for that yet, either. While my guilt may have eased in its intensity, it is still there, smoldering beneath the ashes, along with the self-inflicted punishment that comes with it. Talking to Dunk is one thing, but letting myself be human is something entirely different.

Of course, at the end of the workday I leave the Taylor I am on the crew behind and revert to the Taylor who is fully apart. I do not take my meals in the barn, cannot let myself join the others for fear that if I do, I will come undone. If I take just one step into that room, see Dunk waving me over or Buck sitting there grinning or Kate looking at me with those eyes of hers, my self-imposed exile will crumble to dust. They don't need my company, and I don't deserve theirs. Each night, meals magically appear on a tray outside my room, and I imagine the disappointment on Dunk's face as he lays the tray outside my door. Still, he doesn't speak of it, for which I am grateful.

We go on that way for a while, and I lull myself into thinking I can go on that way forever, that everyone will accept this is the way things are and need to be. Sometimes, thoughts of Kate drift into my mind. Holding her hand. The sweet sound of her laughter. Arguing with her even when I feel like agreeing. The sunlight glinting off her hair in the afternoon sun. Kissing her in the barn. I let myself relive each memory, allow them to consume my senses, until I can feel nothing besides the softness of her skin, hear nothing but the richness of her voice. Then I push them away, rejecting them as I have her.

I take to having my daily shower in the evening instead of the morning, trying to wipe off the grime of the day's work, figuring there isn't much point in bathing in the morning only to be fouled with dirt and sweat within an hour. Of course, it doesn't hurt that my new shower time is smack dab in the middle of dinner, which conveniently allows me to wash and be safely back behind the door to my room until lights out, enabling me to avoid our little community in the process.

That is the theory, anyway. As with most theories, it's only right until it's debunked.

One night, upon returning to my room, I bump into Kate. It is actually more of a slamming into than a bump, as I am working my towel through my damp hair and thus don't see her standing in front of my door. I'm not used to having to watch out for obstacles in the hallway, especially not of the human variety.

The collision sends her stumbling backward, straight into the tray of food she has just finished leaving in front of my door. I stare at her, wide eyed, my brain caught somewhere between absorbing the shock of seeing her for the first time in weeks and apology for practically mowing her down. I see the remnants of my dinner, green peas still wobbling back and forth on the floor.

"Sorry," she says, the sound of her nervousness tearing at my heart. She bends down quickly and begins shoveling the food from the floor back onto the tray. "I can be such a klutz."

I stand there, watching her clean up my mess, the signals from my brain refusing to connect with the rest of my body even as my mind screams at me.

Help her, you moron!

Something clicks and I drop to my knees, silently helping her collect the rest of my ruined dinner. She doesn't look at me, but I hear her breath catch. Little globs of mashed potatoes cling to her fingers, and I hold out my still-damp towel to her. She stands, wiping her hands clean while I finish dealing with the tray.

"You've been bringing me dinner?" I ask, finally looking at her. It isn't really the question on my mind, but it seems safer somehow.

"Sometimes," she admits quietly. "Duncan and I take turns." She shrugs, as if to say it is no big deal, but I know it isn't. To her or to me.

She looks down at my hands and offers me the cleanest part of the towel. "Looks like you might need this back. Wouldn't want to be caught hitchhiking across the galaxy without your towel."

"Yeah," I say, smiling a little at the reference. I take the offering and finish cleaning myself up, then throw the soiled towel down on top of the tray. "I'll take this all back to the barn later. Let them throw my towel in with the rest of the kitchen wash."

"I can take it. If you want?" It is such an innocent question, so seemingly innocuous that I almost miss it. Almost. But it hangs in the air, full of promise, held aloft by the hope that underlies it.

If I want. *If* I want. Of course I want. Many things.

"I'll take care of it," I say brusquely, rejecting her offer and, along with it, her. My rejection is not lost on her.

"Oh."

One simple word, not even a word really, and yet it is like a branding iron to my heart, which will now be forever scarred by her disappointment. The pain of it hardens in my veins, fusing the iron within each blood cell until it forms a shield between what I want and what I need to do.

Be strong, Taylor. Do what's right. For once in your pitiful life.

I square my shoulders and raise my shield, and I stare her down as if she is merely a stranger, an annoying gnat circling my head, not even worth the bother of swatting at.

"Well, I…"

She searches for some sign this isn't the end, but I refuse to let her find it. She swallows whatever words would come next and turns away so quickly I think she might break into a run. She doesn't. She is too strong for that, too proud to show how I have wounded her. But I know.

As she walks away, it is a dagger scraping against my ribs, sticking out of my chest with my fingers still wrapped around its hilt. I have only myself to blame.

I stay in my doorway, staring down that hallway long after she has left it, clutching the doorjamb until my fingers turn white to keep myself from running after her. Eventually, when the voices of the dorm's other residents start to filter in from outside, I scoop up the tray and retreat into my room. Once the door is safely shut behind me, I look down at the ruined tray, and my hand starts to shake. I barely make it over to the desk before the tray slips from my hand, clattering down onto the wood.

I sink down onto my bed, still staring at that damn tray and all it represents. Even in sleep the image follows me, screaming at me to fix it, to make it better somehow. But there is no way to make it better, and that wretched thought haunts me until morning.

Chapter Twenty-three

The next day is perfect, crisp and clean and warm enough to make you think it is spring, and not winter's bitter wind, just around the corner. The crew is practically giddy with it, if a bunch of grown men, plus one who is almost grown, can be considered giddy. They laugh more than usual, tossing clumps of loose dirt around like water balloons as they dig their trenches. The frivolity in the air is lost on me. All I can think about is last night, and all I can do is keep digging harder and faster in some maddeningly useless attempt to keep my thoughts at bay.

I know Dunk is worrying about me, but he has sense enough to keep his mouth shut. I don't need to feel any more guilt than I already do, and I know if he utters a single word I will lash out at him for lack of a better target.

Midday comes and goes before I even know it. Even when the guys stop for lunch I keep on digging, knowing if I stop I will surely break.

"You think if you dig far enough you can escape the entire world?"

I look up to find her there, silhouetted against the afternoon sun, her hands fisted against her hips as she stands over me. Even in her anger, she is the most beautiful thing I have ever seen. I thought I did enough last night to get her to leave me to my worthlessness. That the hurt I caused her and myself might have somehow been worth it. I thought wrong. Here she is, trying one last time, offering one last chance for us both. Yet all I can think is while this is her last stand in defense of me, it is my last chance to push her away forever. The knife twists a little further.

"Or maybe it's not the world you're running from at all? Maybe it's just me?"

I know I have only to lash out and it will be over, and the necessary words blitz my mind, words that will hurt her in ways that will finally prove to her I'm not worth a damn. And yet I can't summon the courage of my convictions, cannot deal that final blow. Coward that I am, I turn back to my digging, trying desperately to ignore the pain that wrenches my heart at the sight of her.

She refuses to take the hint.

"Well? Which is it, Taylor?"

The devil inside cries out to be released, but I fight it off once more, praying it will be the last time.

"Just leave me alone, Kate."

Just go, leave me to my misery. I am not worth saving.

"I have been. We all have been. Trying to give you space, time. But enough is enough."

She is too stubborn, too noble to walk away easily. I wonder what makes her care for me so much. I have brought her nothing but heartache since I arrived, yet here she is, trying to save me. I realize, finally, that she cares for me, and for one too-brief, glorious instant of eternity, the knowledge fills all the empty places inside. But just as soon as it comes it is gone, replaced by the certainty that I'm not worthy of such love. I will only ever let her down, fail her as I failed my family, and the only thing I can truly offer is to push her away. Once and for all.

"I'm so sorry my need to grieve offends you." The change begins. I taste the venom of my words as they ooze off my tongue, feeding off the anger that has been fueling me all day. If she notices, she shows no sign.

"You're not grieving. You're hiding."

I throw down my shovel and pull myself out of the hole and up to stand toe-to-toe with her with such ferocity that she flinches.

Her reaction wounds me, but I know I am going to be torn to shreds before this is all over.

"You can read minds now? Well, that's just fan-fuckin-tastic." I spit the words in her face, clenching my jaw to the point I might actually break a tooth. Kate takes a half step back, her eyes growing wide as her mind tries to comprehend the violence my actions imply. It makes me want to cry, but I press on.

"What exactly am I hiding from, Kate? You? You really think you're worth that much? You really are the center of your own universe, aren't you? You think you're so fucking special that what's left of this godforsaken world should revolve around you! Well, guess what, sweetheart? It doesn't. Get the fuck over it."

Absently, I notice the rest of my crew, who have been taking their lunch over by the truck, starting to edge away, trying to back out of the line of fire. I imagine how horrified I might be at publicly doing this to Kate if I had any shred of decency left. But I have no decency. Not a single drop.

Isn't that the point, jackass?

I can see I have hit home, that she is questioning everything she ever felt for me and wondering how she could have been so wrong. I would gouge out my own eyes to never see that look upon her face, but I force myself to let the image burn into my brain if only to reaffirm I am doing the right thing.

"You can't possibly believe that's what this is about." Her voice is weaker now, her resolve shaken. As her conviction wavers, mine solidifies.

"Isn't it? Ever since I landed on this goddamn farm it's been Kate this and Kate that. You've got your own little cult of personality here, don't you? Duncan, Buck…Zeke."

The name tumbles out of my mouth without thinking, and she pulls back as if I have slapped her. As much as it hurts her to hear it, it hurts me infinitely more to have said it. I have become the thing which I despise the most, that which makes my skin crawl and my guts churn. And as I prepare to inflict the coup de grâce, my soul slips the last few inches into hell.

"Yeah, you had him wound up pretty good, didn't you? All of them. You just leave them salivating after you, teasing them and leading them on, making them think you might give it up before you pull it out of reach. You use 'em and lose 'em, don't you? Well, guess what? I was using you, too. It's been a while since I've had a good fuck, and I figured you might fill that need. But you know what? I don't sleep with—"

The slap lands before I finish, hard enough to knock me back a step and leave the crack of it ringing in my ears. Kate sucks in deep, trembling breaths, and I can only imagine what is racing through her mind. She seems to be in shock, whether from my words or from having hit me, I don't know. I rub my cheek. It is warm beneath my fingers, and I cling to the pain of my swelling tissue lest I beg for her forgiveness. I am a monster of my own making, a victim of my own choosing, but the deed is done. I win. I can see it.

It is a hollow victory.

Not trusting my voice not to break with the first word I utter, I turn away from her, knowing we are done. I stride away, each step carefully composed to exude a strength I don't feel. All I feel is weak. And alone.

When I have put enough distance between us that I am certain no one will know, I let down my guard. My strides ease into a methodical trudge, purposefully carrying me to a nonexistent destination. After a while I find myself at the same hill where Kate showed me the expanse of the farm after my arrival. Unlike the rest of the trees on the property, which are growing bright with the colors of fall, the oak is nearly bare, having lost the bulk of its foliage. The hillside is littered with fallen, shriveled leaves, a memorial to the death of summer. Still, the tree towers proudly over the hill and the farm beyond, a lone soldier manning a watchtower at the end of the world.

I press my palm against its mighty trunk, hoping to absorb even a fraction of its strength, of its resolve. I know I did the right thing, and yet I am consumed with a pain beyond measure. I have obliterated any hope of a future with Kate, just as I intended. But now, faced with the reality of that destruction, I falter.

What have I done?

I had known I had to push Kate away, could not allow myself to be the person she deserved because that would mean a chance at happiness, which I did not deserve. But I had failed to consider what it would feel like not only to let hope die, but to be hope's murderer. I have killed it with my bare hands, strangled the life out of it and felt that life slipping through my fingers, and now I don't know how to live with what I have done.

"Nice try. But I don't give up that easily."

Kate.

By some grace of God or the devil's command she is here, to give me one last chance or to torment me further, I don't know. I cannot look at her, already warring with myself as I am. I want to run from her. I want to run to her. I want to collapse against this tree and stay here until the winter snows come and bury me.

"I'm not worth this." My voice is hoarse, my words merely a whisper, yet somehow she hears, or she already knows. Like always.

"Bullshit."

I look at her. Her eyes shine, boring into me, challenging me to fight her. As long as I am fighting, there is still a chance. My blood rises as my mind churns.

"What do you want from me?"

"I want you to be honest for once. I want to know why you said those things. I want to know why you're pushing me away!"

"I already told you." My words are hollow.

"And again I say bullshit."

The world explodes in a white hot instant, and I am powerless to stop it from screaming forth.

"You want me to tell you how much it hurts, knowing that the last five months have been for nothing? That after all I've gone through I didn't get there in time to save them? That I wasn't smart enough or fast enough or selfless enough to get there to keep them from getting their brains blown out? That if I hadn't been so scared to leave Pennsylvania, if I hadn't decided to wait like a coward for help that I knew deep down was never coming, then I wouldn't have been caged like an animal...and beaten...and forced to listen to those women screaming each night? That if I'd stood up to those fucking bastards, maybe John wouldn't be dead, or Claire, or Melanie, or…"

My words come out in choked sobs. I can't stop them, can't keep my body from shaking as every horrible detail of my failure pours out of me.

"And Tim, who just tried to help us…he wouldn't have been shot…wouldn't have had to die knowing his own brother pulled the trigger. He was only a kid. And my parents…and my brother and… oh God, my little niece…They…oh God…"

Her arms are around me before I can fall, and I cling to her, sobbing and choking, mumbling words and names that I have carried for far too long, baring myself on her altar. I have cried before, have wept for all of them at one time or another, but I have never wept for myself.

It sounds selfish, I know, especially given all the other selfish things I have done and said, and maybe it is. But it is also the most important, necessary thing I have ever done in my entire life.

I don't know how long I cry, or even what all I say, though I know we stay that way for a long while. In the days and weeks that follow, I will fill in the blanks for her, give the names context and the words form and meaning. But in these first few precious hours, she simply holds me, and I allow myself, finally, to be held.

CHAPTER TWENTY-FOUR

Thunder rolled through the farmhouse, chasing the lightning down darkened hallways and thrashing its way through every chamber of the house. The only other light came from the children's searching flashlights and the ghostly glow radiating from beneath closed doors marked: ENTER...IF YOU DARE. It was truly a creepy affair, if you did not know that the thunder was courtesy of a system of speakers threaded throughout the house, or that the lightning was thanks to the magic of a couple of strobe lights set on a timer.

Children were children, and they dared to enter the places they were warned not to go—or at least, they tried to dare. Duncan watched his group of three huddle before yet another closed door, debating which of them would grasp the doorknob in their tiny hand and lead the others into whatever came next. This was their fourth such doorway, and they were filled with an equal mix of anticipation and trepidation, having been through this all before. There was something waiting for them on the other side of the door to be sure, just as there had been the previous three times, something designed to scare even the mightiest of pirates and Jedi Knights. Of course, it was the pirate and Jedi who now wavered in their bravery, which left the fairy princess, in all her pink-taffeta glory, to finally and with a dramatic sigh push the boys aside and bound once more into the unknown.

The haunted house had been Taylor's idea, much to Duncan's, and everyone else's, surprise. In fairness, part of that surprise had come because no one had recognized that the approach of October 31 had meant anything other than November was just around the corner, which meant the first snow would soon be on its way. As for the rest, well, of all the people who would have remembered Halloween, it had been a bit of a shock to have it be Taylor, let alone for her to have suggested they put together an old-fashioned haunted house for the kids.

Everyone had been a bit skeptical when she had broached the idea a week earlier, everyone except the farm's teenagers of course, who embraced the concept with all the enthusiasm of their foregone youth. But Buck had just smiled and nodded his head, and pretty soon Duncan and some of the boys found themselves on official scavenging duty, sent off in search of cotton to make cobwebs and hay for scarecrows and any other supplies that could be turned into costumes for young and old alike.

For nearly a week most other work on the farm stopped. It was not that they could really afford to waste limited resources or to turn their attention to something as frivolous as Halloween. But they needed to show the children, and themselves, that there was something still to look forward to in this life, something beyond the day-to-day. That was how Duncan thought about it, anyway. He did not know if that was why Taylor had suggested it, or why Buck had agreed, but the reason sounded right in his own head, so he went with it.

Duncan stood in the hallway of the farmhouse, listening to the children's screams and shrieks give way to delighted giggles and laughter, and smiled. All the work they had put in over the last week to turn the farmhouse into a ghoul-filled world of frights and fun had been completely worth it. Since it had been Taylor's idea, Buck had put her in charge of the design and construction of the house, and although she had tried to feign indifference at the responsibility, she attacked the task with gusto. She ran the project with the authoritative air of a battlefield commander. Although everyone's ideas were considered, every suggestion heard, at the end of the day she called the plays and expected perfection. Duncan thought she would have made an excellent general.

Of course, a general was only as good as her commanding officer, and Taylor had an excellent CO in Kate. The two had been practically inseparable, ever since the day Kate had confronted her out on that work detail. From that point on, Taylor had been a different person. She still carried a certain amount of sadness with her, still harbored some of the pain that had weighed her down, but she seemed to have found some amount of happiness. She certainly smiled a lot more, anyway.

Duncan held no illusions that most of the goodness in Taylor's life came as a direct result of Kate. There was no announcement, no declaration of intent, but everyone knew that Taylor and Kate were together now. They were fairly private about their relationship, but the little things were obvious enough for anyone who cared to notice. The shared smiles, the stolen looks, the whispered words, the way their fingers would brush when they thought no one was looking. Duncan figured it was not that they were trying to hide anything, but instead that they were simply a little confounded by the newness of it all, and they were protective of what they had found together.

If they thought they were being sneaky, however, they had a lot to learn about subterfuge. No one said anything, but everyone knew darn well that Kate was not sleeping in her own room anymore, at least not most nights. He had not asked, and he silenced any such speculation with a stern glare. It was nobody's business what went on between Taylor and Kate after dark. Not even his.

Chapter Twenty-five

I lie in wait, as still and quiet as possible, despite the tennis racket digging into my backside. I really should have cleared myself a better spot in the tiny broom closet, but it is too late now. I fight the urge to shift as I hear the thump-thump of tiny feet cautiously making their way down the hallway. The children have hushed themselves, trying to sneak up on whatever creepy thing awaits them next. They are about as stealthy as a herd of elephants in a gymnasium, but they try. I stifle a laugh as I picture their tiny faces on the other side of the doorway, eyes bright and wide with wonder and maybe a little bit of fear.

I don't know what possessed me to suggest the haunted house. Probably just some bad beans I'd had for dinner the night before that put a random dream in my head about a haunted house from long ago. My father took me to one when I was little. I couldn't have been more than seven or eight at the time. I remember being so excited, walking nervously down plywood hallways, the lights flashing up ahead, spooky sounds filling the air. I was holding my daddy's hand, and there wasn't a safer or more wonderful place to be. But then some mummy-like monster had jumped down from heights unseen, brushing my arm on the way down, and I completely freaked out. I was hysterical to the point that they had to turn on all the lights while my dad carried me outside, with me screaming the whole time. I remember the mummy ripped off his mask, turning out just to be a pimply faced teenager. He looked horrified that he had scared me so badly. The poor kid.

I have always regretted my reaction to that haunted house, have always felt in some way I ruined a rare and precious moment with my dad. So the day after I had the dream, I suggested the haunted house. Maybe it was my way of reclaiming that moment in time, or maybe it was about giving this group of children, who'd had their childhoods stolen in incalculable ways, something they weren't likely to ever have. Or maybe it really was just bad beans.

The children draw ever closer. I guess they are only a few feet away now, and I crack open the door. They don't see me. They are too focused on the corner around which they expect the next scary beast to come from. I open the door a little wider, preparing to pounce. Two boys are debating in stage whispers who will round the corner first, both of them scared to take the lead but trying hard not to show it. The little princess crosses her arms and sighs, shaking her head in an exaggerated motion at her two fraidy-cat companions.

I chuckle before I can stop myself, and instantly the girl's eyes are upon me. She makes no sound, more curious than scared. I bring my finger to my lips in the universal sign for *shush*, and I nod my head toward the two boys. She looks over at them and then back to me, a slow grin beginning to light up her face. She understands my plan, and she likes it. She steps back, giving me room to emerge from the closet undetected. The boys are still arguing over who will go first, completely unaware of the big, scary monster standing directly behind them. I reach out and put my hands on their shoulders. They freeze. Ever so slowly, they turn their heads back toward me, and I whisper.

"Boo."

The boys scream and go tearing down the hallway, back the way they had come and directly into the arms of Dunk, who is standing with his flashlight at the far end of the hallway. The boys bury their faces in Dunk's arms, peering back at me through their protective shelter. I rip off my mask, and Dunk shines his flashlight on my face, then down at the little princess next to me, who is giggling uncontrollably. Immediately the boys' fear subsides, replaced with groans as they realize they've not only been had, but they've been had by a couple of girls.

"Come on, kids," Dunk says. "Time to join the party."

Three faces beam up at Dunk, and they race outside for the Halloween bonfire that has been set up in our absence. I follow them outside, laughing to myself. The farm's other children, who have already gone through the haunted house, are there, stuffing their faces with s'mores. The whole farm has come out for the party. Sam is strumming a wordless tune on Buck's guitar. Everywhere you look, folks are grouped off in little clusters, laughing, talking. Off to one side, the farm's teenagers are whispering urgently, and Dunk quickly joins them. I can only imagine what diabolical Halloween fright fest they are cooking up.

I grab a beer from an old washbasin filled with ice and twist off the cap with a satisfying hiss. I have missed that sound. I take a long swig, relishing the feel of the frosty liquid sliding down my throat.

"I heard you scored a little victory for feminism."

Two arms settle on my hips, Kate's breath tickling my ear with each word. My heart starts revving beneath my breast, purring like a finely tuned race car engine. I suppress an involuntary shudder. Oh, the effect she has on me.

"Just a little one," I say, struggling to keep my voice smooth and level. "Gotta instill a little bit of the revolution in the next generation."

Kate laughs at that, a throaty, delicious laugh that does nothing for my efforts to keep calm. She squeezes my hip and then lets go, sliding up next to me. I am grateful for the move even as I miss the feel of her pressed up behind me. We stand in silence, content to enjoy each other's company as we watch the party from afar.

"I think the boys are plotting something," Kate says after a while.

They are still off to one side, whispering conspiratorially.

"I can only imagine what they're up to."

"Something wicked, I hope."

I have to laugh at the naughty grin that lights up her face.

"Dunk said they were planning on telling ghost stories later. Maybe they're getting their stories straight."

"Well, I'm going to have to sit next to you. You know, in case I get scared."

"Like anything could scare you," I chuckle.

"There are some things."

I note the change in her voice, so subtle you could have easily missed it. I look at her, questioning. She just smiles, clearly not wanting to discuss it further. I let it go for now, tucking it away for a later time. The night grows colder, the chill beginning to sink into my bones. Once I notice the cold, I can't keep my body from shivering.

"Come on, let's go get warm by the fire," Kate says. She tugs on my shirt sleeve and heads off. I follow, beckoned by both the promise of warmth and the nearness of Kate.

The bonfire has grown crowded, drawing other frigid souls with its toasty glow. We manage to find an open space and squeeze in. Kate presses into my side, and I put my arm around her back, having no choice given the tight space. Not that I mind. Far from it. But Kate and I, through some unspoken agreement, have taken great care over the past few weeks to not make too much of a public spectacle of ourselves, and I am conscious of that even now.

There is no reason for it, really. We are not hiding, neither of us ashamed of what we have become. And yet something is always there, tingling the base of my brain, telling me to take care of this precious, fragile gift I have been given. I don't really know what Kate thinks of the whole thing, whether she would be happy to call a town meeting and kiss me senseless in front of the whole farm. I get the sense she is following my lead, content to let me work out whatever is holding me back, and I am once again overcome by her tender, patient heart.

Kate snuggles in even closer to me, resting her hand upon my thigh, and so, for this night, I decide to stop worrying and just let the night take hold. If anyone notices, they don't let on, and I find myself caring less and less, too focused on how perfectly Kate fits into my side, how her hand burns hotter into my skin than the fire, how our breathing seems to meld together into one breath. In and out, in and out.

All I can think about is lifting her chin and kissing her with all of the passion I can muster. I remember with shocking intensity the way her lips feel pressed against mine, how when we kiss her mouth opens so sweetly to welcome me, the soft moans that come unbidden from her throat. We have spent many nights over the last few weeks like that, kissing and touching until we are too exhausted to do anything more than fall asleep wrapped up in each other's arms.

We have slept together nearly every night, but we have not made love. It isn't for lack of desire on either of our parts. She whispers things in my ear at night. Sweet things. Delicious things. Words that make my heart race and my head spin, make my blood thrum in my veins and my fists clench the bedsheets. Images thunder through my brain, how she looks up at me late at night, her skin glowing beneath the moon's gentle light seeping in through my window, her hair spread out like fire against my pillow. I can feel her soft skin beneath my fingers, impossibly soft, like the finest Egyptian cotton. Her moans fill my ears, stealing my breath.

No, it is certainly not a lack of desire that keeps me from making love to her. And it is me holding us back, of that much I am sure. But something always holds me back, something I do not understand beyond the knowledge I am afraid. Maybe it's the fear I do not deserve her. Maybe it's the fear I cannot make her happy. Maybe it's the fear of opening myself so completely, and of that one last wall around my heart falling forever.

As with how we act in public, Kate seems to be content to follow my lead here, too. I pull back, and she eases up, snuggling into my side and sighing contentedly. I want to tell her, want to explain that it's not her, that I want her so desperately I can barely breathe. But she shushes me before I can speak and holds me tighter, telling me it is okay without uttering a word. Most nights, it is enough to soothe me, to ease the worrying that accompanies my nameless fears, but then, a week ago, it wasn't. We lay in my bed, trying to slow our breath. She exhaled her sigh and nestled in closer, and all I could think was she would misunderstand, mistake my pulling back for rejection, and once again, I was letting her down. I should have known better.

"Stop," she whispers. "You stop that right now."

"Stop what?" I croak.

"Whatever masochistic, self-defeatist absurdity you're flagellating yourself with."

I can't help but laugh. "You certainly have a way with words."

"It's a gift."

"I just...worry."

"About everything. Yes, I know."

"Stop that."

She says nothing, but I feel her lips curl into a smile against my shoulder. She can really be a smart-ass sometimes. Just one of many things I adore about her.

"You know it's not you, right?"

"I know."

"I want you."

"I know. I want you, too."

"I want you so much. You drive me absolutely out of my mind sometimes. I mean completely, stark-raving around-the-bend nuts, with your perfect skin and sparkling eyes and your swaying hips, and all I can think about is peeling off your shirt and—"

"I know, baby. I feel it every time you look at me."

I find her eyes in the darkness. "Then why is it when we're alone like this, and I have you in my arms and my heart is pounding, something always stops me."

A delicate hand reaches up to stroke my cheek.

"You're scared."

"Yeah, but of what? I keep trying to figure it out, but every time I get close it dances out of reach, like a dream."

She kisses my cheek, then snuggles back into my side. "You'll figure it out."

"When?" I ask, my voice carrying more than a hint of a whine. She chuckles at that.

"When you're ready, baby. It'll happen. I'm not worried."

"This must be driving you crazy."

"I will admit to a certain amount of...frustration." She laughs.

"I'm so sorry. I don't mean to be so dysfunctional."

"Don't be sorry," she says, placing a delicate kiss on my neck, and then another. "I have no doubt that when we do finally make love, it's going to have been worth the wait."

That makes me smile. "Really?"

"Oh yeah," she moans, sending a bolt of electricity right down my spine. She leans in closer, her breath tickling my ear. "We're talking fireworks."

Kate's fingers knead my thigh, snapping me back to the present. It is an easy gesture of intimacy, and yet it inflames my senses and ignites my blood. I want nothing more in this moment than to feel her with nothing between us, skin against skin, to take her back to my room and spend the whole night worshipping her. The air rushes out of me with the want of it, and I breathe in deeply to replenish what I have lost. She must feel the change in me because she looks up at me. I do not know what exactly she sees, but she gasps, her eyes darkening in a way I know well. Her hand tightens on my thigh, and I feel her body humming against me. She knows exactly what I am thinking, what I am feeling, and by the grace of God, she feels the same. A slow, sensual grin overtakes her, and I nearly come apart.

The spell is broken by Dunk plopping down next to me in a space I hadn't even noticed had become empty.

"Hey guys, watcha' doing?" he asks innocently. I turn to glare at him, both for interrupting and for what I assume is sarcasm, but soon realize he hasn't a clue. My brain is still having trouble processing the abrupt change in focus. Kate is quicker to recover and pats my thigh lightly before turning to Dunk.

"What have you and the boys been plotting all night, Duncan?"

"Nothing," Dunk says with all the innocence of the devil on holiday.

"Mmm-hmm, right."

"Just a little Halloween fun," Dunk backpedals. "Scout's honor."

"Of course."

My brain finally awakens from its stupor enough to join in the conversation.

"I think it's about time for some ghost stories, don't you?" I am incredibly grateful my voice isn't squeaking like a prepubescent boy's.

Dunk doesn't respond verbally, but the big old grin on his face tells me all I need to know. The party turns to the telling of tall tales designed to delight and frighten. Some have more of a gift for it than others. Buck, of course, is a natural, using his deep baritone to full effect. Margie is pretty good as well, telling the story of the two teenagers down on Lover's Lane who are stalked by the man with a meat hook for a hand. She looks pointedly at the teenage boys around the fire, who are of course oblivious to the clear warning about what happens to kids who have sex in the backs of Buicks.

The big, devious plotting the boys had been doing turns out to be in preparation of their own frightening tale, the story of the babysitter who gets a series of menacing phone calls only to find out the calls are coming from inside the house. Rather than just tell the story, the boys have decided to enact it, with Sam playing the role of the courageous-but-ultimately-doomed babysitter, complete with mini-skirt and long blond hair.

All the while, I am intrinsically aware of Kate sitting next to me, her body still pressed up against mine, though less intensely than before. I only half focus on the stories being told, too attuned to my still-humming blood to pay full attention to anything else. Her hand strokes my knee lightly, a touch that is designed more for comfort than arousal, although the effect is definitely the latter. Kate seems completely focused on the storytelling, and I have no indication whether she, like me, is still thinking about…before. It is not until later, when the stories are all told and the fire extinguished, that I know any different.

After saying a few good nights and giving Dunk a pat on the back for a job well-done, I turn back to Kate. The look she gives me nearly makes my legs give out. It always seemed corny when it happened in the movies, but here I am, my knees feeling like they are made of Silly Putty. She doesn't say a word, just reaches out her hand, waiting for me to take it. She leads me back to my room, the only sounds the rushing of blood in my ears and my labored breathing. I am a total wreck, completely unhinged, yet she is as calm as the sea after a storm.

She enters the room ahead of me, not bothering to turn on the overhead light. I follow, unable to do anything else nor wanting to, closing the door behind me with a soft click. I lean back against the door, trying to gather myself. She has cast a spell on me, and I am powerless against it. She stands in front of my bed, watching me, her eyes softening. Her hands go to the hem of her shirt, and she lifts it up and over, dropping it carelessly to the ground. My breathing hitches. I am overwhelmed by the gesture, by my desire, by my fear. She seems to understand. Yet one more thing for which I am grateful this night.

She approaches me slowly, her fingers sliding between mine. She kisses one corner of my mouth, then the other. So soft. She walks backward toward the bed, and my feet follow. I am caught in her orbit, helplessly drawn to her by a force both awesome and terrifying. She kisses me again, this time her lips meshing perfectly with mine, and I am lost. My hands lift to her face, tangling in her hair as our lips brush again and again. Her tongue flicks mine teasingly, a silent invitation, and I hear myself groan. Her mouth is a haven, warm and wet, welcoming me home. Her hands are at my waist, gripping me, pulling me closer.

She presses into me, and my mind registers a subtle change. I step back slightly, my breathing ragged, searching her eyes in confusion. Finding no answer other than a plea for me to continue, I glance down and discover the something that has changed. My breath catches again. Her breasts stand proud and bare before my eyes. She takes my hand from her face and places it against her chest. I have never felt anything this perfect. I cup her breast gently, the silky weight filling my palm, and she releases a long, shuddering breath. She crushes her lips against mine, our tongues dueling as I press both my hands into her flesh.

"Bed," she gasps. "Need…"

She is already pulling me down as I groan my assent. I follow her down onto the mattress, my hands becoming trapped between our bodies. She is clutching my back, pulling me even further into her, our mouths moving frantically against each other. Her thigh slips in between mine, pressing up into me. I am so wet, so ready, and she is so hot and perfect and…

I still my hands and pull back, breaking the kiss.

I finally understand my fear.

"Taylor?" Her voice is thick with passion, her eyes still unfocused with want, and I nearly give in. I struggle to slow my racing heart. I lean back and slip my hand to her side, unwilling to break contact with her skin but needing my hand to be somewhere less intimate.

"Taylor?" she questions again, by now realizing something has changed. "Look at me."

Her hand strokes my cheek. She searches my face, giving me the space I need to explain, or not.

"It's okay," she says, pressing a gentle kiss to my forehead. "It's okay."

Her acceptance gives me the strength I need.

"I want you," I whisper. "I need you. And tonight I…but I don't want to rush. You deserve more."

"You don't always have to treat me with kid gloves, you know. I'm a big girl, Taylor. I know what I want."

There is no scorn in her words, just a simple truth. I smile, kissing her softly.

"And I know what I want. I want to give you everything. I…"

I want desperately to say the words, to tell her I love her. And I do love her. I know that already. But the words fail me. They are stuck inside, unable to pass my lips. And that is the problem, the reason I stopped. For the first time in my life, I need the words to come before the act. I need to bare my soul before we bare our bodies.

"Kate, I…" Time passes, with me locked in some surreal war inside my brain, fighting to simply say what I know in my heart. Once again, Kate saves me.

"I know."

I don't know how she knows, but I know that she does. She kisses me again, a slow, deep kiss that conveys patience and desire all at once, relieving me of any fear that I, once again, have hurt her.

Exhaustion hits me, and I long for nothing more than to fall asleep in her arms. I reluctantly climb from the bed so I can remove my shoes, taking the opportunity to remove hers as well.

"Do you want…" I nod toward her still bare chest, point to her discarded shirt, feeling uncertain. She glances down, as if she's forgotten that she is shirtless, and then smiles up at me.

"I'm good if you are."

Just because we aren't going to have sex doesn't mean we can't enjoy some quality naked time. I start to climb back into the bed, but she stops me with her foot.

"Uh-uh. This bed is a shirt-free zone."

I grin, shucking off my shirt and slipping back into the bed so quickly she doesn't have time to protest until I am already safely under the covers.

"Not fair," she whines, snapping my bra strap. "There is a definite inequity here."

"Oh?" I say innocently. "Well, we can't have that."

Slowly I reach behind my back and unhook my bra, sliding it off my shoulders and tossing it over the side of the bed, my breasts remaining hidden beneath the blanket the whole time.

"Tease," she laughs, turning onto her side. I slide up behind her, pressing my now naked torso into her back. We both groan at the sensation. It is the most perfect thing I have felt in all my days. She pulls my hand around her side and up to her chest, pinning it close to her heart. Within minutes I fall into a dreamless sleep.

CHAPTER TWENTY-SIX

November whispered its way across Burninghead Farm, and all around the farm the trees showed off their resplendent fall coats, a mixture of scarlet and gold. The month began surprisingly warm, but the air carried a crispness that spoke of a harsh winter to come. The trees picked up on this and, despite the mild temperatures, the ground was quickly becoming littered with fallen leaves. As nature waged the eternal battle between style and substance in its preparation for the cold, Duncan was consumed by the fierce urgency of now.

They had made great progress on the wall that would protect them from the world, completing it on two sides of the farm. They were about halfway finished with the western wall, but it was clear they were running out of time. Winter in Indiana could be unpredictable, and despite the fine weather they were currently experiencing, all it would take was a little breeze from the north coming across the Great Lakes to turn the ground into a frozen tundra that would rival Siberia for its impenetrability. So Duncan picked up his pace, hoping that with a little luck and a lot of hard work, they could outrace the wind.

Duncan was a man on a mission, and he was not the only one. Although they had not spoken of it, his entire crew seemed to sense that time was of the essence, and they worked with a new determination to get the job done. Beside him, Taylor set a hard pace, but she had lost the anger and desperation that had worried him only a few short weeks ago. She seemed content now, working to finish the job simply because it needed finishing and not because she was trying to fight a war she could not win. That made Duncan smile.

They had lost time the day before, only a few hours but time being as precious as it was, the loss had Duncan working even harder today. A new family had found its way to the farm, a man, his wife, and their ten-year-old son, looking famished and exhausted. Buck had spoken to them a while, given them food and water. Eventually, Buck had done what he always did, which was invite them to stay and call all the farm's residents together to break the news.

Duncan was lost in his work and his thoughts and barely heard the pickup crunching the dirt as it pulled up to a stop only a few feet away. Margie jumped down from the driver's seat, closing the heavy truck door with a deceptively soft click. The tightness of her lips told Duncan something was wrong. He hopped up and out of the ditch just as Margie reached its edge. She spoke before he could ask the question, but her words were not directed at him.

"Taylor."

Taylor looked up, shading her eyes with her hand against the afternoon glare. She smiled at Margie. "What brings you out here?"

"Dad needs to see you," Margie said. Her voice was all business, and yet Duncan sensed a certain sadness beneath her words, and it was directed squarely at Taylor.

Taylor's face dropped. "What's wrong? Did something happen?" she asked even as she jumped up out of the ditch to stand next to Duncan. "Is everyone okay?"

"Everyone's fine," Margie said reassuringly. She even gave a hint of a smile, but it quickly faded. "Something…Dad just really needs to see you."

"Is Kate all right?" Taylor asked, still somewhat panicked. Duncan's mind raced over what Buck could need to see Taylor so urgently about, and why it would have Margie upset. Kate seemed like the logical answer.

"She's fine," Margie said, squeezing Taylor's shoulder. "This isn't about her."

Taylor relaxed slightly but her concern remained.

"Then what?"

"Better for Dad to explain. Just come with me, okay?" Margie said, turning back to the truck. "You come too, Duncan," she said over her shoulder.

Taylor looked over at Duncan, but he was as confused as she was. He shrugged slightly and followed Taylor over to the passenger side.

Clearly they were not going to get any answers out of Margie, and they rode back to the farmhouse in silence. Duncan's mind flew through a dozen possibilities, analyzing and rejecting each one in turn. Tension radiated off Taylor, and he could tell it was taking every ounce of her control not to yank the steering wheel out of Margie's hands and demand she give them some answers. Duncan felt the same. Patience was definitely not one of his better qualities.

Taylor sprinted up to the farmhouse when they finally arrived. Duncan was fast on her heels, bursting through the doorway.

"In here," Buck called out, and they ran into the kitchen.

"What's going on, Buck?" Taylor demanded before her feet had even stopped moving. Duncan looked around the kitchen in complete confusion. If they had not been cryptically summoned to the farmhouse, Duncan would not have had any clue that anything was going on. Buck sat with the new man, two half-drunk cups of coffee sitting before them on the worn kitchen table. Duncan was not sure what he had expected, but this was definitely not it.

"Have a seat, Taylor," Buck said with a smile that did not reach his eyes.

"I'll stand, thanks," she answered curtly. "Is everyone all right?"

Clearly Margie's answer to that question had not satisfied Taylor, just as it had not satisfied Duncan. Duncan tried to read Buck's face, but it was an impenetrable mask.

"You meet Adam yesterday?" Buck asked, nodding toward the man at the table.

Taylor gave a terse nod, waiting for Buck to explain something of relevance. "Buck..." she said warningly.

Buck sighed. "Adam's got a bit of a story to tell. Better to let him tell it."

Taylor immediately looked at Adam.

"Well, you see, Kim and I—Kim's my wife—we were huddled up with a few of the other survivors from our town. We had our boy...did you meet him? Well, we were real lucky, all of us making it through and everything. It was a miracle, I'll tell you that."

Adam grew quiet, lost in the notion that somehow his whole family had survived intact, Duncan supposed. Taylor shifted impatiently.

"Oh, sorry. Anyway, a bunch of us were doing fairly well over in Iowa, for a while anyway. Eventually, food started running low, and JJ—he was the leader of our group—well, he started acting kind of crazy. Started thinking folks were stealing food and whatnot, just getting real paranoid. Of course I started thinking that I was the one who was being paranoid, but we had a family meeting one day and Kim felt the same, and we decided we'd best be leaving. A few nights later we took off. I felt bad sneaking off in the dead of night like that, but it seemed better that way somehow. We thought we'd head to Kim's brother's place near Columbus. We didn't know whether he'd made it through the plague or not, but it was someplace to go. We've been traveling for a long time. It's tough with the boy, we have to take it kind of slow, but we wouldn't change that for the world. And then we stumbled upon this place and here we are."

Duncan looked back and forth between Adam, Buck, and Taylor, trying to figure out why they had been summoned to hear that story. Taylor was trying to figure out the same thing, and Duncan watched a tide of frustration and bewilderment ebb and flow across her face.

"I'm glad you found this place and you're safe," Taylor said more compassionately than Duncan would have expected. The question of what in the hell was going on hung in the room like the proverbial 800-pound gorilla. Duncan had never really understood that expression, but it seemed fitting nonetheless. "But why did you call me up here to tell me that? Buck?"

Buck looked up at her, his face a world of concern. The knot in Duncan's stomach grew.

"Tell her what happened in Illinois."

"What about Illinois?" Taylor asked, the tension in her body exploding through her vocal cords.

"Oh right," Adam started nervously. "Well, after a few weeks my son got pretty sick. I didn't think it was the plague, not after all this time, but we were terribly worried. We knew he needed medicine. Luckily, about then we stumbled on a small town that had a group of survivors. They were real nice and welcomed us in, like you folks here, and they had antibiotics and stuff. They were starting to run a bit low on supplies, but they shared with us anyway. I don't know what we would have done if we hadn't found them. We stayed there for about a week and then left. That was about two weeks ago."

Adam stopped again, and Duncan still had no idea what any of this meant or had to do with them. But he saw Buck staring up at Taylor, watching her, so he turned to look at Taylor, too. Her skin had gone pale, as if she had just seen a ghost.

"It's not possible," she muttered.

"Tell her the name of the town, Adam," Buck prodded gently.

"Asheville."

Taylor stumbled backward, the simple word knocking her back with its weight. Duncan, for his part, was too stunned to react to steady Taylor, but she recovered her footing. For an instant, Duncan was consumed by a joy he had not known was possible at the revelation. All hope was not lost. There was still a chance Taylor's family, or some of it anyway, was alive. Duncan did not know he could be this happy for another human being, but he was, and it thrilled him. He started planning the search party in his head, the rescue mission that would bring Taylor's family home.

And that was when it hit him, why Buck was looking concerned. What if her family was still dead? What if she had just been given this gift of hope only to have it dashed again? Taylor had nearly come undone the first time she had found out her family was really and truly gone. Duncan did not think she could survive the loss a second time, even as the person she had become here at Burninghead Farm. Plus, there was the added factor that for Taylor, Illinois was home. If her family had somehow survived, Taylor might not be coming back. Duncan now worried that no matter what Taylor found in Illinois, they might lose her. It was completely selfish, Duncan knew, to be thinking such things, but for this one moment he did not care.

"Are you sure?" Taylor asked woodenly, quietly. "Are you sure it was Asheville?"

"Yes," Adam said, nodding.

"Could you describe it?" Her voice was childlike, and tears began to gather.

"It was like most towns, I suppose. I'm not sure I really know how to describe it. They were all staying at one end, had taken over some houses on this cul-de-sac. On the way out of town there was this really pretty church, with a big white steeple. I remember it because there was this huge stained glass window in the front, of the Virgin Mary kneeling before the crucifixion."

Taylor gasped. Duncan knew without even having to be told what it meant. It was written all over Taylor's face.

"That church is on the east side of town," she said, tears brimming over to meet the stunned smile on her cheeks.

She turned to Buck then. "Buck?"

Buck stood. "Go pack a bag. Duncan, go help Kate out in the barn. She's getting one of the horses ready and some supplies."

Taylor seemed startled by the knowledge that Kate already knew, as Duncan was himself. He figured Buck had his reasons. Taylor ran out of the room, the screen door slamming behind her. Duncan's mind was chaos. He was happy for Taylor, yet he feared losing her. He could only imagine how Kate was feeling.

CHAPTER TWENTY-SEVEN

I race to the dorm, ignoring the burning in my lungs and in my thighs. My mind runs even faster, a blurring mixture of thoughts and memories ground into one beautifully unbearable truth. I know the likelihood is my family is still gone, but as long as Asheville remains, hope remains with it. Despite everything that has happened since the world came to an end, or maybe because of it, I want nothing more than to let hope take hold.

I pack up my meager belongings in a haze. I am outside myself, watching with detached interest what I choose to shove into my backpack and what I choose to leave behind. For some reason, I struggle over whether to bring my towel, putting it in and then taking it back out of my bag, back and forth until finally I zip up the bag, the towel still lying on the bed. I throw the bag over my shoulder and grab Mugsy, safely cocooned in her scabbard, and head out to the barn.

I don't know what I will say to Kate. I want to stay here on the farm and live this new life I have built, that I am still in the process of building. But my family calls to me, pulling at my blood and demanding I finish what I started all those months ago. The real question is what I will do after, once I have either found my family or found my hopes ground out like a cigarette beneath my boot heel. For that question, I have no real answer. My brain is in too much chaos to know anything for certain, other than I have to go.

Kate is in the barn when I arrive, holding Stu's reins. Fitting. The black monolith is saddled up and waiting, and he eyes me in that way of his, as if he knows exactly what I am all about. He stomps his hoof, but he does not seem perturbed like the last time I was here. Instead, he seems to understand the gravity of the situation and has accepted his part in this mission of mine. I am sure I am reading too much into Stu, again, but I am equally as sure I am right about his intentions.

I stand frozen in the dirt and hay, overcome with the reality of all that I am leaving behind. I meet Kate's gaze. I try to read the myriad of emotions I find there. She smiles gently, trying to tell me it is all going to be okay. I take the last few steps to stand before her.

"I have to go," I say.

"I know."

"I have to find out."

"I know."

She strokes my face, and I feel her willing me the strength I need to see this through. And then I know the answer, know without the slightest doubt that no matter what I find in Illinois, I will be coming back. I will be coming home.

"You about ready?" Dunk's voice comes out of nowhere.

"Huh?" I fumble, turning to find Dunk standing a few feet away, holding Goldie's reins. "What's going on?"

"I'm coming with you," Dunk says.

"Like hell you are," I snap.

"Like hell I'm not. You don't really think we'd let you go by yourself, do you?"

"You two plan this?" I ask, looking back and forth between Dunk and Kate.

"It was Buck's idea, actually," Dunk says.

"Well, then he's a fool, too," I snarl. There are too many dangers for me to even consider taking anyone with me, let alone Dunk. I cannot, will not, take responsibility for his safety.

"You're not going alone," Kate says, crossing her arms across her chest as if that settles the matter.

"Not your decision to make," I bark. One look at her, though, and my anger dissolves. "Kate," I say more gently, "what if I run into trouble? I can't be worrying about Dunk the whole time. It could get me killed."

I cringe at how melodramatic it all sounds, but these days everything is life and death. I have been on the road before. I know all too well what dangers lurk in the world outside Burninghead Farm.

"What if you do run into trouble?" Kate asks, her voice barely a whisper. "You need someone to watch your back."

"Yeah, but—"

"Kate's right. You can't go alone."

This time, it is Buck's voice that comes out of nowhere. The irony that I have once again been snuck up on as I am arguing I don't need anyone to watch my back is not lost on me.

"Buck—"

"You're part of our family now, Taylor, and family members support each other. Duncan's going."

I want to bristle at Buck giving me orders, but I can't. I know not only that he is right, that they all are, but that I am grateful for it.

"You don't have to come, you know," I say to Dunk, giving him one last chance to back out.

"I know I don't have to. I want to. Let me watch your back."

I nod, overcome. As Duncan mounts his horse, Buck reaches for my shoulder.

"If you find them, bring them back."

"Are you sure? I mean, we don't even know how many there are."

"It's like I said when you first arrived, Taylor. Anyone is welcome, as long as they don't mean us any harm."

I nod my understanding, and my gratitude. Then I turn back to Kate.

"You know why it's Duncan and not me going with you, right?" Kate asks. I feel her conflict. This is not easy for her. "You'd be panicking the whole time about my safety, and it would only distract you."

"I'll be panicking about Dunk too, you know."

"No, you'll just be worrying about him, and that's okay. Worry will keep you honest. Panic would get you in trouble."

She is right, of course. Still…

"I'll never forgive myself if—"

"Stop," she says, placing a finger over my lips. "Trust Duncan to take care of himself. Not everything in this world is your fault, you know."

I know she is talking about Pennsylvania, that she knows my fear is not just some abstract concept but borne out by experience. "I know that," I say, almost believing it. "But some things are my responsibility."

"Then take responsibility. For Duncan and for yourself. Watch his back. But trust him to do the same for you. Whatever happens after that is no one's fault."

I let her words sink in. There is no more to say, so I turn to mount Stu. Just as quickly as I turn, Kate's strong arms pull me back around. She kisses me with an urgent passion for which there is no response other than to match it. I pour my heart and soul into the kiss, use it to tell her all the things I cannot yet find the words to say.

"Come back to me," she whispers fiercely.

I memorize her face, every line and curve, and then jump up astride Stu. There are no more words as Dunk and I ride out of the barn and toward the front gate of the farm.

We don't get far before I am hit with a need so strong I pull up the reins and turn the big horse around. Kate and Buck have followed us out of the barn and are standing in the doorway, Buck's arm around Kate's shoulder.

"I love you," I shout, my voice booming across the open field. I don't wait for her to reply, turning Stu back around and hightailing it out of Burninghead Farm. I am too much a coward to say it to her face.

Chickenshit.

But at least I have finally told her, and for now that is enough.

CHAPTER TWENTY-EIGHT

Soon, Burninghead Farm fades to just a speck in the distance, and then to nothing more than a memory somewhere over the horizon. We fly due west across open fields and abandoned farmlands, the grasses and scrub overgrown but not overwhelming, more evidence of the earth's newfound dominance over what was once occupied territory. We keep off the highway but near enough to follow its lead. The pavement would be too hard on the horses for them to manage for any length of time, especially at our current speed. Not that I had known that, of course, ignorant as I am about all things equine. To me, taking the horses up onto the pavement seemed the most logical thing in the world. Thankfully, Dunk warned me off the highway, preventing me from what would have been a boneheaded mistake that could have ended our little adventure before it had really begun. I am all too aware that for all my protesting, Dunk has already proved his worth by saving my dumb ass.

We ride the wind, racing against the turning of the planet, and I have never before felt such a sense of freedom. Stu's powerful legs churn up the ground beneath us, and I swear I can feel him reaching down into his heritage, to the days of his ancestors running wild across the plains. This is what horses used to know, back before man conquered them, when they were allowed to simply run free.

I have no idea how long we can keep up this pace, although I am certain it cannot go on forever. The horses, despite their power, are not machines. Even I know that much. I have to trust Dunk to set the pace and slow us down when it becomes too much for our rides. Still, selfishly, I dread the coming of that moment.

Eventually, Dunk slows, pulling back on the reins and easing Goldie into a walk before stopping her altogether. I follow suit, pulling up beside them. Dunk pats Goldie's thick neck and whispers into her ear. She whinnies slightly and stomps her front hoof. Clearly she wants to keep running.

"Easy, girl, easy," Dunk coos, loud enough for Stu and me to both hear. "There'll be plenty of time for that later. For now we need to give you guys some rest."

Stu snorts, as if to say that rest is for beings far less powerful than he and Goldie.

"Come on, Stu, you know I'm right," Dunk says with a chuckle.

It is strange sitting here astride this giant horse, listening to Dunk have a full-on conversation with him. Yet once again, I am taken by how Stu seems to respond to Dunk, how he and Goldie always seem to understand every single word we are saying and answer us back. Finally, the matter appears to be settled enough for Stu and Goldie, and we continue on our way.

Already the sun is starting to slip lower into the sky, and I know we only have a few hours of riding left, if we are lucky, before night claims the day. We ride on in silence, me lost in my thoughts, Dunk seeming to sense my mood. I'm not purposefully ignoring him, but I feel guilty just the same. Still, we aren't college freshmen on some glorified road trip, and I push my guilt aside. Besides, Dunk doesn't really seem to mind the lack of conversation. I notice his head bobbing and weaving in time to some tune I can't hear, and every now and then a little bit of the melody in his head escapes his lips in a low hum.

"We probably ought to find a place to stop for the night," Dunk says after about two hours.

By my calculations, keeping an eye on the mileage signs that mark the side of the highway, we've only made it about twenty-five miles. Truth be told, I have absolutely no idea how far a horse can go in one day, or how long it will take us to reach Asheville.

I sigh my frustration.

"Horses can only be pushed about ten hours a day when we're traveling like we are," Dunk says, having picked up on my disappointment. "Otherwise, exhaustion sets in, and these guys won't be able to make it back."

That thought scares me. I haven't even considered how hard this will be on the horses, and I certainly don't want to do anything to harm them. I realize that it isn't just Dunk's safety I am responsible for.

"Ten hours a day? How far do you think we can get in that time?" I try to sound only mildly curious.

"Well, depending on the conditions, maybe thirty to forty miles a day if we're lucky. We pushed them kind of hard today, but these horses like to run, so we'll see. We just have to be careful."

I quickly figure out that it is going to take us at least another four days to get to Asheville. If stupid were a town, I would easily be its mayor, running unopposed and winning in a landslide. I don't know what in the hell I was thinking. I had just figured I'd take a horse and be there tomorrow. Clearly that isn't going to be the case.

Stupid, stupid.

"I know you want to get there," Dunk says, trying to make me feel better. "And we will. But it's just going to take some time. For now, let's just find a place to make camp. Get some food and get settled in for the night."

We find a small clearing in some woods about a mile farther along, far enough from the highway to hide us. My legs are jelly as I jump down from Stu's back, and my mind flashes to that day riding with Kate, and how she'd had to catch me to keep me from falling. This time I manage to stay on my feet after I dismount. Kate would be proud that I seem to have gotten my horse legs. Dunk goes to work caring for the horses, getting them fed and tucked away for the night. I gather wood for a fire.

By the time I get back, Dunk has finished with the horses and has found about a dozen medium-sized stones and made a small circle for a fire pit. It isn't long before he has a small blaze going, after my own attempts to start the fire fail.

"What were you, a Boy Scout?"

"Eagle Scout, actually."

"Figures," I mutter. "Wish I'd had you with me all those months on the road. Lots of cold nights I wished I'd had a fire and could never seem to get one going for long."

"Yeah, well if I'd been there, I would have whipped you into shape in no time. Starting fires, tying knots, pitching tents, skinning squirrels—"

"Skinning squirrels? What in the hell kind of Eagle Scouts were these? Future Serial Killers Troop 101?"

"Hey, don't knock it 'til you've tried it. Squirrel is good eating."

I gag at the thought. A hearty laugh erupts from Dunk's throat, and I can't believe how gullible I am.

"Asshole."

"Well," he says, still chuckling, "thankfully Franny packed us a lovely assortment of cornbread, dried food, and a few canned goods, so no squirrel tonight." He rummages through one of the supply sacks.

We fix our dinner, and the scent of the cooking food, wafting over the fire, has my stomach growling. Soon we are digging into hearty helpings of Spam and beans.

"Mmm, tastes like squirrel."

I nearly spit out my dinner, laughing. Dunk keeps his head down, focused on his food, but I see the smile tweaking the corner of his mouth. I laugh again. Dunk can be pretty cheeky when he wants.

We make quick work of our dinner and the cleanup, burying our refuse and packing away our cookware and supplies. We opt to not unpack our tent, preferring instead to lay out our sleeping bags directly under a blanket of stars. It will be cold overnight, of that I have no doubt, but the temperatures are not yet frigid. Besides, there is something comforting about being stretched out with the sky as our ceiling, seeing stars that have only returned now that the glare of man's lights are no longer polluting the nighttime sky.

"Do you think they're up there watching us?"

I am nearly asleep, soothed by the rhythmic twinkling of the stars, and it takes me a minute to respond. "Who?"

"All the people we've lost."

I look over at him. He is bundled up in his sleeping bag, staring up at the great big sky.

"You mean Heaven?"

"Maybe."

I finally understand his meaning. I turn back to the stars.

"When I was a kid, I had this cat. His name was Billy. He wandered into our yard one day, all dirty and scrawny. My dad was worried the cat was feral, but he was just about as sweet as a cat could be. All he ever wanted to do was curl up in your lap. He was my best friend."

This many years later, the thought of that cat still tugs at my heart a bit.

"But even when we took him in, he was pretty sick. We did everything we could for him, but in the end…we just couldn't let him suffer anymore. I cried for days. One night, my dad took me outside and pointed up at the stars. He told me about the constellations, about the Big Dipper and Orion and the others. Then he searched the sky for a while until he found this one particular star. It wasn't as bright as the others, but it flashed in the sky like it was winking at me. He told me the star was Billy, keeping an eye on me from Heaven. I asked him why it was twinkling, and he said Billy was trying to let me know he was up there, watching over me. Any time I was missing him, all I had to do was look up at the sky and look for that winking star, and I would know Billy was there."

Dunk doesn't say anything, just keeps looking up at those stars.

As the silence lingers, I find myself growing embarrassed. "Sorry. That was a really hokey story."

"See that one there? Next to that really bright one?" He asks me after a while, pointing up to the sky. "That one's my mom and dad."

I smile, my embarrassment vanishing. "That's a good star, Dunk."

He seems pleased at that, and I watch his eyes fall slowly closed. I lie back, watching the stars, until sleep claims me.

Early the next morning, we break camp and begin again, heading ever west. We quickly develop a pattern of riding for a few hours and then resting the horses, then beginning again. When we are hungry, we eat. When it gets dark, we make camp. We are blessed with mostly good weather, although it turns noticeably colder by late the second day, and that first night under the stars turns out to be our last. From that point on, Dunk and I share a tent at night.

The days pass, and I barely even notice when we cross into Illinois. The road is quiet, and I am thankful we do not run into anyone along the way, living or dead. Not a single body litters the roadside, at least as far as I can see. But every now and then, death soaks the air, and I am reminded that things are not always as they appear. We stay south of Chicago, not wanting to take the risk even though it would shave at least thirty miles off our journey.

On the seventh day, just past noon, we enter the city limits of Asheville, Illinois.

Chapter Twenty-nine

Gray storm clouds lumbered high above, menacing and full of intention. The air was heavy with the threat of rain, as if the skies would open at any moment and wash Duncan and Taylor away, along with any trace they had ever existed. All morning, they had been dogged by thunderheads, yet the rain had not come. As they sat astride their horses, staring up at the front of Taylor's childhood home, Duncan was grateful for the patience of the rain.

The house was statuesque in its stillness, its whitewashed siding gleaming against the foreboding sky. Seasons had come and gone from this place, leaving behind an overrun lawn woven with decaying leaves. Heavy drapes were drawn inside the windows, as if someone had tried to fend off death by shutting out the world. On the front porch, a set of wind chimes rang out a tune orchestrated by the wind, a last-ditch attempt to welcome visitors to a place long abandoned. This house, which Duncan could imagine once standing majestic and proud, now stood only in mourning.

Life had not flourished at the home of Taylor's parents for a long, long time. Of that, Duncan was sure. Taylor's parents might not be dead, of course, but Duncan knew they were, just the same. There was an emptiness to this place, a conclusion to be drawn by the absence of the telltale signs of existence. By the set of Taylor's shoulders, Duncan knew that Taylor knew it, too.

Taylor dismounted, still staring up at the crest of the roof, lost among the ghosts of her past. Duncan followed silently, not wanting to intrude in any way, wanting simply to be present. Without looking back at him, Taylor offered him Stu's reins, dropping them into Duncan's hand on a blind assumption that he would catch them, which he, of course, did. She headed off around the side of the house, so Duncan followed, being sure to keep some distance between himself and Taylor. She disappeared at the back of the house, and Duncan paused. He was unsure of himself and unsure of what Taylor needed of him beyond caring for the horses. Minutes passed and still he waited, wondering where she had gone and even whether she was planning on coming back. That thought, and the uncertainty it created, got his feet moving. He headed toward the back of the house, bringing the horses along behind.

Duncan rounded the back corner, and there, beneath a large walnut tree scarred from the years, he found Taylor kneeling in the grass, her head bowed before two wooden crosses. He knew without needing to read the names carved into the makeshift grave markers. At long last, Taylor had found her parents.

Duncan felt the weight of Taylor's grief descend upon him, as he watched her shoulders shake as she wept upon the graves of her parents. It reminded him of his own grief, which he had thought long buried in the many months since he had dug his own parents' graves, at least until that first night with Taylor under the stars. He still did not know for sure what had triggered it, what it was about those stars that had brought up memories of his parents or his need to be comforted. But Taylor's story had comforted him, and that night he had fallen asleep feeling closer to his parents than on any night since their passing.

Duncan led the horses over to the back porch of the house, tying their reins loosely to the railing. Slowly he walked over to where Taylor knelt, not wanting to startle her but hoping his nearness would comfort her somehow. She did not acknowledge him, but he knew that she knew he was there, and that was enough.

He read the names on the markers, the simple act offering up both his respects and a prayer for their souls. Taylor reached out a hand, touched the swollen grass before her, clutching then releasing her fist upon one grave, then the other. Her sobbing subsided, replaced with what, Duncan did not know. He watched as she kissed her fingers and then reverently transferred the kiss to each of the markers, a clear good-bye. Then she stood and turned toward him, full of power and grace. Duncan thought she might push him away, might retreat to that dark place that had consumed her for so long. But he could see in her eyes none of the darkness he feared for her. They held sorrow to be sure, but her face was open, a mixture of grief and peace, as if she could finally let herself rest. Clearly, her parents had died months ago.

Duncan risked reaching out a hand and settled it on her shoulder, still unsure of how she would react even to such a tentative offer of support. She reached her hand up and covered his, squeezing it gently in gratitude. In that moment, Duncan knew that no matter what else they found in Asheville, Taylor would really and truly be all right.

"They must have died early on," she said quietly, turning back to gaze down upon the final resting place of her parents. "Back when folks were still burying their dead."

"Then there's still hope," Duncan offered.

"Yeah. My sister's place is about a mile from here. We should head there next."

"Don't you want to go inside?" Duncan asked, nodding toward the house. "There might be things you want to take with you. Mementos and such."

"No," she said wistfully, staring up at the house one last time. "Let it rest in peace. I have my memories. That's enough."

Duncan nodded, knowing that Taylor had found all she had needed to find. He untied the horses, and they mounted Stu and Goldie, heading off toward her sister's home.

This time Duncan did not wait by the side of the house when Taylor went around back. This house, too, was devoid of life, and they knew what they would find. Just as at her parents' place, two makeshift gravestones marked the backyard, crosses of wood lovingly etched with the names of Taylor's sister and brother-in-law. Taylor's ritual was the same, and Duncan gave her time to weep upon their graves. She offered them her final kiss good-bye and turned back to Duncan.

"My brother lives on the other side of town," she said, taking the reins back from Duncan.

"Do you want to wait a while? Take a break or something?" Duncan feared racing off only to find one more gravesite, and along with it the end to Taylor's entire family.

"I'm fine. But thanks. Unless you think the horses need a break?"

Duncan thought Taylor was simply in denial, that she was beginning to shut down despite what he had thought earlier, but he soon realized her concern for the horses was real. As long as she was feeling concern for something, Duncan reasoned, she was still doing okay.

"No, I think they're fine. We can go if you're ready."

They headed off toward Taylor's brother's home, and the last of Taylor's hope for her family.

It took more than an hour to reach the far side of town. They rode past home after home, storefront shops and churches, all of which showed absolutely no signs of life. Although the town looked like a bigger version of the one he grew up near, it reminded him more of the ruins of some long-lost civilization he had studied in school than a once-thriving town. Wherever the group of survivors was that had helped Adam and his family, Duncan could see no sign of them.

They reached the outskirts of town, where there were fewer houses and more open land. On a street called Maple, about halfway down the block, they found Taylor's brother's home. This time, Taylor did not dismount at the front of the house. She barely even paused before leading Stu around to the back. Unfortunately, the change in ritual did nothing to change the outcome. Four graves awaited them in the back, the wooden crosses rising up from the earth, silent witnesses to the end.

Taylor slid down from Stu and made her way over to the graves. Duncan dismounted and took hold of the horses, giving Taylor her space. He looped the reins over a low but sturdy branch of a nearby tree. This was truly the end, then, Duncan thought, saddened even though he was not surprised. He mourned for Taylor's family, mourned for Taylor. All he could hope for now was that these graves would bring her more than despair and heartache. That somehow, someway, they would allow her to get on with her life.

Taylor rose from her knees, and Duncan took his cue, softly approaching. She remained facing away from him, her attention focused on the four grave markers. He squeezed her shoulder, letting her know he was there.

She looked up at him weakly, her face a mask of anguish. She worked to regain some sense of composure. Duncan could feel her willing herself to take control, to realize that nothing had changed, that they had known this was going to be the result as soon as they had found her parents' graves. That the peace was in the knowing.

She drew herself straighter. "I'm okay."

Duncan nodded, releasing her.

"What do you want to do now?" Duncan asked. "Should we keep searching for the survivors Adam talked about? Try to find out what happened?"

She stared off into the distance for a long moment, and Duncan wondered if she was saying good-bye to all that she now knew she had lost. She turned back to him.

"We head home. There's nothing left for me here."

He wondered if maybe they should wait, allow Taylor to take more time given all that had happened, maybe try and get some answers from the survivor colony. But then he wondered what he would want to do if it had been him in Taylor's place, and he realized he would feel the same as she seemed to feel. The only answers that mattered were the ones she had found in the graves of her family. The details were not important now. He handed her Stu's reins.

"We should find some place to bunk down for the night, before the rain lets loose," he said as they walked back around toward the front of the house. Taylor started to reply but her words died as a man with a shotgun stepped directly into their path, his gun pointed square at Duncan's chest. The only thing that surprised Duncan more than that shotgun was what came out of Taylor's mouth.

"Nate?"

CHAPTER THIRTY

I stare into the face I have known since childhood, that now seems unrecognizable and unbelievable and yet familiar and real all the same. This is my family, and it has survived. It has not all been in vain.

"Taylor? My God…"

His voice is scratchy and disbelieving, his eyes worn and bloodshot. He lowers the shotgun, still gripping it tightly as if it is the last thing he has to hold on to. I can tell he has lost weight even though he's always been skinny, and rough, patchy stubble lines his face. He never could grow a proper beard.

"Nate?" I say again, trying to get my brain to accept that he is really here, standing in front of me, alive.

"Taylor? Is that…are you really here?"

I lunge for him, flinging my arms around his neck and squeezing with every ounce of strength I have. I need to know he is real, touch him with my own hands, feel his lungs expand and contract, his heart beat. He returns the embrace, wrapping his arms around me, the shotgun now held loosely in one hand. We have never been all that close, our ages and temperaments too similar for us to appreciate our differences, but none of that matters now.

"My God," he says. "My God."

I pull back, just enough to see his face. I study the lines and memorize the features, as if he will disappear at any moment, and all

I'll have left is the image scratched into my mind. Tears spring up in his eyes. I have only once seen my brother cry, and I can't help the tears that answer in my own eyes.

"Look at you. You look pretty good for a survivor." He strokes my cheek, pausing to trace the scar under my eye. His eyes crinkle, as if he realizes he might have spoken too soon.

"Best diet ever," I say breezily, trying to shuffle past his discovery. We might not be close, but he can still read me like a book, and he nods. There will be time for details later.

Dunk coughs, announcing himself.

"Oh, Nate, this is my friend Duncan. Duncan this…this is my brother, Nathan."

"Nate," my brother says, reaching out his hand.

"You can call me Dunk."

I smile at that.

Nate glances at the horses. "Where in the world did you come from, Taylor?"

I laugh. "It's a long story."

"I'm sure it is," he says with a chuckle. He sobers. "We thought you'd gotten caught by the bomb."

"I got out just before. Was trying to make my way here. I…I got hung up. But I finally made it."

"Mom and Dad would be proud."

I have to know. "What happened, Nate?"

"Mom and Dad were already sick the last time they talked to you. They didn't want to worry you. We took care of them as best we could, but…Well, you know. They went about the same time. I was grateful for that. I buried them underneath that old tree. I thought Mom would like it there."

Of course it had been Nate. My heart sinks at what it must have been like for him. I see recognition on Dunk's face. He understands better than I ever will what it means to bury your parents with your own two hands.

Nate tells me how our sister got sick next, but she lingered, even after her husband had gone. Nate had buried them, too. Nate's wife and young son had fallen last.

"But the graves," I say, remembering. I search his face for some answer. "There were four graves. You have a headstone."

"Oh, Taylor, I'm so sorry," he apologizes. "Lily begged me to do that. She didn't want her mom and brother to think we abandoned them."

"Wait," I say, struggling to put the pieces together. "You mean...Lily?"

"She didn't get sick. She's alive, Taylor."

The image of that little girl's face fills my mind, and relief washes over me.

"Come on." Nate turns on his heel and strides down the street. Dunk and I hurry after him, anticipation surging in my blood. We reach the end of the street, which dead ends in a cul-de-sac. And there, peeking out of windows and screen doors, are the survivors of Asheville.

Nate is already calling out to them, telling them it is okay, that Dunk and I are no threat. Slowly they come out into the world to meet us, uncertain but full of hope. They are young and old, mostly men and a few women, a microcosm of the residents of Burninghead Farm. And there, among the children hiding nervously behind adult legs, is my niece. I haven't seen her in more than a year, and with everything she has been through, I wonder if she will even remember me. But as her eyes settle upon my face, recognition dawns and she shoots forward, all hesitation gone. She runs straight into my arms, and I scoop her up in a mighty hug.

"Hey there, sweetheart," I sigh into her hair, holding her close. Her arms tighten around me, and for the first time in a long time, I offer up a silent prayer of thanks.

The next little while is a blur of hellos and handshakes, and before I know it, we're sitting around in lawn chairs, drinking and eating and talking. To the casual observer, it might have seemed like a typical neighborhood barbecue, except for the warm beer and stale potato chips and the lack of any real food. They'd managed to siphon off enough gas from abandoned cars over the months to run a couple of generators, but food had become a problem. They had exhausted their rations for the day, so the real food would need to wait for tomorrow.

"There's just not much left to salvage around here," a man named Bill says, taking another swig of his beer. "There's gas enough to leave, and water, but without a place to go…"

"Better to try than to stay here and starve." This from Simon, whose frustration is obvious.

"You know we can't," a woman named Sharon says, glaring at Simon. "Not with the children."

"You'd rather they die here?" Simon retorts.

Clearly this debate has been raging for some time, and everyone is entrenched in their positions.

"No one wants to die, Simon," Nate says finally. He stares off after Lily, who is running in circles with the other children, chasing imaginary butterflies. "The choice is the same today as it was three weeks ago. We stay here and wait for the food to run out completely, or we go out in search of something we might not be able to find. Neither option is good, but we're going to need to choose one sooner or later."

"I think we can help," I say. All attention turns toward me. "With a destination, anyway. You can come back with us."

"Come back where?" It is Nate who asks the question.

"Burninghead Farm. In Indiana. That's where we came from," Dunk supplies.

"That's where I've been, Nate. Not the whole time, but for a while." I rush my words, desperately needing to apologize for my failure. "I spent months walking, Nate. I thought you all were dead, that Asheville was gone—"

"It's okay, Taylor," Nate assures me, but I do not hear him.

"But then I found out people had survived, and I came to find you. I'm sorry I wasn't here sooner—"

Nate comes over to kneel before me, taking my hands in his own. "You're here now. That's all that matters."

I swallow hard and accept his words as truth. He doesn't forgive me, because he doesn't need to. He is telling me there is nothing to forgive, and with that, I am finally able to begin to forgive myself.

"So this farm of yours…" Bill says, trying to lead the conversation back.

"Right," I say, swiping the tears away. Nate stands by my chair, his hand resting on my shoulder. "We have a pretty big survivor colony there, nearly fifty of us. We're pretty self-sustaining. The man who runs the place, Buck, has things set up well."

"And anyone is welcome," Dunk adds.

"Would there be enough room for all of us?" Sharon asks hopefully.

"It'll be tight, but we'll find a way. Buck and I talked about it before we left." I look up at my brother. "Come back with us."

Nate surveys the small group, which has grown to include everyone as the conversation has gone on. Scared yet hopeful faces look back at him. Clearly Nate has become the leader of this little band. My heart swells with pride.

"Okay then," he says finally, the decision made. "If we're going to leave here, then we've got a lot of work to do. We'd best get some sleep and start early tomorrow. We'll meet up at eight to start planning."

The party breaks up with everyone returning to their respective quarters. Dunk and I go with Nate and Lily once Dunk has settled the horses in around back. After nearly a week on the ground, it feels good to sleep in a real bed, even if I am shoved into the wall with my niece pressed in beside me. Lily insisted that I sleep in her bed, and I couldn't have said no if I had wanted to. The look on Nate's face told me all I needed to know about how much Lily missed her mother, and so for a night I become her surrogate mom.

Shortly after dawn, the group begins making its preparations. It is quickly decided that given the children and the cold, we will need to drive to Burninghead Farm. That proves to be much less difficult than I might have imagined, with the stockpile of gas they'd stored. I know that driving will be too fast for the horses to keep up, but I push that thought off to the side, deciding to worry about it

later. Dunk goes out with Simon and another man to requisition two
large vans to accommodate everyone, while everyone else works
to pack up a few possessions and the remainder of their supplies.
It takes two days to get everything ready, mostly so the children
have enough time to adjust to leaving behind what they have grown
used to, and we decide to leave early the next morning. The vans
sit ready in the cul-de-sac, looking like a gypsy caravan with their
burdens of bags and boxes strapped to every square inch of their
roofs.

"Taylor, come out front," Nate shouts to me from outside the
house. I push open the screen door to find the best surprise of my
life. Parked next to the vans is an old, beat-up pickup truck with a
horse trailer big enough for Goldie and Stu.

"Dunk mentioned he was worried about getting the horses
back, so I sent one of the guys out to the Johnson place to borrow
one of their trailers."

Leave it to Dunk to take care of things. Thank God Kate and
Buck had been stubborn enough to insist that Dunk come with me.
Even though I had been worrying about the horses, I had never even
considered mentioning it to Nate or thought of using a trailer to
bring the horses back.

The next morning we leave Asheville, heading for home. What
had taken Dunk and me nearly a week takes our traveling caravan
a matter of hours. I ride with Dunk in the pickup, Stu and Goldie
tucked safely away in the trailer.

As the miles fly by, I think about all I have gone through, all I
have seen and all I have done since leaving DC. My father's voice
over a broken phone line, John and Claire and Melanie and the rest
I could not help, the terrible things Jacob did to me, Tim dying in
my arms, that old woman I buried behind her home, the nameless
places where I found brief respite and the nameless faces who tried
to hurt me, the smell of rotting flesh near the cities and the serenity
of the open fields where crops wasted away, all the days I wanted
so desperately to give up but kept pushing on…These things are
no longer stones in the wall I use to defend myself, but are the
foundation upon which I will build my future.

When I arrived at Burninghead Farm, I thought it would be like any other place I had passed through on my journey home. The journey was my only purpose, my rules were my only guide, and Mugsy was my only friend. I was not looking for anything more, but I found it all the same. I found a new home, and a family, and a woman who made me dream of something better, when I no longer believed such a thing was possible. And now, finally, I understand what Kate said to me about choosing hope over fear. Survival means nothing if you don't have something to live for.

With each mile, every fear and doubt I have held all these months slips away, until I am left with only anticipation of what the future holds. I kept my promise to my father. I came home. And I believe wherever he is now, he is smiling down on me. Hope has staked its claim firmly in my soul, hope for a life after the fall. Now, all I have to do is live it.

By early afternoon, we pull up to the farmhouse of Burninghead Farm, and I can't wait to celebrate.

CHAPTER THIRTY-ONE

I am half out of the truck by the time Dunk brings the pickup to a complete stop next to the farmhouse. I half expect the entire farm to be waiting for us when we arrive, hailing the return of the conquering heroes and all that, though I know my fantasy is completely ridiculous. Within moments, however, the people of Burninghead Farm have taken note of our arrival and one by one head up the hill to the farmhouse. Nothing stays a secret on the farm for long.

I scan the faces of the farm's residents, desperate to find Kate. I see Buck coming up from the direction of the dorm wearing a proud grin. I keep scanning the crowd, searching each face in turn until, at last, I find her. She seems to spot me at the same moment, and our eyes meet in one of those little bits of forever we always seem to share. I feel whole again.

I move as if in a trance, slowly at first, almost afraid I will scare her off with the intensity of what I feel. But in my heart I know she feels the same, and when she starts running up the hill toward me, my mind knows it, too. I start running. We collide halfway down the hill and she jumps into my arms. I never want to let her go, but I also know, finally, that we have the possibility of forever in front of us, for however long forever might be, and that our days are no longer numbered by my clumsy, stupid heart.

I pull back to study the face I know so well, that I have spent countless hours memorizing in the night. Her eyes glisten with unshed tears, and she smiles a smile that could light up a thousand starless skies. I press my lips to her forehead, drinking in the feel of her skin beneath my lips.

"You came back to me," she whispers.

"I love you." It is the only response that seems appropriate or necessary.

She smiles anew against my cheek. "I love you, too."

"I must look a wreck," I say, entirely too aware of my filthy clothes and the dirt permanently embedded in my skin.

"You're perfect. I don't even mind the smell."

I laugh at that and cup her cheek, her skin warm and soft beneath my fingers. "There's some people I want you to meet."

She eyes me curiously, but I shake my head, sliding my hand down to hers and lacing our fingers together. We walk back up the hill to where Dunk and the others are waiting. Buck is already there welcoming everyone, and he envelops me in a giant hug while Kate and Dunk embrace warmly.

"Welcome home," Buck says.

He steps back and returns to Dunk's side. Just then Nate and Lily approach, and I can tell by the twinkle in Buck's eyes that he has already been introduced. Lily's hand is tucked snugly in her father's, and she looks up shyly at the way Kate's hand is similarly tucked into mine.

"Kate, I'd like you to meet my brother, Nathan, and my niece, Lily."

Her head whips around toward me, shock and joy evident in her expression. Fresh tears spring up, this time slipping freely down her cheeks. She turns her attention to Lily first.

"Hi there, Lily," she says, bending down so they can see eye to eye. "My name's Kate. It's a pleasure to meet you."

Lily smiles and holds out her hand in official greeting. I hear Buck chuckle from over my shoulder.

"You're pretty," Lily says, and Buck chuckles a little louder.

"Thank you, so are you."

Kate rises again and hugs Nate, whispering something I can't hear but which makes Nate smile.

By this time, the rest of the farm has arrived, and Buck launches into his traditional speech to welcome the newcomers. After he finishes and people have had some time to introduce themselves, Buck turns to his daughter.

"Seems like we're going to need a place for all these fine folks to sleep."

"We'll need to double up now, but it shouldn't be a problem," Margie says. "Help me, Kate?"

Kate agrees, and though I am loath to let her go, I know there are too many important things that need attending to for me to be entirely selfish. At least for now.

"Taylor, why don't you and Nate come into the house for a bit?" Buck says. "Let's have a chat."

Nate looks down at Lily, who is still clutching his hand.

"Probably better if it's just us grownups," Buck says meaningfully. He bends down to Lily. "Why don't you go down with Duncan and find your room? I'm sure Kate will pick you out a good one."

Lily asks her dad for permission, and he nods.

"It's okay, sweetie."

She slips her hand out of Nate's and immediately latches on to Dunk's.

"Come on, kiddo. Let's see what trouble we can get into."

She giggles at that and heads off with Dunk down to the dorm. Once they are out of earshot, I turn to Buck. I wish I could read Buck's mind. Maybe he just wants to talk through some of the challenges we will have integrating the new folks into farm life, but I doubt it. We follow him into the kitchen of the farmhouse.

"You want some coffee?" Buck reaches for three mugs without waiting for a response. Seems like every conversation with Buck starts with coffee.

"Actually, would you mind if I used your shower? I'm sure it's chaos down at the dorm." Despite what I assume to be the importance of whatever Buck wants to talk about, I just can't stand the stink radiating from my skin for a second longer. "And maybe we could burn these clothes later."

"Sure thing. I'll have someone grab you some fresh ones."

I head up to the bathroom and quickly strip, kicking my ruined clothes off into the corner, trying to put as much distance as I can between me and them. I step into the shower spray, groaning in delight as the pressurized water pelts my skin. A shower has never felt this good. I scrub and rinse and repeat, to the point where my skin glows pink even under the muted light of the bathroom. When I step out of the shower stall, a fresh set of clothes sits folded on the sink.

I dress quickly and head downstairs, Nate's and Buck's muted voices echoing down the hall.

"Well, you look much better," Buck says, smiling.

"Much. Thanks."

Nate smiles at me, too, but it is clearly forced. I look back and forth between the two men. They've been talking in my absence, and whatever they were talking about, it isn't good.

"What's going on, Buck?"

"Why don't you have a seat," he responds, sliding a mug of steaming coffee in front of one of the empty seats at the kitchen table. I sit down and wait, ignoring the coffee for now.

"I was just filling your brother in on the farm."

"Is there a problem?" I ask, concerned that maybe Buck is unhappy I brought so many people back with me.

"With them coming here? No. Absolutely not."

I look to Nate, who confirms Buck's statement. "We're fine here, Taylor."

I blow out the breath I didn't know I'd been holding, but the pressure in my chest settles down in my stomach. "What is it then?"

Buck fiddles with his coffee mug, as if he is unsure of where to begin.

"Zeke paid us a visit while you were gone."

The words slam into me with such force they might as well be a Mack truck.

"What? When?"

"A few days ago."

I thought Zeke was simply a bad chapter in our lives, one I would never need to reread.

Damn it all to hell.

"What happened?"

"He showed up late in the afternoon with his boys in tow, and some new ones."

"How many?"

"He had five with him. I got the distinct impression there were more of them, somewhere."

So Zeke's little pack has grown.

My mind flashes back to the morning Buck sent them packing, the morning I tried to run away. The same morning I went toe-to-toe with Zeke and dared him to try something. A man like Zeke doesn't need much in the way of provocation, but I'd gone and done it anyway.

What in the hell was I thinking?

"He didn't come back because of you, Taylor," Buck says. I don't know how he knows what's in my head, but he does.

"What happened?"

"Oh, he put on this show about wanting to come back to the farm, how he'd learned his lesson and would play by the rules. I didn't buy it for a second, and he knew it. He got mad, of course."

Buck grins at that, like it is some amusing tidbit instead of profoundly serious.

"Buck…"

"We chased them off, Taylor. It was no big deal."

"If it was no big deal, then you wouldn't have brought us in here to tell us about it," I say angrily. Realization strikes me. "And you did bring both of us in here. Why? Nate doesn't know Zeke."

Buck peers down into his mug, like maybe he'll find some answers there.

"You think he'll be back," I say flatly.

Buck nods slowly. "And I figured Nate should know what he and his folks are getting into," he said, looking over at Nate apologetically.

Nate's eyes hold more understanding of the situation than they should. "He tell you about Zeke?" I ask him.

"Yeah," Nate answers. "And I know Zeke's kind all too well. We had run-ins with some boys like Zeke, men who think they can take whatever they want from whomever they want. It wasn't pleasant."

I file that information away to ask him about later. I wonder just what my brother has been through that I don't yet know.

"How'd you chase them off?" Zeke could've taken Buck in a heartbeat, and I am surprised by his restraint.

"He wasn't really prepared to do anything. After they dropped the pretense of wanting to come back quietly, which didn't take long, he just ran his mouth."

"What did he say, Buck?" When he doesn't answer, I press him. "Come on, Buck. You didn't bring us in here to shoot the breeze. Tell me what he said. Tell me what really happened."

Buck sighs. "He spouted his same old lines of crap. The details aren't important. You know the gist. Zeke believes he should be running this place, that this farm rightfully belongs to him. He said that if I couldn't see that, then he'd be back to take what I wouldn't give him. Then they left."

Buck rises from his chair, walking over to refill his cup. He turns and leans against the counter.

"They didn't *just* leave."

"Well, no…" Buck says, grinning. "Kate pulled a shotgun on him."

"What!"

"Don't worry, it wasn't just her. Some of the others noticed me talking to Zeke and rode in to the rescue," he says proudly. "But Kate was the first."

"Jesus, Buck—"

"You should have seen her. All fire and teeth. I think ol' Zeke must've pissed himself for the fright she gave him."

As angry and scared as I am at the thought of Kate taking on Zeke—yet again—I can't help grinning at the image of her making that asshole squirm.

"Exactly," Buck says, seeing the look on my face.

I sober quickly.

"I'm sorry, Nate." My brother is thoughtfully sipping his coffee. "Maybe I shouldn't have brought you all here. This isn't your fight."

"Like hell it isn't," he says forcefully but without anger. "I've had enough of people like Zeke. These guys think they can dominate through fear and intimidation and brute force. Damned masters-of-the-universe types, who think other men are there to be conquered and women are there to be controlled. But they don't get to inherit what's left of the world just because they think it's their birthright. Not as long as I'm still breathing."

Buck nods. It's clear he likes Nate, and I couldn't be more proud of my little brother.

"You know I didn't want this, Taylor," Buck says. He is sad, but resolved. "But I think we're going to need to finish it."

"Then we'd best get ready," I say, my own resolve hardening in my veins. "Do folks know?"

"Not everyone. Not everything."

"We should tell them."

"Tomorrow. We'll tell them tomorrow. Let them have one last night of peace."

We talk a while longer, making some preliminary plans. There isn't much we can do to secure the farm. It is too big, and without the wall finished, there is just no way to prevent Zeke and his men from getting in. Still, with three sides of the farm protected by the wall, we know at least when they come, they will have to come in from the north. It isn't much, but it is something.

Eventually, we make our way down to the barn for supper. I can smell the makings of an elaborate meal as we near the building, and my stomach does jumping jacks. The barn is packed with folks chowing down, especially the newcomers from Asheville. I catch sight of Dunk, who waves us over to where he, Kate, and Lily are seated. There really isn't any room left for us, but by the time we get there, Dunk has gotten everyone to squeeze together enough to fit us in. Buck and I sink down next to Dunk, and Nate settles in across from us beside Lily and Kate.

"Everything all right?" Kate asks, reaching across the table to squeeze my hand. "You all were gone a long time."

"Everything's fine," Buck answers for all of us. "How'd the move in go?"

Kate doesn't miss the change in topic, and she looks over to me. I squeeze her hand in response, and she nods imperceptibly, understanding that I will tell her everything later. Given her part in the run-in with Zeke, the news won't come as a surprise.

We are barely settled when three plates of food magically appear before us. I look up to find Franny hovering.

"Now don't go expecting this kind of service all the time. But I figured y'all would just spend the night gabbing away, completely forgetting that I can't get my kitchen cleaned up until everyone has eaten. Speaking of," she says, staring down at me, "seems to me I have you to thank for all these extra mouths to feed and the dirty pots and pans that come with them, so I'll be expecting to see you later for KP."

With that, Franny sashays away, leaving me slack jawed. The thought of what that kitchen must look like is scarier than any Freddy Krueger movie.

"She's kidding," Dunk says, trying to reassure me, and himself. He looks to Buck for confirmation. "Right?"

Buck laughs and starts in on his dinner. I look to Kate, hoping she will tell me I am worrying about nothing, but she just shrugs.

"Oh man," I grumble, going to work on my own supper.

Later, Buck tells me Franny had only been joking. I remain unconvinced, especially since every now and then I see Franny poke her head into the room, holding up a large pot in her hand and grinning wickedly at me.

We finish our suppers and chat about the day. The move in had gone well. Every room is now filled up, with most everyone sharing. It isn't long before dinner gives way to a full-blown party, despite the fact it isn't Saturday. There is much to celebrate. I have never danced so much or laughed as hard as I do this night, and it all feels perfectly normal and exceptionally right. This is my life now, and it truly is worth living.

I am running on joy and adrenaline, but even that can't sustain me forever. Exhaustion finally grabs hold of me, so suddenly it rocks me on my heels. Kate, who has been off somewhere chatting with some of the farm's new residents, is at my side in an instant.

"I think it's time to get you to bed," she says, wrapping her arm around my side.

"Yeah. Sorry. I don't know where this came from."

She frowns at me, like I am completely daft for apologizing for being exhausted. She leads me to my room, good old 39, but pauses outside the door.

"Now, you know we had to double up to accommodate everyone," she says hesitantly.

I nod at her dumbly. All I can think about is climbing into my bed and sleeping for a week, with Kate tucked safely in my arms. Her point is lost on me.

"So, you know that means we all have roommates now."

I still don't see what she is driving at. I really am dense sometimes.

"I have a roommate now. And so do you."

Understanding knocks me upside the head. We have roommates. There will be no sleeping with Kate in my arms anymore. I am now very cranky.

"Who?" I demand, even though it isn't that person's fault, even though it really doesn't matter who it is.

"See for yourself," Kate says, turning the doorknob and leading me through the doorway.

I stumble into the room, frustrated and fatigued, only to have those feelings replaced by confusion. The room is empty aside from Kate and myself. More confusing is that the two single beds that had previously occupied opposite sides of the room are now pushed together into one double bed, complete with an appropriately sized comforter.

Kate grins nervously.

"I don't understand. Who…"

Another whack to the head. A lazy smile creeps up my face.

"You mean…you?"

"Surprised?"

I feel like I'm going to burst.

"Is this okay?" she asks, still nervous but growing more confident at my reaction. "I just thought—"

"It's perfect."

"It just seemed—"

"It's perfect."

"Because if you don't want—"

I pull her into my arms. "It's *perfect*," I say again, this time whispering into her ear. She finally relaxes, looping her arms around my neck.

"I just figured if you were going to have to bunk with someone, it should be with the woman you love and who loves you back."

I kiss her then, not having the words to tell her just how much she is loved, how brave she is, how she has saved me and brought joy and peace and hope back into my life, or how I will spend the rest of my life trying to make her happy.

We are both breathing heavily when the kiss ends, and she gives me a deliciously wicked smile.

"Still tired?" she asks devilishly.

I grin and step back to close the door, giving her all the answer she needs.

CHAPTER THIRTY-TWO

W inter had officially come to Burninghead Farm. Snow had not yet fallen, but Mother Nature had delivered the first hard freeze of the season, leaving no doubt as to her intentions. Duncan sat huddled on the porch of the farmhouse, his hands wrapped around a steaming mug of coffee. He had grown accustomed to coffee of late, no longer minding its bitter flavor. It seemed to fit his mood these days.

Duncan stood and stretched, shaking out his legs, trying to restart the flow of blood. He grabbed his rifle, slung it over his shoulder, and began to pace the porch, still gripping his mug. Sentry duty could be mind numbing if you did not keep moving, and the last thing Duncan wanted to do was let his guard down.

Buck had set up the sentry system the day after Duncan and Taylor had returned to the farm. Three guards per night, with a system of repurposed church bells to warn if and when something happened. Buck's news about Zeke's return had sent shockwaves through the farm, or at least most of it. It was clear to Duncan that a few people had already known what had happened, including Taylor and Kate. For a while Duncan had been mad they had not told him. That they had not trusted him. But eventually he had let it go, deciding he was being childish. What he needed to do was focus on the problem at hand, namely, the threat to the farm. And so Duncan had been the first to volunteer to serve as a sentry.

It was a man's job, and Duncan did not take the responsibility lightly. He was well-acquainted with a rifle, having been taught by his daddy to hunt when he was only twelve, as his father had been taught by Duncan's grandfather. He was a good shot, but he knew there was much more to pulling a trigger than the accuracy of your aim. You never picked up a gun you did not intend to fire, and you never pointed it at anything you did not intend to kill.

Duncan had volunteered for extra shifts, although Buck would not let him take as many as he had asked for. Duncan was frustrated by that, although he understood it. Too many shifts keeping watch could drive a man crazy, make him hear noises that meant nothing and see things that were not really there. That was how accidents happened. Or worse yet, a man could go the opposite way, grow complacent from too many nights of nothing happening. Neither possibility was good.

Still, Duncan stayed frustrated. The need to do something gnawed at him. It was building up inside him, this nervous energy born of waiting for something to happen and feeling impotent against it. With work halted on the wall on account of the weather, the only outlet Duncan had for his growing anxiety was guard duty, which sometimes felt more like doing nothing than something. All he could do was wait, wait for Zeke to come back, wait for something—anything—to happen. And Duncan was tired of waiting.

It was not that he wanted Zeke to come back, or that he wanted a confrontation over the farm's future, but he knew it was coming. They all did. Zeke said he would be back, and Buck had ordered armed sentries posted for a reason. It was not a question of *if* a fight was coming so much as *when*. The inevitability of it hung in the air, in the stillness of the trees and the way the moon rose ominously overhead. And if it was coming, Duncan just wanted it to get here already and be done with it, one way or another. It was time for a reckoning.

But night after night, nothing happened. Duncan paced the porch of the farmhouse, watching and waiting and finding nothing changed. Even when he was not on duty, he found himself pacing over near the barn or outside the dorm. Still watching. Still waiting. And it was making him crazy.

It was an itch deep beneath his skin that he could never reach, that prickled and burned so far down it made his whole body twitch and ache. The only thing that helped was to keep moving, to walk the farm and scan the horizon and know, when the time came, he would be ready. He would see them coming. He would warn the farm. And he would stop Zeke and his men from destroying all that he loved.

He would stop them.

Duncan stepped down from the porch, extending his pacing into the less confining ground around the farmhouse. The grass, which had been alive and spongy beneath his boots only a few days ago, now crunched and shattered with every step. Duncan was once again reminded of how quickly things could change. Just when you thought you had everything figured out, that you understood the world and you knew your place in it, something came along to blow apart all you had carefully constructed. Control was an illusion, a trick of the mind and sleight of hand wielded by a faceless master magician. Duncan was just the lowly magician's apprentice, one without any real chance of mastering the magician's secrets or taking over the act.

It was hard to accept that tomorrow was Thanksgiving. Duncan knew that Franny and Mrs. Sapple and a few extra helpers had been working for days in preparation, baking pies and shucking corn. A few of the men had even managed to shoot some wild turkeys on the farm's western edge, and while it would not be enough to truly feed the entire farm, everyone would get a taste of the traditional turkey dinner. Still, it did not feel like any Thanksgiving Duncan could remember. Maybe this was the way Thanksgiving would feel now, after the plague, though Duncan did not think so. It seemed to Duncan it should be better somehow, like they had more to be grateful for here in the after. And maybe some folks felt it was better, but not Duncan. Instead, Duncan was consumed by the irony that as they prepared to celebrate all that they were grateful for, Zeke and his men were preparing to try and take it all away from them.

Up until now, Duncan had managed to retain his sense of self and his optimism. While the plague had stolen away his family and his childhood, he had rebuilt his life on Burninghead Farm and found a new family here among the ruins of the world. Life was vastly different than it had been before the plague, but in some ways, it was also entirely the same. You still worked hard, treated others as you would want to be treated, paid respect to those to whom it was due, and tried to help wherever and whenever you could. Those were the lessons he had grown up with, the lessons of before, and they carried over into the new world.

There were dangers to be sure, people who had allowed their desperation to push them into doing things which would have once been unthinkable to them, and other people—bad people—who no longer felt bound by society's rules once civilized society had vanished. Duncan had known those truths when he first arrived on the farm, before Zeke had begun demanding the world be remade in his own image, before they had begun building the wall, and even before that day sitting out on those rocks with Taylor, when she had told him the story of Pennsylvania. But Duncan had convinced himself that was the exception and not the rule, that most people were inherently good and would not go out of their way to hurt anyone, and that somehow Burninghead Farm would be immune from the dangers that lurked beyond the farm's boundaries. Despite some doubts along the way, Duncan had believed the life he had built would last forever.

And now Zeke and his ilk were threatening everything.

Duncan felt his anger rising. He had never known such bile, had never thought himself capable of this thing that had begun welling up inside of him the day Buck had told the farm to start preparing to face Zeke's threat. But Duncan's outlook, as well as his illusions about the world, had begun to unravel. In their wake came a churning storm that fired his blood and left him unable to think of anything but stopping anyone who dared threaten what he had built. No matter the cost.

Duncan climbed back up onto the porch and leaned his gun against the house's exterior wall. He glanced down at his watch. It was nearly three a.m., time for the next shift to come and replace him and the two others keeping watch. Not that it mattered. Duncan knew he would not be sleeping that night. No, like every night, he would stay awake until dawn broke over the eastern horizon, as he watched and waited for the beginning of the end. Only when light had cast its first full shadows across the farm, chasing away the stealth of night and, with it, Zeke's ability to take the farm by surprise, would Duncan finally fall into a restless sleep plagued with demon-filled dreams.

CHAPTER THIRTY-THREE

I awake to the sound of bells. At first I think it is part of a strange dream I've been having, the result of too many mashed potatoes and that extra piece of pie Kate and I snuck out of the kitchen late last night. But as I climb out of the dream and toward consciousness, the clanging of the bells grows more distinct, and I recognize them for what they are. This is no dream. The nightmare we have been dreading has finally come to life. The distant sound of a gunshot confirms it.

I can barely hear the shouts out in the hallway over the thudding of my heart.

"Baby, wake up," I whisper urgently into Kate's ear, shaking her.

She wakes with a start, blinking up at me in the darkness, trying to get her bearings. Realization dawns.

"Oh God."

Kate scrambles from the bed as I quickly slip on my already laced sneakers. Like others on the farm, we have taken to sleeping nearly fully dressed in preparation for the inevitable. I grab Mugsy and slip her securely over my shoulder. Kate is already at my side by the time I finish. She squeezes my hand, and I kiss her quickly, stealing a moment we can't afford.

I love you. We will survive this. We will still have forever.

We each have specific tasks to accomplish, and they will be taking us in different directions. I hate that I won't be with Kate to protect her, but I am grateful she will be heading away from immediate danger.

We flee the room and run straight into an orderly chaos. People are everywhere, some evacuating, some trying to wake up others, and some heading to other assigned jobs. Everyone has a place to be, and they are going. Fear thickens the air, making my limbs heavy, like I'm swimming against the current in a river of mud. With one last squeeze, Kate lets go of my hand and runs down toward the children's rooms. She, Margie, and a few others are responsible for gathering the children and leading them off the farm. They will head east toward the wall then follow it north, using the trees as cover, until they reach an open section and can escape. With any luck, they will miss Zeke and his men, who we expect will head straight for the heart of the farm—the dorm—from due north, not wanting to pin themselves against either the western or eastern wall.

I head outside, where I am to make my way over to the barn and help free the horses. Better they run free than be taken by Zeke or caught in the crossfire. I reach the open air and sprint toward the barn. It is nearly pitch black, the clouds obscuring both the moon and the stars, but my vision adjusts quickly. Muzzle flashes explode in the darkness from up near the farmhouse, lighting up the night like a fireworks show gone horribly wrong. Gunfire thunders across the farm, the echoes mixing with angry shouts and strangled cries. I can hear Rusty barking frantically off in the distance. I pray someone grabs him before he gets himself shot. Dozens of fast-moving shadows line the horizon, and some of them are already heading my way. My heart lodges in my throat, choking me as it pounds frantically against my windpipe, and I gasp for air. *Oh God.*

Time spins wildly out of control, speeding and slowing as the ground lurches up before me. I am back in Pennsylvania, running and stumbling through the woods, broken and bleeding, pursued by brutal men with murder in their hearts. Tree branches tear at my arms, sulfur assaults my nostrils, the coppery tang of my own blood seeping from my lip fills my mouth. I fight to right myself, to shake the memories from my skin and nose and throat. All around me, guns keep exploding and people keep shouting, and I struggle to find my way back to the present.

You're not in Pittsburgh. You're on the farm. You're under attack. *Now move!*

Adrenaline surges, snapping me back to reality. I am running again, faster than before, my legs hammering the ground. As I reach the barn, a horse comes flying out into the night, nearly running me over. Franny is already there and has begun throwing open the stall doors and chasing the horses outside. I take the other side of the barn and follow suit. I find Stu's stall and open it. He whinnies bodily, clearly agitated. I have no doubt he knows what is happening. I run into the stall and clap my hands at him, trying to chase him out. He bolts for the entrance to the barn, only to pull up in the barn door. He turns and eyes me, stomping his foot once as if to tell me to get a move on.

"Not this time," I say sadly. "But you need to go."

He refuses to move, and so I shout. "Go!"

With a final snort, he turns and races out the door, soon followed by the remaining horses.

"That's all of them," Franny yells to me as she comes running up. We can hear the shouting outside getting closer. "We've got to move."

We are supposed to flee west once we have finished freeing the horses, then north and off the farm. The plan is to get the children and elderly off the farm and away from Zeke and his men. It is simple numbers—there aren't enough guns to go around, and not everyone can shoot them anyway. There is no sense in leaving the farm's most vulnerable to be killed or used as hostages. The other women will leave, too, not because they can't fight, but because of the things that will happen if Zeke catches them. Things I know all too well.

But I have no intention of leaving. I refuse to save myself when others are still in danger. I refuse to let others pay the price for my survival ever again.

"Go, I'll be right behind you," I say, shoving Franny toward the barn door. She is not so easily fooled.

"You're not coming."

It is a statement, not a question. It does not require an answer. She hugs me tightly before pulling back. "Be safe." And with that she runs out the back of the barn and into the night.

I run out the opposite door and back into the fray. I have not yet seen Zeke, but his men are everywhere. They run wildly, whooping and hollering as they shoot off their guns. It seems like many of the farm's residents have fled to safety as they were supposed to, but others remain, running across the farm. Some are being chased, but others are fighting back. As many shots as are being fired, it doesn't seem like Zeke's men are actually firing *at* anyone. He'll need slaves for his new world order. So the fighting stays hand-to-hand, at least until one of Zeke's men uses the barrel of his gun to knock someone to the ground.

My heart stops as I see Kate being chased by one of Zeke's men, and I fight off another flashback. She has a lead on him, but he gains on her quickly. I chase after them and watch in horror as he catches her. Her scream pierces the night. He grabs her from behind and tackles her to the ground. She is kicking wildly and scratching at his arms, desperately trying to break free. He laughs as he wrestles her beneath him. I pull Mugsy out of her sheath with murderous intent. I must scream, because his head snaps up to see me charging at him.

It all seems to go in slow motion.

I am thirty feet away. He sits back on his knees, with Kate still pinned beneath him.

Fifteen feet away. He raises his gun. I raise Mugsy over my head as I run.

Ten feet. He takes aim.

He is going to beat me. I swing at him anyway.

He never gets off his shot.

As I swing Mugsy at his head, he doubles over, and the bat arcs directly where his head should have been. I am moving with such force that it takes several more feet for me to bleed off my speed and turn around. By the time I do, Kate has pushed the man off and is scrambling up from the ground. I reach her side quickly. The man is curled up in the fetal position, holding his groin and crying out in agony. It all happened so fast, I missed Kate kneeing him in the crotch just before he would have pulled the trigger.

Kate stares down at him, her eyes blazing. Rage fires her, and she kicks him in the crotch again, this time her foot making contact with such force I can hear the bones crack in the hand covering his damaged genitals. She pulls her leg back to kick him again, but I stop her. She looks at me as if seeing me for the first time. I kick his gun away from him.

"Damn it! What are you doing here?" I scream at her, grasping her face in my hands.

"One of the kids was missing. I couldn't leave her," Kate says, smiling sadly.

I pull her back into my arms, praying like hell she is a figment of my imagination.

"Well, isn't this touching?"

Zeke has arrived. He stands there, an evil grin tugging his lips into a sneer, a shotgun resting on his shoulder like a big game hunter posing for a photo over the body of the rhino he just slaughtered. He has five men with him. We are surrounded, and suddenly I remember what it feels like to be locked in a stall with no way out.

They round up thirteen of us and quickly relieve us of whatever weapons we have. Mugsy is tossed into a small pile of tree limbs and shovels. The farm grows quiet as the shouting and gunfire die off. Zeke has about twenty men in total, all armed with shotguns, rifles, or handguns. They push and shove us into a line and order us to kneel with our hands clasped behind our heads.

Three more men come running over from the dorm.

"Well?" Zeke asks.

"It's empty," one of the men answers. "They're all gone."

"Fuck!" Zeke shouts, throwing his gun to the ground. His men look more than a little nervous as Zeke paces angrily. Finally, Zeke slows, reaching down to pick his gun back up. When he straightens, he seems as calm as a Buddhist monk. That scares me more.

"So Buck decided to flee instead of fight, eh?" he says, eyeing each one of his hostages. His gaze stops on me. "Figures."

For once, I don't take the bait.

"Zeke!" Another man runs up. He is clearly out of shape and takes several gasping breaths.

"What is it?" Zeke snaps.

"One of the boys spotted some people trying to sneak a group of kids off the farm."

"So?"

"Well, they have a good lead on us, but we can catch them—"

"Leave it."

"There were women—"

"Leave it."

"But Zeke—"

"I said leave it," Zeke growls, like he is ordering a dog to let go of a bone. "We don't need to deal with a bunch of rug rats right now. They won't get far. We'll round them up later."

He walks back over and stops in front of Kate.

"Besides, we've got some women right here," he says sickly, reaching out to brush the hair out of Kate's face. She yanks her head back as if she's been burned. He grasps her chin, not liking that she recoiled from him. He leans down close to her face.

"You and me have some lost time to make up for."

I start to move, to try and do something even though I know it is futile, but Kate beats me to it, spitting in Zeke's face. He springs back, rage building as he wipes the globule from his cheek. I know he is going to smack her, and I race to figure out how to adjust my body so I can deflect the blow when it comes. But to my surprise, he holds back. I am grateful for that, but when I see the fury in his eyes, I know that rage will build until it explodes, and it will happen when he is alone with Kate.

Zeke steps back to address all of his captives.

"This farm belongs to me now."

His men cheer, a few of them shooting their guns into the air once again.

"That means everything on it belongs to me. You all belong to me. You will live by my rules. Trust me when I say you don't want to find out what happens if you choose to disobey."

He walks back and forth before us, eyeing each one of us in turn.

"You can thank Buck for this. This place should have been mine from the start. Buck was never strong enough to do what needed to be done."

He pauses. He stops in front of me, but I refuse to look at him. I won't give him the satisfaction. I gave in to Jacob, at least in the end. I refuse to give in ever again.

"The old world is dead, and it's up to us to build a new one. There's no room for weakness. Weakness degrades the whole, and it must be eliminated."

He begins to walk the line again.

"Survival requires us to obey the basic laws of nature. Food, water, shelter, procreation. Everyone has to do their part."

He stops in front of me again, and this time I meet his eyes.

"Those who won't do their part have no place in my world."

Like a steel trap, he clamps down on my arm and hauls me up to my feet. Distantly, I hear people gasp and Kate cry out, but I am focused on Zeke. He drags me out to the center of the crowd and throws me back to the ground. He circles me like a wolf preparing to devour its prey. I rise to my knees and follow him with my eyes. He comes to a stop in front of me, and he cocks his shotgun.

"*You* have no place in my world," he says, baring his teeth.

I fight the urge to shrink away as I stare down the barrel of his shotgun. If I am going to die, then I am damn well going to do it with a little bit of dignity. For myself, for Kate, and for everyone else. I stare up at him, defiance burning bright. That pisses him off, and his evil smile fades.

"You ready to die?" he asks, trying to bait me. I square my shoulders.

That's when I notice a series of dark shapes off in the distance behind Zeke, getting closer by the second. I try not to let the hope show on my face.

The cavalry has arrived. But if I don't buy myself a little time, they will be too late, at least for me.

"You know, Zeke," I begin slowly, trying to stall, "killing me isn't going to be as satisfying as you seem to think it will be."

His gun falls a little.

"Oh yeah?" he says smugly, although I hear the slightest bit of curiosity in his voice. "How's that?"

I try to keep him going as the quickly moving shadows edge closer.

"There's a lot better ways to prove your point."

His gun drops a little further.

"Like what?"

"Well, you can kill me, that's true. But the whole reason you hate me is I represent the opposite of everything you believe. And killing me won't fix that."

"You're just stalling because you don't want to die," he says dismissively, the gun coming back up.

"Of course I don't want to die," I say quickly, desperate to regain his interest and that of the rest of his men. "But that's not the point. See, I'm this big ol' dirty dyke who won't accept her proper role, right? And even worse, I make other women reject men. Reject people like you. And that's just not right, is it, Zeke?"

"It's disgusting," he agrees.

"I'm the worm in the apple, and you need to cut it out."

"Yes."

"Or you could make the worm work for you."

His eyebrows furrow. I risk a quick glance past him. They are almost here. Just a little longer.

"Work how?"

"All any woman needs is a good man, and she'll know her place, isn't that right? Well, maybe you just need to prove it. Make me the example of how it all should work."

He finally gets where I'm going. He sneers. "I wouldn't touch you if you were the last woman on earth, you filthy whore."

I smile wickedly. "Good. Because I'd rather die than let you touch me, you fucking pig."

His momentary shock at my response is replaced by a vicious anger. "Say good-bye, bitch."

"Good-bye, bitch," I snarl.

"Hold it right there, Zeke," Buck shouts, startling Zeke and his men. They spin around to come face to face with Buck and about twenty of the farm's residents with guns cocked and ready. Nate is with them. Dunk is there, too, his eyes blazing against the darkness. Zeke's men bring their guns up. It is a standoff.

I let myself breathe for the first time, being careful to stay as still and quiet as possible as I continue to kneel on the ground, seemingly forgotten. Buck's plan had been to stay hidden with his men until Zeke and his boys had made it down to the dorm to find everyone gone. The rest of the farm's residents were to escape, some unseen, but with some acting as decoys. We had figured that Zeke would not know just how many people were living on the farm now, and therefore he would see people running but wouldn't realize Buck and his men were missing, lying in wait. Buck had thought they'd be able to sneak up on Zeke in the confusion and overpower him, before he had hostages. Unfortunately, Zeke's men had been quicker than Buck had anticipated. But Buck and his men had been out there watching, waiting for the right moment to strike.

"Don't do this, Zeke," Buck pleads. "Just take your men and go."

"I'm not going anywhere, old man," Zeke says almost gleefully. "This farm belongs to me."

"It never belonged to you, Zeke. That's always been your problem. You think you can bully your way through life taking whatever you want. But that's no way to live, son."

"I'm not your son!" Zeke explodes.

"But that's how I always treated you. Like family. You were always welcome here."

"You cast me out."

"Because you wouldn't live by the rules—"

"Your rules, not mine."

"Zeke," Buck says sadly, shaking his head. "No good can come of this. Why don't you just take your men and leave. We'll forget this ever happened. If it's food you need, we'll give it to you. Just let us live in peace, and we'll do the same for you."

Zeke spins, and I have no time to brace myself. He grabs me with one hand and drags me up to my feet, pressing the end of his shotgun into my temple. Buck's eyes widen in horror.

I can hear commotion behind me, and out of the corner of my eye I see Tony trying to hold Kate back. Tony clamps his hand over Kate's mouth as he drags her off to the side. They move unnoticed by Zeke and his men, as they are too focused on the continuing standoff. I am just grateful Kate and the others are now out of harm's way.

"Please don't do this, Zeke," Buck says, begging for my life.

The cold metal of the gun presses deeper into my temple. Zeke is growing more agitated.

"You threw me out!"

"Don't do it," Buck says even as he raises his gun at Zeke. His eyes dart over to me, and I silently plead with him to end this.

Take the shot, Buck. It doesn't matter. Just take the shot.

I don't want to die. Not now, not after everything I've done and fought through to get here. I crane my head, finding Kate's eyes in the darkness. If my death will buy her life, it is a price I am willing to pay. I know it's not fair, and I know it's not what she would want, but I am too selfish to think any differently. I cannot bear to live without her.

Zeke's men tighten their grips and Buck's men do the same. Faces strain tight with tension, cutting across the quiet that descends. No one seems to dare to move, or even breathe. Eyes shift nervously between Buck and Zeke, who are locked on each other. Finally, someone moves. I don't see it, but I hear the snap of a twig, followed by a shot ringing out across the silence.

It is impossible to tell who fired, but my heart stops as Buck staggers backward. Guns lower as Buck drops his gun and clutches at his side, trying to stop the dark patch that blossoms across his shirt. Two of his men are at his side in an instant, while the rest of the men from the farm jerk their guns back up angrily. Zeke's men follow suit, and the standoff resumes. Buck steadies himself, then brushes off the hands that have been trying to help him. Reluctantly the men step back, and Buck straightens, still pressing his hand to his side.

"Enough, Zeke," Buck says weakly. He is gasping for air. "That's enough now."

Zeke says nothing, but his grip on me loosens. The gun moves away slightly, too, though I barely notice. I stare at Buck, who seems to be growing a little stronger. Buck's men cast worried glances at their leader, while Zeke's men seem to be growing more nervous by the second.

"I'm okay," Buck tells his men. "It just nicked me."

Buck's words bring some measure of relief, enabling his men to regain their focus. That, plus Buck's shooting, has a clear effect. Zeke's men are beginning to waver.

"Come on, Zeke. Let the girl go, and walk away."

For a moment, I think Zeke might actually listen, and his grip slackens a little further. But then, for reasons passing understanding, Zeke explodes. He pushes me forward, releasing his grip completely. I flail to the ground, turning in mid-fall to see Zeke bring his other hand up to the shotgun and point it squarely at my chest.

There is no time for my life to flash before me. I have a split second to wonder whether I will feel any pain before the end. Then I hear the gunshot.

Chapter Thirty-four

Duncan watched as Zeke's eyes widened in surprise before his body fell to the ground in a heap. He barely remembered pulling the trigger.

He glanced down at Taylor, who was staring at Zeke's now-lifeless body. She looked up at him finally, her shock clearly evident. He could only imagine what she was feeling. Zeke had almost killed her, but Duncan had stopped him. If it had not been for the smoke curling off the barrel of his rifle, he might not have even believed he had fired the shot. But as he watched the smoke rise lazily into the night, he knew. And he was glad.

Duncan looked back to the ground and watched absently as blood seeped into the grass from beneath Zeke's corpse. He idly wondered how long it would take for the earth to erase the bloodstain.

The world froze around him. He looked up and looked straight into Buck's eyes, but he couldn't read what he saw there. Something akin to sadness and pride, with a little bit of horror mixed in, Duncan thought. He would have to ponder that later.

Buck stared back at Duncan for a bit longer before turning his attention to Zeke's men.

"It's over," he said quietly. Duncan thought Buck was speaking more to himself than to Zeke's men. "You men can walk away, no one will stop you. But if you ever come back you will be shot on sight."

Zeke's men glanced around at each other and then started to backpedal from their fallen leader.

"Leave your guns on the ground," Buck ordered.

It took a minute, but one by one they complied. Each man slowly set his gun down where he stood, as if he was afraid that any sudden movement would get him killed. Then the men turned and fled north, back the way they had come onto the farm, leaving Zeke's body where it had fallen.

Duncan settled his rifle down at his side, keeping his focus on the fleeing men. Eventually, he looked back to Taylor, who was slowly getting up from the ground. Kate rushed past him and was at her side in an instant, helping her up. Duncan watched Kate frantically check Taylor over for injuries. He was glad they had each other. Maybe now he would be able to have someone someday, too.

"Sam, Tony, go follow them and make sure they leave without delay," Buck said. The men nodded and headed off after Zeke's men, along with a few other of Buck's men in tow. Duncan thought about following, too, but for some reason his feet refused to move.

"Now we need to get everyone back," Buck said, smiling slightly. Duncan watched as a few of the men set off east for the kids, and west for everyone else. Nate led the charge to go bring back the children.

Those who remained behind were suffering a combination of shock and exhilaration. Some stood in stunned silence, while others began chatting nervously. Duncan kept off to the side, his eyes once again drawn down to Zeke's limp body. For some reason, Duncan half expected to not find it there, like a bogeyman in a horror movie who dies but is not really dead. He did not notice Taylor and Kate approaching him until they blocked his line of sight. He looked up. Kate quickly wrapped her arms around him, hugging him like he was a long-lost relative she had not seen in a dozen years. He thought about hugging her back, but he could not seem to get his limbs to work. He just stood there, letting Kate hug him.

She pulled back, and Taylor stepped up to fill the void, although she did not put her arms around him. He was a little relieved by that, although he was not sure why. Instead she reached up and squeezed his shoulder.

"Thank you," she whispered, her eyes full of tears. He could not understand why there would be tears, but he nodded anyway.

Shouts filled the air, and they all turned to find Buck lying on the ground. They sprinted toward him, Taylor and Kate pushing their way to his side. Duncan hung back slightly, his brain fuzzy and unable to comprehend what was happening. He could hear the words, but it would be hours before he could fully absorb them.

"Hang on, Buck. We're going to get help," Taylor said urgently. She was kneeling at his side, gripping his hand tightly. Kate was pressing someone's shirt into the wound at Buck's side. Even in the faint morning light, which Duncan finally noticed creeping across the ground, Buck looked pale.

"It's okay. I'm ready," Buck said shakily.

"But we're not. Please, Buck," Taylor pleaded.

"Yes, you are. More than you know."

Taylor's head dropped to her chest.

"They're gonna look to you now."

Duncan watched as Taylor looked back at Buck, her eyebrows knitted together.

"Why me?"

"Take care of them."

"Come on, Buck. You have to fight," Taylor begged. Tears streamed down her face.

"Not everyone can be saved," Buck whispered, smiling softly. "Sometimes...the best you can do is die at peace."

"Are you?" she asked, her voice breaking. "At peace?"

Duncan waited for Buck to respond, but he never did. His eyes stayed open, staring up at the early morning sky. Taylor reached over and ran her fingers gently across his eyelids, closing them. Duncan turned, following Buck's sight line toward the horizon, where he was met with the most stunning sunrise he had ever seen.

CHAPTER THIRTY-FIVE

Five months have passed since Zeke's attack on the farm, and the earth is beginning to awaken from its hibernation. Leaves are sprouting from barren branches, and the air carries that particular smell that always seems to announce the coming of spring.

We buried Buck behind the farmhouse, next to his wife. She died in the plague, but her last wish had been for Buck to help as many people as he could, which is exactly what he had done. His legacy is Burninghead Farm, which we recently renamed Burninghead, Indiana.

We buried Zeke, too, but the location of his grave isn't worth remembering.

Just as Buck said, the farm looked to me after his death. I still don't understand it. There were plenty of people more qualified to take over for Buck than me, and it seemed only right that the leadership role would have fallen to his daughters, Margie and Franny. But they declined, saying there was more to running Burninghead Farm than actually understanding how to run a farm, and that Buck had chosen me. I was responsible for the farm and its residents now, they said. For some reason, that thought didn't scare me as much as it might have not so long ago.

We took in more folks over the winter, people who either stumbled upon the farm in search of a new life or who had been sent our way. Buck's rules remain in effect. Anyone is welcome, as long as they don't mean us any harm. Everyone is entitled to their privacy. Everyone pitches in. It wasn't long before even tripling up in the dorm wasn't enough, and we made plans to begin building small cabins as soon as the ground thawed. We began construction in March and things are progressing quickly. Ten homes have been finished. They don't have plumbing or electricity, but no one seems to mind. Kate and I moved into our home a few weeks ago, the community insisting we take the first one. Rusty moved in with us. He has rarely left my side since Buck died.

I proposed to Kate one winter evening, out beneath the full moon. It was a magical night, the whole farm coming out to find a pristine snowfall blanketing the landscape. We made snow angels in the moonlight with some of the children, while others made snowmen and threw snowballs. I had been planning on proposing for a while, and as we stood beneath the stars, looking out across a field of angels in the snow, the time seemed perfect. Thankfully, she said yes. We made plans to wed later in the spring. It won't be official of course, since there is no such thing as official anymore, but one of our newer residents is a former notary who is working up a whole system of record keeping that will include marriage licenses. Kate and I will be the first to receive a license. It will be stamped with the seal of Burninghead, Indiana.

All in all, time has been good to us. Supplies have run short with all the new people, but the coming spring brings new hope for food. With so many people, we decided to create a town council to help make decisions. Kate, Margie, Tony, and Mrs. Sapple all sit on the council, as does my brother. Nate and Lily are doing great, and every day I am reminded how blessed I am to have both my old family and my new one together and safe.

Dunk is a bit quieter these days. He still works hard, still talks and jokes and even plays guitar on occasion, but I think he's lost the last of his boyhood. He took Buck's death pretty hard, and it took him a while to open up about it. When he finally did, he said it was a little like losing his dad all over again. Truthfully, I think killing Zeke had an equally profound effect on Dunk. He has never spoken of it, at least not to me. Kate tells me, though, that Dunk's been spending a lot of his free time with a girl named Charlotte, who came to the farm with Nate's group. Maybe he'll find in Charlotte what I found in Kate.

I have taken over the weekly guitar lessons, playing Buck's old Martin every Wednesday afternoon. During the winter we held the class inside the farmhouse, but today we are huddled on the porch. It is really still too cold to be outside, but it is such a beautiful day, and the children begged, so I caved. They have me wrapped around their little fingers, and they know it.

I am about to play another song when the distant sound of a diesel truck catches my attention. I stand and look to the horizon, and see not one but an entire convoy of what look to be military vehicles approaching from the north. Kate comes up next to me, and I don't have to say a word.

"Come on kids, let's get you all inside," she says. A few of the adults whisk the kids away. There have been rumors of a convoy of official military vehicles bringing supplies in from the west, and seeing is believing. I don't expect that representatives of whatever government is left mean us harm, but still, better to move the children indoors. The others know what to do if there is trouble ever again.

I step off the porch and await the convoy. As I wait, I hear the screen door open and close behind me. Kate steps up next to me, sliding her hand into my own. Whatever this is, I know we will face it together, and I draw strength from that knowledge. I am sure that elsewhere on the farm word is quickly spreading about the convoy. It won't be long before the rest of the farm comes up to see what all the commotion is about.

The convoy pulls up to a stop in front of the farmhouse. Truck doors open, and dozens of men in fatigues jump out to stand beside their trucks. A man from the lead truck approaches us.

"Sergeant Stafford, United States Army, ma'am," he says by way of introduction. He removes his sunglasses and squints against the sun's glare. I don't miss the helmet and bulletproof vest he wears, nor the rifles his unit carries. They make me nervous, but I sense no hostility coming from the sergeant or his men.

"The name's Taylor, please. Ma'am is reserved for Mrs. Sapple."

Kate chuckles beside me.

"I'm sorry?" Sergeant Stafford says, not getting the joke.

"Never mind. What can we do for you, Sergeant?"

"Well, ma'am. It's what can we do for you, not the other way around. We're part of an advance scouting unit, sent ahead of our main platoon to see just where we're needed most."

"The military dropped off the face of the earth nearly a year ago, Sergeant," I say meaningfully.

"Yes, ma'am. It took us a while to regroup. I'm sorry about that."

I eye him for a moment. He seems sincere.

"It's good to see the military is back up and running," Kate says, stepping in while I study the convoy behind the sergeant. The volume of weaponry concerns me, even though I know it wouldn't make any sense for them to be traveling cross-country without some means of defending themselves. There are still a lot of desperate people out there.

"Yes, ma'am," he says, turning to Kate. "Federal government, too. It's based out of California now. There were a lot more survivors out west than out here. But now that the government and military are back up and running, those of us the brass can spare are pushing east. We've got some supplies with us, if you need them."

I ponder his comment about troops *the brass can spare*. I can only imagine what it must be like in the coastal cities, although something tells me that's not what he meant. I push that thought aside for now. Supplies are a far more pressing matter, but I also know there are other survivor colonies in much worse shape than ours.

"We'll take a few things if you've got them, but all in all we're doing pretty well here. Save the bulk of it for those who really need it."

He nods at me appreciatively. He looks around the farm, sweeping his gaze over the construction and farmland, as well as all the people making their way up to the farmhouse.

"We've been traveling for nearly four months now, stopping to help where we can. There are so many people struggling to get by."

"It's a hard world, Sergeant. But you already know that, don't you?" I say.

He nods again. "Can I ask you two something?"

"Of course," Kate answers for us.

"We've been through hundreds of encampments, full of cold, tired, starving people. Yet you folks seem to be thriving. What's the secret?"

I think about it for a moment. I feel Kate beside me, squeezing my hand. I see the children's faces peeking out at us through the windows of the farmhouse. I hear the chattering voices coming up behind us. I feel the golden sun shine down upon my face and the warm breeze kiss my skin. I look into Kate's eyes, and she is smiling at me, and I know she knows my answer.

"Hope, Sergeant," I say, turning back to him. "Hope and hard work and community, with just a dash of luck sprinkled in."

My answer seems to make sense to him, and he smiles.

"The main platoon should be through here in the next month or so. They're working to restore power in this half of the state. Once it's back up, it'll be staffed full time by army personnel. I'd say you should have electricity in the next couple of weeks."

"That's excellent news. We've got solar power but it's a big farm and getting bigger all the time."

"Well, we can leave you a supply of gas, if that'll help?"

"That would be much appreciated. We've got crops to raise, and it'd be much easier if the farm equipment had something to run on besides spit and willpower."

He laughs at that. "Is there anything else you folks could use right now? Anything at all?"

I glance over at Kate, and I honestly can't think of anything more I need. She seems to have other ideas, though I have no idea what. "Well, there is one other thing, Sergeant."

"Yes?"

"We've been telling the children about this wonderful place called Disneyland," she says, her eyes twinkling in the sun. "You think the Army could get that back up and running anytime soon?"

God, I love this woman.

The sergeant laughs again. "I'll see what I can do."

"Where are you heading to next?" I ask.

"Farther south and east. Another group is heading north into Michigan later in the week."

"There are plenty of people out there in need of help," Kate says. "Hopefully, they can hold on a little while longer."

"Yes, ma'am," he agrees. He looks around again, seeming to notice the children in the windows for the first time. "We found some kids about a hundred miles back. I have no idea how they survived this long on their own. We've been through a couple of survivor colonies since then, but I didn't feel right about leaving them there. Those people, even with our supplies, are barely getting by. But you all seem to be doing well here..."

Kate squeezes my hand, and I nod my assent. Not that there had been any real question. She answers for the both of us. "We'll be happy to take them in."

The sergeant walks back to speak to one of his men, who nods and walks farther back into the convoy.

"There's four of them. Three boys and a girl," he says as he walks back up to us. Over his shoulder I see the other man help the children down from one of the trucks. They are clearly tired and hungry, but their eyes are wide and full of innocent wonder.

"Sergeant, anyone is welcome here. Anyone at all. We'll make room."

Kate leaves my side and walks over to the children. I can't hear what she says, but I don't need to as I see the smiles pop up on their faces. She is like a healing potion for their sad, tired little hearts. It is her gift, and not just for children. She certainly helped heal my heart.

The sergeant, who was watching, too, turns back to me. "Thank you, ma'am. We should be heading out now. There's still a lot of country to get to."

"Good luck, Sergeant," I say, reaching out to shake his hand.

"Thank you, ma'am. Oh, ma'am?"

"For heaven's sake, would you please call me Taylor?"

"No, ma'am," he says, grinning. "What should I call this place? In my report."

"You're standing in Burninghead, Indiana. Population one hundred thirteen. Well, one hundred seventeen now."

"There's no Burninghead, Indiana on my map, ma'am."

I smile. "There is now, Sergeant. It's named for the man who gave us a chance to build a new life together. Some things are too important to forget, even after the end of the world. Don't you agree?"

About the Author

Robin Summers began her writing career in high school, thanks to an insightful (and a little bit pushy) English teacher who, having decided that Robin was not living up to her potential, gave her extra, non-graded homework over winter break: to read Douglas Adams's *The Hitchhiker's Guide to the Galaxy* and Helene Hanff's *Q's Legacy*. In those pages, Robin discovered how far good writing and a vivid imagination could take a reader, and she has been writing ever since.

Robin is an Illinois native who works in public policy in Washington, DC. When she is not writing, she can often be found rooting for Da Bears and her beloved Cubbies.

Robin can be contacted at *robinsummerswriting@gmail.com*. Her website is *www.robinsummerswriting.com*.

Books Available From Bold Strokes Books

Firestorm by Radclyffe. Firefighter paramedic Mallory "Ice" James isn't happy when the undisciplined Jac Russo joins her command, but lust isn't something either can control—and they soon discover ice burns as fiercely as flame. (978-1-60282-232-0)

The Best Defense by Carsen Taite. When socialite Aimee Howard hires former homicide detective Skye Keaton to find her missing niece, she vows not to mix business with pleasure, but she soon finds Skye hard to resist. (978-1-60282-233-7)

After the Fall by Robin Summers. When the plague destroys most of humanity, Taylor Stone thinks there's nothing left to live for, until she meets Kate, a woman who makes her realize love is still alive and makes her dream of a future she thought was no longer possible. (978-1-60282-234-4)

Accidents Never Happen by David-Matthew Barnes. From the moment Albert and Joey meet by chance beneath a train track on a street in Chicago, a domino effect is triggered, setting off a chain reaction of murder and tragedy. (978-1-60282-235-1)

In Plain View by Shane Allison. Best-selling gay erotica authors create the stories of sex and desire modern readers crave. (978-1-60282-236-8)

Wild by Meghan O'Brien. Shapeshifter Selene Rhodes dreads the full moon and the loss of control it brings, but when she rescues forensic pathologist Eve Thomas from a vicious attack by a masked man, she discovers she isn't the scariest monster in San Francisco. (978-1-60282-227-6)

Reluctant Hope by Erin Dutton. Cancer survivor Addison Hunt knows she can't offer any guarantees, in love or in life, and after experiencing a loss of her own, Brooke Donahue isn't willing to risk her heart. (978-1-60282-228-3)

Conquest by Ronica Black. When Mary Brunelle stumbles into the arms of Jude Jaeger, a gorgeous dominatrix at a private nightclub, she is smitten, but she soon finds out Jude is her professor, and Professor Jaeger doesn't date her students…or her conquests. (978-1-60282-229-0)

The Affair of the Porcelain Dog by Jess Faraday. What darkness stalks the London streets at night? Ira Adler, present plaything of crime lord Cain Goddard, will soon find out. (978-1-60282-230-6)

365 Days by K.E. Payne. Life sucks when you're seventeen years old and confused about your sexuality, and the girl of your dreams doesn't even know you exist. Then in walks sexy new emo girl, Hannah Harrison. Clemmie Atkins has exactly 365 days to discover herself, and she's going to have a blast doing it! (978-1-60282-540-6)

Darkness Embraced by Winter Pennington. Surrounded by harsh vampire politics and secret ambitions, Epiphany learns that an old enemy is plotting treason against the woman she once loved, and to save all she holds dear, she must embrace and form an alliance with the dark. (978-1-60282-221-4)

78 Keys by Kristin Marra. When the cosmic powers choose Devorah Rosten to be their next gladiator, she must use her unique skills to try to save her lover, herself, and even humankind. (978-1-60282-222-1)

Playing Passion's Game by Lesley Davis. Trent Williams's only passion in life is gaming—until Juliet Sullivan makes her realize that love can be a whole different game to play. (978-1-60282-223-8)

Retirement Plan by Martha Miller. A modern morality tale of justice, retribution, and women who refuse to be politely invisible. (978-1-60282-224-5)

Who Dat Whodunnit by Greg Herren. Popular New Orleans detective Scotty Bradley investigates the murder of a dethroned beauty queen to clear the name of his pro football–playing cousin. (978-1-60282-225-2)

The Company He Keeps by Dale Chase. A riotously erotic collection of stories set in the sexually repressed and therefore sexually rampant Victorian era. (978-1-60282-226-9)

Cursebusters! by Julie Smith. Budding-psychic Reeno is the most accomplished teenage burglar in California, but one tiny screw-up and poof!—she's sentenced to Bad Girl School. And that isn't even her worst problem. Her sister Haley's dying of an illness no one can diagnose, and now she can't even help. (978-1-60282-559-8)

True Confessions by PJ Trebelhorn. Lynn Patrick finally has a chance with the only woman she's ever loved, her lifelong friend Jessica Greenfield, but Jessie is still tormented by an abusive past. (978-1-60282-216-0)

Ghosts of Winter by Rebecca S. Buck. Can Ros Wynne, who has lost everything she thought defined her, find her true life—and her true love—surrounded by the lingering history of the once-grand Winter Manor? (978-1-60282-219-1)

Blood Hunt by L.L. Raand. In the second Midnight Hunters Novel, Detective Jody Gates, heir to a powerful Vampire clan, forges an uneasy alliance with Sylvan, the Wolf Were Alpha, to battle a shadow army of humans and rogue Weres, while fighting her growing hunger for human reporter Becca Land. (978-1-60282-209-2)